PART-TIME
DEVDAAS

PART-TIME DEVDAAS

Rugved Mondkar

Srishti
PUBLISHERS & DISTRIBUTORS

SRISHTI PUBLISHERS & DISTRIBUTORS
N-16, C. R. Park
New Delhi 110 019
editorial@srishtipublishers.com

First published by
Srishti Publishers & Distributors in 2015

10 9 8 7 6 5 4 3 2 1

Cover design: Sanjay Gauraha

Dedicated to

The Mother,
The Father,
The Sister
& Her...

Some of this actually happened...

Acknowledgements

There were times when as a little boy I would make up stories about myself, simply to entertain people and get kicks out of it. Then came a time when lying and making up stories didn't satiate the itch of telling stories in me. This book is an attempt to derive a bigger kick by entertaining you, my reader. Thank you for picking up the book. I hope you love it.

I am eternally thankful to all the beautiful people around me who in their own way have helped me make this book happen.

My parents who have provided me with stable supply of *Roti, Kapda* and *Makaan*, and making me the person that I am.

My sister Rucha - the sweetest thing that has ever happened to me. Vishwarath my brother-in-law – my brother from another mother.

Anuja Gondhalekar, for literally kicking me to write this book, for being the most patient sounding board, for all the creative inputs, for being the first reader, for tolerating my erratic emotions which were all over the place during the writing of this book, and for being everything that you are. Thank you.

Sushant Tungare, Ameya Masurkar, Mithil Khadke, Akshay Vaidya and Apeksha Belsare Anavkar – the most amazing five people who made my growing up years so beautiful. Thank you for all those memorable days. No words can explain how much I miss you guys.

Rutuja Mane Vaidya, Riddhi Khadke, Manali Vaidya, Namrata Narkhede, Purva Chaudhary, Gargi Lad, Apurva Vaidya, Manish Narkhede, Ranjit Gupte, Nachiket Kambli, Sagar Deorukhkar – the friends who are the victims of the random spurts of my story telling. Thank you for your mad belief in me.

My family and friends for the never-ending love and insane support. Thank you, all you lovely people.

Vinayak Kulkarni – thank you *Kaka* for helping me promote the book.

Super talented Sanjay Gauraha for the cover design and Rukmini Chopra for posing for the cover.

Team Srishti for patiently clearing my doubts, believing in the content and making this book happen. Thank you for all the support during the process of publication.

Wish you all Love, Peace and Happiness..!!

2012

Godrej / 85163, a steel key.

I kept staring at it as I stood at the door. The door to my first apartment. Rented, yet mine. The happiness that I had anticipated somehow managed to bunk the moment, but I had to bear with it. It was strange considering I had gotten the independence I always starved for – no questions, no arguments, no screaming roommates, no chaos. Nothing at all.

Then in a moment, the fact that I was going to be alone began to sink in and suddenly the world around me went silent. All I could hear was my broken wailing self, wishing life had an option to undo things. Life had changed drastically from jostling in crowded local trains to travelling alone in my car. I was so alone that it had been more than a week since I had heard my own voice.

"Arjun?" A voice called my name.

"Hmm," I turned around startled and saw a girl's face framed by the grill of my neighbour's door.

"Maa told me you'd be coming," she said. "Is everything alright? You look a little flustered."

"Ahh, no, I'm fine. Just trying to figure out which is the key to the first door," I blurted foolishly, barely managing a smile.

"Cool, our doorbell has conked out so knock if you need anything... Oh sorry, I am Aditi," she closed her door with a smile that stayed with me.

I turned the key and opened the door, Thanks to my producer Rocky, I finally had my own sea-facing apartment in Bandra. I could see the sun rise from my bedroom while the living room had a perfect view of the sunset. Right from the open kitchen to the flawless marble flooring to the brick-wall-finished walls – everything was just as I had wanted. Almost everything in life was in place. The only thing missing was her, without whom my life was as empty as the apartment I was standing in.

The two bean bags and a coffee machine were my only companions. I made myself some coffee and sat on the Italian style window. The view of the setting sun from the living room looked mesmerizing.

The door bell rang.

"Do you mind if I bug you for a while?" Aditi grinned.

"Not at all. Come on in! Will you have some coffee?" I asked.

"I don't mind."

I made a cup for her while she made herself comfortable on one of the bean bags.

Aditi – dusky skin, bee-stung-luscious lips, dazzling smile, blue and red streaked hair, multi-coloured nail paint, black thumb ring, pierced nose and a slight accent. The scissor cut, navel revealing singlet threw just the right amount of cleavage at the viewer plus her track pants made sure her curves were justified. Pure hotness. Nineteen years old, not more than that, I thought to myself.

"You do know you need to fill this place up, right?" she said looking around the emptiness.

"Yeah, the movers will be here with my stuff," I handed her the coffee mug.

"You know the girl who lived here before you? Arrgghh... Class one bitch! Never even smiled at me!" she said animatedly as she juggled between talking to me, sipping the coffee, and typing messages on her phone at rocket speed.

The orange light of the setting sun coming from the window made her skin glow. The fizz she had in her was infectious.

"So?" She gazed at me, then trying to find words, she asked, "What do you do?"

"I'm an ass..." I gobbled up the rest of my sentence realising I was no longer an assistant director. I smiled to myself re-registering the change in my mind. "I'm a director."

"Holy fish! A director? Like a real film director?" she bounced with excitement.

"Ya, a real film director. I'll be starting my first film soon."

"Is it a romcom?" She had a twinkle in her eyes as she said that.

"Yes." I smiled. "What about you?"

"I'm studying. FYJC Arts, at Nationals. I wanna be a journo. Sounds like a fun job, right?"

Sixteen years old? A voice yelled in my head as I did the math; she looked too old for high school.

"Oh, that's nice," I said lamely.

"Hey what's your BB pin?" she asked, noticing my Blackberry and added me immediately.

Her purple blackberry suddenly started buzzing.

"Hey I gotta go, I'll catch you later?" she sprung up and rushed to the door.

Minutes later, my Blackberry pinged. It was her.

"It wAs nIcE mEEtiNg yOu... M glAd mY dAd rEntEd yOu ouR apaRTmEnt... hAVe fUn... M jUs a PING!!! aWaY iF yoU nEEd aNythiNg" followed by smileys, a grin, eyelashes, and a hug.

"Likewise." I replied.

By night time, the movers had moved in all my stuff – the sofas, the bed, my writing table, the photo frames, everything. The apartment had now become a house – a messy one. It had been a long day and I had no strength left to unpack. I crashed on the haphazardly dumped bed and almost instantly fell asleep. I was dreaming about a narration with Shah Rukh Khan when my phone began to ring. I cancelled it a couple of times but it continued ringing. I realised I was dreaming and I had to wake up to answer it. It was Radhika. I checked the time. Why would she call me at midnight?

"Hello?" I said groggily.

"Happy birthday, kiddo!" she screamed into the phone.

"Couldn't you find a more annoying hour to wish me, Didi?" I said. "Thanks anyway."

Since we were kids, Radhika had not once missed wishing anyone in the family at the stroke of midnight. The birthday bum also had to read the long letter she wrote followed by the cutting of the cake and hunting for the gifts she hid in the house. In spite of her being married, her juvenile excitement was intact.

"Done moving into the new house?"

"Hmmm..."

"How is it?"

"It's really good," I said.

"Are you alright? You seem quiet."

"Yeah... that's because it's 12 at night. I'm sleepy and you won't stop talking."

"Same old Mr Snappy! I miss you Poncho. Come back to LA na."

"Me too. I wish I could come back."

"How are you holding up?"

"I'm fine. How's your grizzly husband? Is he still always hungry?"

"Don't ask! If he could, he'd eat in his sleep too," she said grumpily.

"How's Kiara?"

"She's good. Achha listen, Did you speak to her?"

I'd seen that question coming. "No."

"Why? You promised me you would."

"Didi, I really need to sleep. Please."

"Go, get lost, you dog! Take care, okay?"

"Yes I will, kiss Kiara for me."

"Ya, I love you."

"Love you too, Didi." I hugged my phone for a while after I hung up.

Happy birthday to me! Happy *thirtieth* birthday to me. Shit, I'd turned thirty.

My birthdays didn't exactly excite me but the date meant something to me. I had hit most of the goals that I had set out to score.

An apartment – rented, yet mine. Check.

A car – though not a Land Rover. Check.

Being a successful film director – A three film contract with the biggest studio in the country. Definitely check.

Married to Hrida...

The year 2001 changed my life in more ways than one and if there was any *kasar* left, 23rd October of that year completed it. Diwali had always been special for me. The only thing I hated about it was the crackers. I never understood why people spent money to buy smoke and noise. Everything else was fun – dressing up, wearing the traditional kurta (which sat in the wardrobe for the rest of the year thereafter) and visiting the local temple where a crowd gathered religiously, as if it was one big date fest.

Early that evening, my dad woke me up and asked me to get ready as he wanted me to go shopping with him. Shopping with dad was always painless, unlike with Radhika or Mom. Zip zap zoom and he would be done; as a consolation, I would get bagful of stuff for myself too. I wasn't sure where dad intended to shop that day since the stores we usually went to were on the other side of the city. He suddenly parked the car and asked me to get down. I squeaked with joy as I saw him enter a bike showroom. I ran behind him.

"Baba... if you are joking... this is not funny!"

"Consider it a bribe to not drop out of engineering," he said and smiled at me.

And there it was – the blue 200CC mean machine.

"Zero to sixty in seven seconds flat," the sales guy was saying.

In those days, when guys my age used 100cc bikes which made fart-like sounds, this baby was a total boner. How cool could anyone's father get!

"Thank you so much, Baba," I said hugging him.

"You are welcome. Now, will you tell your mom about this?" he said, sounding genuinely scared.

Later that evening, I picked Shashank up. To me the world seemed different that day – my very own bike was something that I had wanted ever since I had learned to ride. When you are constantly around someone like Shashank Sachdev, you are without a doubt invisible. Six feet tall, athletic body, fair skin, stubble or a dimple if clean shaved with floppy hair – girls would never notice a five-feet-seven-inches tall anorexic frizzled-haired guy like me. I would always end up feeling like his sidekick, so the bike was without a doubt an ego boost for my shallow self esteem. We aimlessly rode all over the city. I was just beginning to feel like the hero of my own story when Shashank got a call from some girl named Neha who asked Shashank, who in turn asked me to take him to the Greenwood Park Coffee Shop where she was waiting for him. I realised my time of being a hero was nearing an early end. All the way to Greenwood Park, I whined about how irritating it gets to listen to his moronic conversations with girls, so I declared that I'd drop him and leave. But by the time we reached, Shashank had cajoled me to wait.

As we entered the coffee shop, I saw three girls sitting in the cafe. I quickly peeked at all three of them. There was a fair one, whom I simply glanced at assuming she was Neha. The other two were of my interest as I would probably spend the next two hours or so staring at them or listening to them. One of them was dark-complexioned, with a look on her face which said *"My mom has asked me not to talk to guys so I'll mace you even if you so much as look at me."* The other one was dusky with a cute smile. She got up as we entered and straightway hugged Shashank. He introduced her as Neha. I was merrily surprised. Then I looked at the girl I had overlooked. I cross my heart and swear to die, but I literally observed her in slow motion – fair skin, pink lips, no lipstick, small dark brown eyes carved with just eyeliner, long eyelashes, layered brown hair, a groggy voice and the smile that left me breathless. There was something about this girl that all of a sudden made me feel numb. Hrida.

As expected, Shashank disappeared with Neha, but I had no complaints. I was thinking of what to say that would not make me look like a fool when Hrida spoke.

"Hey your eyes," she said staring into my eyes,"They are beautiful."

"Thanks," I said a little embarrassed.

"What exactly is the colour?" she came close to me and my heart started pounding. "Shit! They are olive green!" she said.

"Yeah, the only saving grace on my face, rest is just a disaster." I giggled.

"If you are fishing for compliments, then I must add that you have a great smile too."

"Nothing like that." I started grinning.

"Yes, confirmed it *is* pretty amazing." She said and winked. Suddenly all my nervousness disappeared.

"You don't seem to like wearing a sari," I said.

"Arrgghh, I hate it. I had to wear it because of these fools." She looked at the third girl, "I'd any day prefer pulling up a pair of denims and a tee. Festival or no festival."

The third girl got a call from her mother and had to leave. The evening couldn't get any better for me.

"So what's with the auntie? What's her problem?" I asked about the third girl.

"Nothing's wrong with her. She is just not used to hanging out with guys."

"She literally punched me with the look in her eyes," I said and Hrida started laughing.

My phone rang. It was Shashank. It better be something important, I thought. I picked up and he asked me to meet him near the fountain just around the corner. He asked me to bring Hrida and the other girl along with me. As we reached near the fountain, I saw Shashank on his knees in front of Neha and he was holding something in his hand which looked like a ring to me. I have to agree it was romantic with the multi-colour fountain behind them and the music that was playing, but it was by far the cheesiest thing I had ever witnessed in my life. I buried my face in my palms. Hrida on the other hand was thoroughly enjoying the scene.

"She said *yes*, she said *yes*!" Hrida said jubilantly as I saw them hugging in full public view. Yukk, couldn't Shashank have found any other place? I thought, but I didn't mind as Hrida was holding me by my arm.

I made a puke face at Shashank. Neha seemed really happy as she hugged Hrida.

"Someday, it'll be you," he said to me.

We started walking towards my bike. Shashank and Neha held hands as they walked. Hrida and I followed them. She seemed exceptionally happy too. I started the bike and Shashank jumped from behind. As we began to leave, Neha hugged him again. Hrida smiled at me.

We sat in silence. Shashank was probably thinking about Neha and I couldn't stop thinking about Hrida. She was different from the rest of the plastered Barbies I had met or dated. She was fun and honest. She cracked jokes and laughed at them herself. She was carefree and the zing with which she talked simply amused me. I wasn't sure if what I felt for her was love or not, but I knew one thing for sure – I had to meet her again.

2009

I sat there as Hrida walked out of the cafe. I watched her go till she disappeared out of my sight. She left me with the same numbness that I had felt when I had seen her for the first time on Diwali seven years back, only this time I felt bitter emptiness inside me. Shivers went down me as reality began to sink in. I left my bike at the cafe and began to walk. A riot of conversations broke out inside my head.

"How could she simply leave?" Voice One asked.

"Because you asked her to?" Voice Two said.

"But why didn't she refuse??" Voice One asked.

"You begged her not to." Voice Two said.

"Didn't she feel anything when she left. After all, we have been together for seven years??" Voice One asked.

"Maybe she didn't really love you." Voice Two said

"Does it mean that I'll never see her again, no calls, no messages, nothing?" Voice One asked.

"Yes that's pretty much what you asked her to do," Voice Two said.

"Fuck!!! What have I done!" Voice One Screamed.

I rang the doorbell and stood blankly staring at the door till she opened it.

"Arjun yaar, its one a.m.!" Devika whined. I stared back with wet eyes.

11

"Hey, what's wrong?"

"I broke up with Hrida," I said and hugged her.

Cut to 1994:

In the year 1994, my dad was transferred to Mumbai. Radhika chose to stay back in Pune to complete her last year of school with her friends. I barely had any friends in Pune and staying away from Mom and Dad was never an option. But I hated everything about Mumbai – the traffic, the crowds, the weather, and especially the rains. However, I had no option but to make peace with the fact that I had to stay there forever.

I was admitted in the same school my dad went to. I saw his name on the board written against '*School captain-year 1966*' and understood why he had been so happy about the school. It made me smile with pride.

I was made to wait on a bench outside the principal's cabin. Beside me was a girl named Devika. The supervisor came out with a list and took us to a class on the first floor. 'VI A' I read on the plate as I followed him into the class. The supervisor introduced us to the class teacher and left. Miss Anita Singh – 27 years old, unmarried, beautiful, fair, round face, big black eyes, shoulder length hair, a bit on the shorter side but great figure and she wore the sari below the navel. She introduced us to the class and then asked them to welcome us. Devika inched towards me in nervousness as the class said, "*Welcome Devika and welcome Arjun*" in a synchronised tone.

That year we were to only two new students in the class, so we were the obvious targets to be bullied. During recess on our first day, someone emptied a water bottle on Devika's desk and she unknowingly sat on it wetting herself. Everyone laughed at her. Seeing Devika embarrassed, I quietly went to the loo and splashed some water on my behind. Noticing my wet pants, the kids forgot about Devika and began pestering me. But as long as they left Devika alone, I was okay with it. Ever since that day, Devika and I were always there for each other. I was the fourth boy on roll call and she the fourth girl, so we were made to sit beside each other. We would talk for hours, walked home together. We even went to the same tuition classes. It did not take very long for school to be fun for me.

Devika was some kind of smiling knight in shining armour coming up with solutions to all my problems. It had been fifteen years since then and not much had changed. I wished Devika would come up with something that would pull me out of my misery. That night Devika spooned me to sleep.

2001

*H*rida. Everything about her was so stupefying that all I could do that night was lie in bed and let her thoughts spin in my head. It was 2 a.m. and I was still awake, reliving every moment of that evening. It was as if she had plastered a permanent smile on my face since then. I don't know when I finally fell asleep that night; all I remember is that I kept seeing her smiling face, she holding my hand with her warm hand, and saying yes as I proposed her. It was phantasmagoria of sorts in a good way. I had dated quite a few girls, but none of them had rendered me this useless. That one evening with Hrida had turned my life upside down.

I woke up in a daze the next morning and the smile was still there. I heard someone in the kitchen. It was my dad making breakfast.

"Baba, why are you up so early?"

"Making sure yesterday's little stunt of ours doesn't cost me a month of sleeping on the couch." I guessed that Mom wasn't speaking to him. "Come, chop some onions for me."

"I love you dad, and so does she; she'll be fine by the end of the day," I said as I started peeling the onions.

"I love you too son, and so does she, and that's the problem," he said patting my cheek.

There was silence for a while, and a nudge from dad startled me.

"You okay, buddy?"

"I think I am in love!" I mumbled.

"You bet you are, with a baby like that anyone could fall in love." I wondered how he knew about Hrida. I soon realised that he was talking about the bike.

"Now if you'll excuse me, I have to win back my love before it's too late," he said as he gave finishing touches to the coffee he had brewed for Mom.

"Greetings, your highness..."

I heard him say as he entered their bedroom.

I decided to talk to Radhika.

Waking Radhika up from her sleep before time was like twisting a Rottweiler's ear; you could rest assured that you would be ripped apart. I contemplated for a while before I tapped her hand to wake her up. She was fast asleep.

"Didi, listen na, I need to speak to you," I said lying down beside her, poking my finger into her cheek this time.

She opened her eyes and stared at me acrimoniously, but I had to talk to her so I decided to put a up a brave front. She turned her face away to the other side.

"Radhika... come on ya... you can sleep the whole day," I begged her to wake up.

"Poncho, get lost before I slap you," she said furiously.

"This is serious ya, Di, I think I am in love," I said desperately.

"All you care about is your sleep, you don't love me anymore!" I whined. She pulled me towards her and started patting my head, forcing me to sleep.

"This would be the hundredth time in the past nineteen years that you've fallen in love." I figured it was useless to talk to her. I hugged her back and lay there. I had to talk to someone. Raghu.

When my calls and messages to Raghu went unanswered, I decided to go to his place and talk to him.

Raghu's dad and my dad were childhood friends. They had gone to the same school and had pretty much done everything together.

"We have had all our 'firsts' together," they used to say with pride.

Our moms joked about how they even planned their kids so they could go to school together. Raunak Uncle was the most adorable guy I'd ever known. He had fair skin, blue eyes, grey hair, and at a hundred and twenty kilos was a heavy man. He bear hugged me as he opened the door.

"Where's Raghu?" I asked in a low voice as I gasped for breath.

"Locked up in his room," he said.

"Kaka... I'll see you in a bit," I said and entered Raghu's room.

"Whaaaattt? Did I sleep with you and forget to call you back or what? Why are you stalking me?" Raghu snapped at me.

"Why aren't you returning my calls, man?"

"Got stoned man... got this new stuff; it's heavy. What's wrong?"

"Nothing's wrong, just wanted to speak to you."

"Heard Sachdev pulled a Shah Rukh Khan yesterday."

"Fuck, you should have been there. Major cheapness," I cringed.

"I bet you this *bhenchod* will be sniffing someone else's ass in ten days," he said scoffing.

"Do you remember 'Dangling Deepa'?" Both of us were in splits.

"God, she was one scary floozy. I mean come on, she was an inch taller than Sachdev!" he said trying to control his laughter.

"No wonder he got all pansy for her," I said.

"I'm sure she would have had a bigger banana than him."

We were rolling on the floor now.

For years, Shashank's love affairs had provisioned us with months of laughter. There was always some or the other trait about his girls that left us roaring with laughter. From the juvenile Anandi who spoke childishly, to the *burkha*-clad Afreen who never showed her face in public. Not to forget *totli* Tulikaa who called him That-hank – they were all hilarious. I have to agree that Neha was doubtlessly Shashank's best score till date. For Shashank's sake, I hoped she'd stay.

"There is more to the evening," I said trying to sound as casual as I could.

"Oh yes, I heard." It didn't amuse me a tiny bit when he said that, "Neha's friend?" he asked.

I knew Shashank had sensed something on the bike and must have told him. Then it struck me that if he had told Raghu, he would have in all possibility told Neha about it. What if she told Hrida? My heart sank. Why couldn't he just keep his mouth shut for once.

Two regulars, I mimed to the waitress inside the cafe through the glass wall while Raghu and I sat at the open air table. Raghu elbowed me to check out the girls sitting at the next table. A while later I saw the girls giggling and smiling at him. The one and only thing I hated about being with Sachdev and Raghu was that I was freaking invisible to the girls when they were around. I had thought girls were only attracted to hefty guys, but this bastard was an inch shorter than me, had fair skin, was baby-faced, and oozed everlasting charm.

Neha got down as Shashank parked his bike; Raghu made our patented 'tight ass' face at me looking at her ass. I just smiled as she was too close. Shashank slapped him hard on his back before he sat on the table. He must have seen Raghu's *hornithologic* expressions. Neha was looking even better than she had in a sari. The pink ganji she wore revealed ample cleavage and just a bit of her love handles. The dark blue heavily stonewashed jeans just made the flawless hour glass figure look better.

"Neha, meet Raghuvir my boyfriend, Raghuvir meet Neha my girlfriend." Shashank introduced them to each other.

All through the time we spent with Neha, Raghu and I kept observing her, looking for any form of impairment or deformity in behaviour which would be in tandem with rest of the nuts Sachdev had dated. We found none. She was flawless! Raghu and I exchanged a look. I hoped Sachdev would not screw up.

"So?" she turned to me with an impish look. "I heard." I stared at Shashank with rage and threw a cigarette box at him.

"Hey I didn't say what!!" Neha exclaimed.

Everybody started laughing at me. A bit embarrassed, I only smiled.

"Don't worry, you'll be the first one to tell her when she comes back." She smiled reassuringly, "Only if you want to, that is."

"Back? From where?"

"She left for Kerala with her parents for vacation this morning."

"For how long?"

"Not sure, but a week I think."

Shit a week? A voice yelled inside me. I had thought I would speak to her that day itself, now I suddenly had seven days to kill. I helplessly looked at Shashank, Raghu and Neha; they were happily making some random plans I didn't care about. All I cared about was meeting her, and she was seven days away from me. Hrida... I thought of her and the smile sprung back on my face.

2001

It had been six days since Hrida had gone, In those six days I had bunked college and spent most of my day either playing Counterstrike at Raghu's place, or being a third wheel and watching movies with Shashank and Neha. Nights were especially difficult. I would kill time by drinking sneaked out whiskey from dad's liquor cabinet or coffee at the James Coffeewala. Hrida was all I thought of. The more I thought about her, the more I felt crazy about her. The pathetic cheesy emotions which I had always despised were now flowing through my body.

At the dinner table that night, there was pindrop silence. I had an intense itch of pulling off an A. K. Hangal but the visual of three heads dissecting their food earnestly demotivated me. I quietly joined them. Mom was still not speaking to dad and that meant my house was a silent zone. Dad tried everything from making morning coffees to cleaning his cluttered wardrobe to going to the gym every morning. But nothing had worked. Lost in my thoughts, I was stirring the soup to death when Dad broke the silence and decided to shoot a few charming lines at my mom using my young able shoulders.

"Did you know our offspring is in love?"

Radhika pinched me and the excruciating pain brought me back. I saw Mom staring at me irately.

"In... in love with my bike," I spoke attempting to recover from the pain.

Dad looked at me disheartened. I realised I had flushed Dad's brilliant attempt to strike a conversation with Mom. Everyone except dad began to giggle. Dad slapped my leg and Mom patted his cheek. Finally there was peace at home after almost a week.

That night Radhika and I snuggled between mom and dad in their room.

"Good I bought him a bike, at least he will have something to impress the girls with," Dad said to Mom thinking we were asleep. "He doesn't have my charm, you know."

"Don't say that, he has your smile," she pinched his cheek by stretching her arm across us.

"And your lips..." Dad said and began to lean towards Mom.

"Poncho run!" Radhika screamed and we ran out of there room laughing.

I wished there would be never-ending love between me and Hrida, just like there was between my parents.

Next afternoon, I was still sleeping and beside me, a nine hundred and thirty page fat engineering mechanics book made itself so comfortable that it had pushed me to the corner of my bed. A vibration below my crotch woke me up. It was a message from Neha. I turned to read it and landed on the floor. The book looked as though it was dancing victoriously. I kind of forgot the pain when I read the message. *"She is back."*

"I have to meet her. Please do something..." I begged.

"I am meeting her with rest of the girls in the evening... we are going for a movie..."

"Can I come please? We'll make it look like a coincidence."

"OK fine... I'll buy a ticket for you and message you the time..."

"You are my hero..."

"We are watching Bhoot, Screen 4, seat no. B-19, I've left your ticket with the security with your name behind it." Neha messaged me diligently.

"I'll be there. I owe you one." I replied.

It was a brainless idea but I convinced myself that I had no other way to see her that day itself. It was dark inside the theatre and I was twenty-five minutes late, so had to cross ten people and bear their *"kya yaar tum bhi, dekh ke chalo na jara, ouches, uffs"* to reach my seat. I tried to be discreet and waited for her to notice me. I stuck to my plan watching the hideous camera angles and listening to loud thuds and tolerating the infant screeching *right* beside me, I tried to look at her from the corner of my eye, but she looked more interested in Urmila rotating her head and whimpering. So I decided to play her part, and act surprised. As I turned to give my performance, the lights went on for the interval and I was staring right into eyes of *'the third girl'* who detested me.

The plan wasn't working so I decided to abort the mission. The interval was nearly over and the crowd was walking back in. I carefully walked down the aisle, making sure she didn't see me. As I walked towards the exit gate, a voice called my name out. *Hrida.*

"Oh hi!" I said and I began my performance.

"Too scared to watch the complete movie?" she asked me as she slurped her cola.

What was once a one-time exercise now became a routine. In the following days, Neha became my tipper, messaging me the locations and time and I would magically appear there.

"Linking road, Bandra, 12 p.m." and I was there, to buy clothes for my sister.

"Crawford market, near Badshah, 3 p.m." and I would be there to buy some pav bhaji.

I would simply cling to her for the rest of the day. The girls would walk ahead, and me and Hrida would be on our own chatting and laughing. As the days passed, my reasons became more lame. Malls, cafes, parks, local trains, at the bhel puri stall outside her college – whereever they went, I was there with one of my reasons in my pocket.

I was so obsessed with following Hrida that I had completely forgotten that I was due for a KT paper which was a day away. Raghu acted all paternal and dragged me to the college library along with him. I had no intention in making peace with engineering mechanics. I cursed the day my dad force-fed me the engineering seat. I could never understand how mugging theory of trusses or study of concurrent forces would help me become what I actually wanted to become; all that *gyaan* was for the bespectacled great souls who slogged their asses and wore the blisters of engineering like a medal and graduated only to do their MBA and work for companies which sell washing powder and other such mundane products to the world. I wasn't ready to be one of the educated fools. I was determined to run away. '*Someday,*' I said to myself, but for now, I wanted to run away from the library before its noxious, damp, fungal air choked me to death.

"I am leaving; it's been three hours and I think I'll get passing marks tomorrow," I said as I stood up. The shrill squeaking of the chair made enough noise for all the medal bearers to give me foul stares.

"Sit down or I'll kill you," Raghu said half whispering and gritting his teeth.

"I have to go. It's almost six!" I began to collect my stuff. *Why hasn't Neha messaged yet,* I thought.

"I am not allowing you to make a fool of yourself anymore; you have hopped enough in your poop," he said as he tussled with me to force me to keep my stuff back.

"What the hell do you mean?" I loosened my grip.

"Poncho, you are blind but the world is not. You are stalking her, man!" he said furiously pulling at my bag.

"No... I am not." I couldn't even convince myself when I said that. "Do you really think so? Did she say anything?" I asked in panic. *Whatever happened to playing it cool with the girls,* I said to myself.

"No, but Sachdev and I have been meaning to tell you to slow down before you scare her away."

"God! What have I been thinking?"

"You should rather ask her out directly than behaving like a psycho."

"I'm scared, man"

"What? Are you expecting *her* to ask you out?" he went back to his reading.

"I wish," I said and rested my head on the table.

An incoming message vibrated my phone. Raghu snatched it from me and read the message, "It's an unknown number," he said and passed the phone to me.

It read: *"Its past six thirty. I think Neha forgot to message you today. I'm still waiting outside my college – Hrida"*

'You really wished it, didn't you?' Raghu said smiling.

We ran out of the library making a lot of noise, leaving the medal bearers infuriated.

It took me forty-five minutes to reach her college. I could see her sitting on a bike parked in front of the college. I hopped off the bike as Raghu parked it at a distance behind her. Turning back, she smiled at me biting her lower lip trying hard not to laugh. She was glowing even in the gloomy light of the tube light. There was a moment of silence with both of us quietly smiling at each other. For the first time in nineteen years, I could literally feel my heart beating. People say it's butterflies in the stomach, but for me, it was a hurricane inside me making me unstable beyond limit. Blushing, I tucked my hands in my pockets and stood there staring at her, unable to speak. There was this mojo about her that gave me the same numbness every time I saw her. Everytime she smiled, with me, at me, for me, I was in a daze.

"I was worried I wouldn't get to see you today," she said and began to laugh.

I just continued blushing.

"It's okay if he smokes around me. Why does he have to stand a mile away?" she said looking at Raghu. I whistled to call him and he joined us.

"I don't mind riding triple seat," she said

"Oh, no, I'll take a rickshaw," Raghu said.

"You take the bike, I'll collect it later," I told Raghu.

"Ya ya, sounds perfect. We'll take the train," she said before Raghu could object.

The train station was a kilometre away. We walked instead of taking a rickshaw and her hand rubbed mine a couple of times. I had this intense urge to hold it, but Raghu's words were screaming in my head: *"do not scare her away."* So I resisted.

"How did you know?" I asked.

"I'm offended!!" she said.

"What do you mean?"

"Do you think I was so dumb that I wouldn't figure out your little arrangement?" she asked, really looking offended. I just smiled.

"I knew it since the pav bhaji day at Badshah."

"That early?" I asked shocked, as she laughed.

"But your appearance at the theatre was flawless. When I thought of it at home, I was quite amused at the coincidence."

"You thought about me?"

"Big deal!" She shrugged.

We jostled our way into a crowed local train. It's relatively easier to enter a gents compartment with a girl in tow. She negotiated a place to stand at the door with an uncle. I stood in front of her with both my hands on her sides. I was barely a few inches away from her face, but I ignored noticing her proximity to me. I had to look away, because looking at her meant being scarily close to her face.

"You smell nice," she said.

I turned to look at her and we ended staring in each other's eyes, smiling.

"*Beta station aagaya, aage jao warna utar nahi paaoge,*" the uncle brought us back to reality. We hurriedly got down.

Hrida lived minutes away from the train station. She asked me to go, but I insisted on walking her home.

"Heard you have a paper tomorrow," she said

"From whom?" I asked

"I have my sources too, you know," she winked.

"Have you been even keeping tabs on me?"

"Well, not exactly. I sometimes filter out what Neha keeps talking about," she said and smiled.

"Hrida..." I said as she looked at me, "I think I am in love with you." I was shit scared but I had to tell her how I felt.

There was a long silence till we walked to the gate of her building. She turned towards me and said, "Is it okay if I give you the answer tomorrow?"

"Okay, I'll wait for it," I said with a grin.

"All the best for your paper," she said as she left.

Having exams on your birthday is like divine punishment. Even if you are least bothered about the paper, people around simply stonewall you from any possibility of fun. The paper went clean as it came because I spent most of the time drawing margins and numbering the pages. I painstakingly wrote the answers to the questions I knew the answers to and then only the questions to ones whose answers I had no clue of.

I submitted my paper an hour-and-a-half before time. The professor raised her eyebrows but I was more interested in what was about to happen eleven kilometres away.

I tried calling Hrida but she cancelled the call. I checked the watch, It was 4 p.m., *Must be in class,* I thought. *I'll wait outside her college.*

I reached her college in twenty minutes. *"I'm waiting outside, near the PCO."* I messaged her. She didn't reply. Four cigarettes and an Aarey lassi later, I called her again. It was 5.30, and she cancelled the call again. Another forty-five minutes later, when almost every student in the college had left, I messaged her *"Where are you?"* She didn't reply. I called Neha and she told me Hrida hadn't come to college that day. I messaged Hrida again *"Hey, Neha said you didn't come to college today, hope you are okay?"* I waited for another thirty minutes outside her college for her reply before leaving.

It was past eight when I reached home. I went straight to my room and locked myself up.

"I'm waiting for your reply" I messaged her, but there was no reply again and I was going paranoid. I spent next two hours fretting about what might have happened to her. I had called Neha, Shashank, Raghu and anyone who could have any info on her. No one did.

It was at 11.45 p.m. when I got a message that read: *"I have a boyfriend. I'm sorry I should have told you sooner. Hope your paper was good."*

She didn't know it was my birthday, yet she had given me a gift. And that's how my nineteenth birthday came to an end.

2012

Winters in Mumbai can get chilly. Not as painful as Delhi or Pune, but cold enough to prompt Mumbaikars to pull out the warm clothes who otherwise are happy sweating all year. Eighteen years in Mumbai, and I had forgotten what real winter chill felt like. So even in the not so boastful low temperature of fourteen degrees, I cuddled under the quilt. The noise of my phone whirring on the side table woke me up. It was 7 a.m., It was a message from her.

"Open your door..."

It took me a while to pull myself out of the bed. I sauntered into the living room, my eyes half open, still trying to acclimatize with the awake world. I opened the door. There was a small box neatly gift-wrapped in white shiny paper, pink hearts of different sizes, and tied with a blue ribbon. Inside the box I found a four-inch long soft toy wearing a light blue t-shirt on which was written *'Binny Rabbit'*. Under it was a letter which read.

On this day, when god chose to send you to this planet,
I ask him to bless you with love, happiness and infinite
reasons to smile. I hope in all these years you've realised
that your smile makes a lot of hearts skip a beat.

Love, Aditi

The gift and the letter thing was a little too mushy for a thirty-year-old me, but I have to agree it brought a smile on my face. Me smiling had become a rare phenomenon. I had strictly reserved smiling for professional purposes.

After my return from LA, I had changed my number so it was going to be a quiet birthday. No calls, no messages and no expectations. I made myself a mug of coffee and sat at the window. The window had instantly become my favourite place when I first walked in; it was so spacious that even an ogre could stretch himself to take a nap. The view from the window was amazing. The yellowish light of the rising sun dispersed in the morning haze spread over the sea. I could see gently swaying small fishing boats docked at the makeshift pier, small huts with hanging fishing nets on the roof lining the shore, people jogging on the sea front, and children waiting for their school buses. Sipping on the coffee, I looked around the house. It resembled the storeroom of a shopping mall stacked with boxes stickered uniformly. The reality of living alone began to sink in.

I began to unpack the boxes. Curtains, bedsheets, clothes, utensils, more clothes, the microwave, buckets, and toiletries began to jump out. The house now resembled one raided by the income tax department. I opened the last box, and stared at it. It contained memorabilia of the seven years of my relationship with Hrida. I took the box and came back to the window. Going through the gifts we had given each other was like reading the synopsis of the life we had spent together. The photo album she made me on one of our anniversaries had a compilation our snaps with her comments. From an uncountable number of soft toys we had gifted to each other; dozens of love letters she had written; bus, train, and movie tickets of the special days we spent together; and hundreds of Polaroid snaps taken at parties, pubs, picnics, college festivals, and birthdays. There were music CDs she had made to cheer me up or for the dance parties we organised, a string of my guitar that she broke trying to play a song for me, and her handkerchief with which she had wiped a gaudy lipstick she tried at a shop (I had stolen it from her). There was a bag containing twenty-one gifts and a note with each one of them for my twenty-first birthday. It had a miniature whiskey bottle and a note *"what I can do to you, she can't;"* a pack of condoms and a note *"I know you won't need it but just in case to be safe;"* a t-shirt that said *"sold to the young lady besides me;"* and a pair of biking gloves with a note *"till the time I learn to ride"*.

I stopped looking at it.

It brought Hrida back to me. I could clearly relive my days with her. Her eyes which could read my thoughts, her enticing smile that left me with a whirlwind inside me, her kisses which made me feel loved, her warm hugs that made me feel wanted, her smell that made me long for her, feeling of her fingers gripping my hand, her touch that made me feel alive, It all came back. I had to stop. I hurriedly dumped everything in the box. It had been three years since I had broken up with her and I was still holding on to these things which only brought me pain. I had asked her to leave me forever. But I couldn't accept the fact that I had to live the next forty odd years of my life without her. I had to forget her. In a fit of rage I took the box to the dry area, threw in a crumpled newspaper, cracked the seal of the whiskey bottle and emptied half of it into the box and set it on fire. I watched every single thing burn. Tears started rolling down my face when I saw flames beginning to engulf a photo of us, first my side of the photograph and then gradually Hrida's face disappeared in fire. I broke down. It was the first time since the break up that I had cried. I gulped the remaining whiskey and threw the bottle in. I stood by it, crying for the fifty-six or so minutes that it burnt. But not anymore, I promised myself. In the past three years, I had scourged myself enough out of guilt. I had hurt too many lives in my pursuit of self-destruction. I had kicked away all the people who loved me. I didn't know how long I would live or who I'd live with, but I decided I was going to be happy.

I typed a number on my cell and stared at it. After musing for about twenty minutes, I dialled the number. When you behave like a jerk it, takes time to accept it, and it takes even more time to say sorry if you don't have enough guts in you. It took me two years to accept it, but I wasn't going to waste any more time to apologize. The caller tune at the other end died when no one answered. I waited for a moment and dialled again, a hideous voice again screamed at me to copy the caller tune later continuing to a song.

"Hello?" finally someone picked up, "Hello?" the voice said. I kept quiet.

"Hello?"

"Is it okay if I say sorry over the phone?" I said.

"Poncho?" Raghu said.

"How have you been man?" I said with a choked voice. There was a long pause.

"Happy birthday!" he said, his voice strained. "Where are you?"

"Below your office. Leave right now, we are going for lunch," I said commandingly. "I mean, can you leave right now?" I said correcting my tone.

He began to laugh.

Raghu had been working with his dad at his construction firm after completing his engineering. I took a chance and found him there. Raunak Uncle had a dream that one day Raghu and I would run his company, but as I said, I had hurt too many people.

I got out of the car as I saw him walk out of the lobby. Formal wear, leather shoes, gelled hair and a paunch. He had changed a lot. We hugged tightly and he even kissed me. If you want to feel what actual love is, hug someone who has really missed you and you'll know. He gave me a hearty punch in my stomach. I almost fell down with the impact.

"*Bhenchod*!" he said "How are you?"

"Less of a jerk than the last time we met," I smiled trying to conceal the pain.

"I missed you, man," he said.

"I missed you too... was just busy hating life."

We sat in the car.

"You look so fucking fit. Your filmy friends are getting to you?"

I laughed. "What happened to you? You look like Raunak Uncle's bonsai version."

We laughed.

The amount of things I had missed out on in the past years was unbelievable. I parked the car outside Cafe Gulshan in Matunga. The *kheema pav* and *bun maska* was our staple diet during college days.

'Milds right?' He asked as he bought a pack of cigarettes.

'No, I've quit!' I smiled.

'You are fucking with me, aren't you?'

'No, I'm serious. Its been nine months now.'

'Fuck, who *is* doing all this to you man!'

Lambu the waiter recognised us as we entered. I wondered who would name a four-feet-tall man Lambu. Whoever did so was cruel. We sat at our old corner table.

"*Do kheema, char bun maska, do* Thumbs Up," Raghu ordered.

Lambu repeated the order in a squeaky voice and left.

Back in the days, we called it the *durbean table*. It had a clear view of the main gate of the college across the road. We used to rate girls on ten and then those girls would have the privilege of getting hit on by us after college. Every morning before going to college, *Gul ki cutting chai* with the daily update on the girls was a must.

"Six, Nine, full ten, and four," Raghu murmured as he stared at the girls walking out of the gate. I smiled.

"Long time man," he said reminiscing our days. I nodded my head.

"So... tell me about her," I said noticing his ring. Radhika had told me about his engagement.

Lambu came back with our order.

"She is lovely..." he lit a cigarette. "Really nice, you know after all the Poojas and Priyankas and the XYZs, I really needed a Ruchika," he said as the smoke escaped out of his nostrils and mouth. There was a glint in his eyes when he spoke about her.

"After a while I figured I was incapable of finding myself a real girl to marry, so I just got it arranged," he shrugged and pushed the cigarette into the ash tray.

This came from a guy who seven years ago in a drunken debate with some random guys at the adjoining table at Pyaasa had declared, *"Jis din iss Raghuvir Joshi ne khudko arranged marriage ke hawale kar diya, usi din is gand pe Chutiya tattoo kar dena..."* pointing to his bare white ass.

"She is like my anchor, she like completely neutralizes me when I get out of hand." He began to laugh.

"I'm really happy for you man." I was glad that God had made someone to tame this crazy bastard.

"When is the wedding?" I said.

"23 December," he smiled wryly.

"Wow, that's close!" I called for the bill.

"I'm so happy you are back. I would have shot you had you missed the wedding like you missed Shashank's." He slapped my hand.

"Where is he?" I asked as I picked up the bill.

"Bangalore. Fuck, he is bloody pissed at you."

"He should be, for if it were me, I would have slaughtered him." I paid the bill.

"He is coming on the 21st. Let's do something."

"*Pakka.*"

As we came out of the cafe, we caught each other staring at the girls at the college gate.

"Good old days!" he said.

"Good old days!" I repeated after him and sat in the car.

2009

The noise of falling utensils woke me up in the morning. Two pigeons had rampaged the kitchen. I fought them with a frying pan in a half-sleep half-scared state. After winning the war, I came back to the bedroom and sat on the bed trying to restart my brain. Reality hit me hard. *I had broken up with her. I would never get to see her again.* I checked my cell phone; three missed calls from mom and Radhika each, and a message from Dad. Nothing from Hrida. It was really over. The riot in my head broke out again and not knowing how to deal with it, I went back to sleep.

At four in the evening, sleep finally decided to give up on me and I was left staring at the ceiling fan. I wondered if it could hypnotise me and make all the hurt disappear. After staring at it for don't know how long, I zombie-walked myself to the wash basin. Devika had left a post-it on the mirror

Good morning, chicken is on the menu today,
you'll have to microwave it, in case you need
an after meal hit there is a joint in the soap case in
the loo. I'll be back by 6, stay alive till then.

Love, Dev

I found a beer in the fridge, so I skipped the chicken which had sacrificed its life for me. I planted myself on the couch and put on the TV. Each and every channel had the dumbest of characters wearing awfully gaudy costumes, psychotically talking to themselves, plotting lamest of conspiracies like adding extra *namak* to the daal made by Savita, Kavita or Babita and making orgasimic faces after screwing the daal. One of the channels showed a promo of a show which had completed three thousand episodes. Who the fuck cares, I wondered. The people watching it abuse it; the actors, the directors, the spot boys, even the writers who write it, abuse it. I know it because I had assisted on one such production.

"Shooting a show after it loses its plot is like trying to have sex after losing erection," the director had said to me. Then who the bloody fuck cares? Actually no one does, and that is how this country works, I concluded.

I switched the TV off and got back to staring at things. Devika was terribly organised with her stuff. Her dad's job kept posting him in different cities every year, so after the second year of college, against her parents' wish, she chose to live in Mumbai with her grandparents. Since then, she hardly lived with them. It had been more than six years that she had been living alone, so the house hardly had anything that gave a familial feel to it. Right from the chillum with its holder to a two-feet-long, four-and a-half litre bottle of Chivas 12 in the showcase, everything was purely Devika.

Back in our college days, Hrida and I had spent many afternoons at her place. *Hrida.* And she was back in my thoughts. I went through every single thing I had said to her. I felt an inexplicable level of rancidness inside me. I was through with the beer and its alcohol content wasn't enough to daze my thoughts about her. I opened another bottle and gulped three hundred millilitres of the beer. One thing I had learnt about myself from my excessive college drinking days is that it took exactly ten minutes for the alcohol to kick in. So I pushed in another two hundred millilitres and caved in on the couch. One, two, three... I began counting numbers, trying hard not to let her thoughts kick in before the alcohol did. Would she be feeling the same pain? Did I actually mean nothing to her? Forty-eight, forty-nine, fifty... she'll come back, don't worry. No she won't; remember how you begged her not to? At seventy-four, I stopped counting.

"Seventy-five, seventy-six, seventy-seven..." Devika continued. I turned realising I had been so lost in counting out loud that I didn't notice her standing beside me.

"How long have you been standing here?" I asked.

"Since thirty-five," she said staring at me. "So it has come to this now?"

She turned to leave, I caught her right hand and pulled her close and held her hand against my face. I hugged her and rested my face on her belly. She leaned and kissed my hair.

"Give it a month, you'll feel better," she said as she stuffed the bowl of chicken in the microwave, "Trust me, the first month is the toughest." She began to place the plates on the dining table.

"Later it's a cake walk." She said as the microwave beeped.

"Come, let's eat."

I sat staring at the floor; she pulled me up by my arm.

"You should have called mom," she said as she stirred the chicken with the ladle.

"You spoke to her?" I said.

"Ya she called me in the afternoon." She served me the chicken, "She said that Uncle found your bike in Greenwood Park in an abandoned state."

"I didn't abandon it. I had parked it there yesterday," I snapped back. "Fuss is their fuel, they can't live without it."

"How did you get a rickshaw at night?"

"I didn't." I tried to avoid giving rest of the details.

"Then?"

"I walked"

"You walked eleven kilometres?" She began to laugh.

"I think I should start growing these at home," she said smiling naughtily as she licked the Rizla to tape the joint. I lit my joint and pulled in a long drag and shrugged as a reply to her. She pulled in a long drag as she caved in on the couch beside me.

"Do you think she ever loved me?" I asked but she didn't say anything. I got up from the chair and came to the edge of the open air gallery overlooking the Eastern express highway.

"Do you think I'll land up on the highway if I jump from here?" Then calculating the distance I said, "If I take a run up all the way from the living room?"

"I think you should open the main door. You'll get another five feet for your run up," she said trying to control her giggles.

She rose from the chair and walked to me. She gently clutched my hand, "Don't worry, you will be loved," she said and kissed it.

I put my arm around her waist and rested my forehead on her shoulder. Thank God for Devika! The hurt and the pain had been pacified for a while. But how would I forget her? What was I going to do?

The door bell rang.

"It's past twelve, who the hell can it be?" I said, flinging the joint out of the balcony. It hit the compound wall. *Ouch!*

"Your Dad. I called him," she said as she went to open the door. "You have to go back home some day. We are not married, you know."

She opened the door.

The 'abandoning the bike and disappearing act' pushed my parents to ground their twenty-seven-year-old son for a month. In a way it worked for me because all the calls from work or friends would be filtered by mom, so I didn't have to explain my 'deserting life' act to anyone. I stayed locked up in my room all day. I would eat my dinner in my room too. After Radhika got married, I was the one my mom would hound with her questions, calls and restrictions. "You'll know when you have kids," she silenced all my protests.

One day, late in the afternoon, I heard my mom speaking to someone. From her tone and excessive cordiality, I could tell it was a girl. She screamed my name to call me.

"It's Devika..." she said, then covering the mouth piece of the phone she threatened me "...you better behave yourself or next time I'll chain you." No matter how old you are, you'll always be sacred of your mother's angry eyes and god had given extra scary touches to my mother's eyes. "Hello," I said.

"Be ready by eight. Kartik and I will pick you up," she ordered.

"Where are we going?"

"Raghu's arranged a party for Shashank."

"For what? Oh shit!" It was 19 December. Shashank's birthday.

"You didn't wish him, did you?

"Hang up," I said.

"Bye, be ready..." She said "... and the party is a surprise, so don't blow it up."

I dialled Shashank's number but it was out of coverage area. Birthdays weren't a big deal for us, but since the time Shashank went to the US for his MBA, there had not been one decent party we had attended. Now when he was back we decided to throw him a party. It had been in planning for months, but after the break up my brains had been too fried to remember anything.

Kartik picked me up at quarter to eight. Devika wasn't in the car. He told me she wasn't ready so he picked me first. His car was a cherry red 1994 Ford Crown Victoria. It looked like one of those cars used in New York as cabs. I wondered where he'd gotten it in India from. He told me he had worked on it in his father's garage and fitted it with some random sports car engine which he bought as scrap. The doors made queering noises and seats were damp. Its interior smelled like it was an address to a rat's grave. I daringly sat in the car.

'So, Arjun, how do you like my baby's roar, *haan*? He asked attempting a weird accent while he inhumanly throttled the car. To me it felt more like a buffalo's snore than a roar.

Kartik, like his car, was of random make. Five feet six inches in height and dairy milk brown in colour, he was partly bald and had the rest of the hair cropped like an army cadet. He had a paunch too. Devika had been dating this bozo for five months. When we first met him, all of us took turns to go to the loo to laugh. Whenever in conversation with him, I had an acute itch of mimicking his fake accent, but for Devika's sake, I behaved myself.

Devika was waiting at the gate when we reached. For an instant I thought I saw Kartik actually slurp his drool off his lips when he saw her, but I don't blame him because for the first time in all these years, even I checked Devika out. A knee-length blue off shoulder dress made her look even fairer. A black belt with red stones on the buckle, red stilettos with a clutch completed her outfit. Highlighted cheek bones, blue eyeliner combined with pink eye gloss and the extra something that she did to her naturally pouting lips made them look more luscious and kissable. She was truly drool-worthy. She hugged me as I got out of the car. She smelled awesome. She sat in the front and I took the seat behind Kartik.

"Why are we leaving the city?" I asked as the car swerved on to the highway.

"Because the party is in Khandala," Devika replied.

"Wow!" I fist pumped.

"Isn't it great?" Kartik said, clearly missing the sarcasm.

Devika slapped my knee as I chuckled. It was going to be a highly enjoyable two-hour ride, listening to awkward gear shifts forcing the car to wail like an animal being butchered.

I cursed myself for taking the back seat as the car's air conditioner only cooled the front of the car. I was so cooked that anyone could have easily taken a bite of me. I looked like I had taken a shower with my clothes on. I was never sitting in that car again, I promised myself. Finally, the beats of the music could be heard from the farm house. I jumped out of the car as soon as it halted and walked to the desk at the entrance.

"Arjun..." I told the bouncer at the entrance.

"Stag for now, sir?" he winked at me checking my name on the list.

"Yes," I said realising it was the first time in seven years that I was walking alone to the party.

Raghu saw me and came running to me with a bottle of tequila and pushed a nice sixty millilitres shot down my throat. He pulled me inside while Devika and Kartik followed us.

The party pimp had done it again – poolside dance floor, open bar, more girls than guys, empty rooms and mind blowing music – everything typically Raghu. Our college friends, long lost girls from school, their friends from college, chat friends, Facebook girls, random girls, girls we met at the events we worked on, and even the girls we met at James Coffeewala and Pyaasa were there. This bastard had been in touch with every single one of them. I have to confess that for a minute I felt like a hungry man in a free for all cafeteria. But the happiness didn't last for long.

"Where the fuck is Hrida?" Raghu asked as he pushed another shot of tequila in my mouth. I didn't say anything, and a girl pulled Raghu on the dance floor. I headed straight for the bar, and swigged down a mouthful of whiskey.

As Shashank entered, a spot light followed him on the dark dance floor and led him to the cake. The lights came on and there were screams and *woohoos* wishing him. The girl he had brought with him fed him the cake. The tequila and the whiskey had begun to kick in. The volume of the music increased and the lights began to move faster. Raghu pulled me on the dance floor. I flicked a bottle from the bar and followed him. Shashank kissed me as soon as he saw me. I couldn't tell if it was the music or the whiskey that was intoxicating, but I didn't care as long as it kept Hrida's thoughts away from me. One more sip directly from the bottle and my body began to move, the substandard downmarket moves breaking out of me. Within minutes I was dancing alone in the middle of the dance floor. A cheering crowd circled me. Raghu and Shashank joined in; I looked for Devika and pulled her in too. Kartik followed us. The world around me began to spin. I gazed at the people around. As the music got wilder, I emptied the bottle, took a deep breath and closed my eyes. Hrida was smiling at me saying she loved me and that she'd kill me if I ever went away from her.

"I love you too..." I slurred.

I felt my hands holding a female body by the waist. Her hands cupped my hands and her body began to sway with mine.

"Just be close to me, always..." I said, my eyes still closed.

"I will," the girl said as she turned around facing me. I opened my eyes. My hands still feeling her body slid further down her waist. Her face was an inch away from mine. I blinked my eyes twice in the hope to register her face, but I could only see her blurred image. I suddenly felt lip-glossed lips kissing me; strangely even in the loud music I could hear her breathing heavily. It took a few minutes before I reciprocated. She let me loose for a second, looked at me and then caught my hand to pull me away from the dance floor. The music began to fade. I was out of the party. And the kissing and gnawing of our lips began again.

"Poncho, what the hell?" Raghu's voice whispered in my ears. The girl was now biting my neck.

"*Chutia*, are you fucking out of your mind," he asked in a hissing voice. "What if Hrida finds out?"

"Nothing will happen, she's already left." I giggled. Shashank joined us.

"What do you mean she left?" Shashank said.

"She is gone. Out... of my... life." I whipped my hand in the air like a sword.

"He is zonked; I'll take him upstairs." Shashank began to pull me by my hand.

"I broke up with Hrida," I said pulling back my hand.

"You what?" Raghu yapped. "Why?"

"What happened?" Shashank asked in a relatively less agitated tone.

I silently walked away.

"Hello boss? I asked why?" Raghu asked.

"She fell out of love with me."

2001

I dialled Raghu's number and left a missed call, a standard procedure of intimating each other. Why waste two rupees fifty paisa on a call? Five minutes later, he came down with the cake. It was twenty minutes to midnight. I started my bike and hit the highway rather than taking the alleys and pulled the throttle realising we were not going to make it to Shashank's place before twelve. I quietly enjoyed the cool December night air brushing my face. I caught Raghu's eye staring at me in the rear view mirror and raised my eyebrows to ask what happened.

"What does he do?" Raghu asked.

"Who?" I tried to sound as oblivious as possible.

"You know..." he ate the rest of his sentence.

"You know who?" I said adjusting the mirror for the conversation.

"The boyfriend," Raghu asked sounding more uncomfortable than I would have been.

"I don't know, and actually I don't care." I raised the speed.

"You should at least know whom you are competing with," he held me by the shoulder as I braked for a municipal corporation funded crater.

"There is no competition, Raghu. She has a *boyfriend* that means she is *not available*, so there *is* no competition." I said as I made a sharp turn to enter Shashank's complex.

"But this is ridiculous man, shouldn't she have told you earlier?" Raghu said getting off the bike as I parked it.

"Look, it was my mistake." I was surprised at my defensive tone. "But it's over now. Honestly I've forgotten about her," I lied. "Anyway, it's Sachdev's birthday, so let's not botch it up with my *chuttadgiri*. Seriously, I'm fine." Raghu stared at me knowing I was lying.

"Hurry up, just two minutes left." Raghu said and poked the candles in the cake. I lit them with my lighter while Raghu rang the door bell.

"Happy birthday, Slutty... Happy birthday oh dear Slutty..." we began to sing as Shashank opened the door. We made him cut the cake at the door itself. Raghu plastered most of the cake on his face and I followed.

"Put some more," Neha whooped.

"Hey, you are here too? Swift move, Slutty." Raghu elbowed Sachdev and hugged Neha.

I froze when I saw Hrida sitting on the couch. It had been twenty-two days since I had seen her. She was wearing the same purple t-shirt and black jeans that she had worn the last time I had seen her. The only additions were her hair that she had pulled back with a hair band and her eyes carved with *kajal*.

Shashank cut the cake that Neha had gotten for him. She gifted him a shirt and ordered him to wear it. He obediently went to his room and came back wearing it. I occasionally peeked at Hrida from the corner of my eyes trying to avoid direct eye contact.

"Arjun, Rageshwari misses you very much." Neha said noticing me stealing glances at Hrida.

"Who?" I asked confused.

"Your sweetheart ya... the girl you were eyeballing in the theatre that day?"

"The Third Girl" I said to myself. Everyone began to laugh at me. I looked at Hrida sheepishly. She smiled at me forcing my heart to jump in the ribcage. Her glowing face, her eyes trying to figure out my thoughts, that mischievous smile, pink kiss ready lips, and then, *I have a boyfriend!* Her voice screamed her message in my head. It was getting unbearable to be around her. I was sure I would do something nasty. I messaged Raghu asking him to wrap up. Raghu looked at me; realising my discomfort, he stood up stretching his back.

"Let's go honey, I won't let these monsters bully you anymore," he told me as everyone laughed.

"Wait I'll drop you." Shashank said. "Let Hrida go with Arjun... they stay close by." Shashank's arrangement had stunned me a little so I didn't see it clearly, but I think he winked at Raghu while Neha and Hrida exchanged a look.

I started the bike and Hrida climbed on it as if it were a horse, first standing on the foot rest with her left leg and then throwing her right leg across practically wobbling the whole bike. She clenched the shaft behind her with both hands. I could see her face in the left mirror. In the right mirror, I saw Neha clutching Shashank's arm and jumping up with a smile as we left. There was something cooking.

I exited the complex compound and took the highway. It was twelve-thirty and the temperature had dipped significantly. A smile popped up as the cool air swept Hrida's face. For the next seven minute or so, there was fluttering sound of wind and my eyes shuttling between concentrating on the road and looking at Hrida's smiling face in the mirror. If it was one of the Priyankas or Poojas, I would have made my move, but with

Hrida, it felt horribly wrong to keep looking at her knowing that she had a boyfriend. Just one more time I convinced my high-principled self. As I shifted my eyes from the road into the mirror, I gawked right into the big dark brown eyes. She smiled at me and I looked away.

"You know I owe you a humongous apology, right?" she said. I peeked at her again, defying my mind's ethical authority.

"For?" I decided to show my resentment by using bare minimum words to reply.

"Ruining your birthday?"

"You didn't," I said with a straight face.

"Hmm." I knew she was looking at me, but now the lovelorn moron inside me insisted on acting pricey, so I concentrated on the road. A few more minutes of silence passed before she spoke again.

"I have to tell you something... about the message I sent you that day."

"There's more?" I said sarcastically. I hated the fact that she had a boyfriend and no matter how many explanations were given, the fact that she would not be mine would remain constant and that was killing me.

"Yes," she said attempting to look through my hostility. "I've been thinking about talking to you for a while and..."

"Thinking for twenty-two days! Is the decision finally made?" I cut her short and took a turn into the by-lanes of her locality.

"I'm sorry. I should have explained it to you earlier," she said quietly.

"Oh please, don't bother. I'm used to getting jerked by girls like you," I snapped back.

"Girls like you? What the fuck is wrong with you" I wanted to smack myself, but it was too late. I was fuming ever since

that ill-fated day. I had contemplated the use of all ways – from messaging, to calling, to mailing, even writing a letter to vent out my anguish but the male chauvinist pig who owns point one percent stake in my brain did not permit me.

Finally I saw a frown on her face that satiated my itch to piss her off.

There was dead silence on the bike and dogs were barking in the background. I stopped near her building gate.

She left without saying anything. I started the bike as she entered the gate. Halfway into the building, she walked back.

"The boyfriend I told you about... he doesn't exist for me anymore," she said.

"Wh...what do you mean?" I asked as my brain only processed the words *boyfriend... doesn't... exist... anymore...*

"Too late, you had your chance to know the details," she smiled snobbishly and left.

I stood there experiencing happiness, frustration, confusion and love...all at the same time.

I tried her number, but it was switched off, so I called Shashank. He cancelled the call. I had to know what was happening. In desperation, I called Neha, but she didn't answer either. Shashank sent me a message which read *'Rghu'*. I called Raghu.

"Where are you guys?" I almost yelled.

"I'm standing outside the car," he replied.

"Where is Sachdev?"

"Inside the car..." he paused "...snogging"

"Bang the door and pull him out... I'll meet you guys at Pyaasa."

"I'll try." He hung up.

Pyaasa was a round the clock bar opened by Bada Anna in the memory of his younger brother Chota Anna who had died in a car crash. Since its opening thirty-five years ago, Bada Anna's only motive in life was relieving people of their miseries by getting them drunk. At night Pyaasa had a special management for the customers. The cops stood guard at the gate of the compound making sure no one interrupted Anna's social service. The three floors of the bar made sure every miserable, unhappy, dejected soul coming to Pyaasa's doorstep quenched his thirst. Subbu the special 'captain' who stood at the door made sure regular patrons got their regular seats on the top two floors which overlooked the lake.

After waiting for over an hour on my bike, my back began to hurt. I dialled Raghu's number for the sixth time, but before the call could connect, Shashank's car pulled up at the gate. The boys along with Neha got down. I was a bit bugged seeing her.

"How many?" Subbu asked.

"Four," I said.

"Ladies there no?"

"Yes, Subbu, thirty-four number *dena* please," Raghu said.

The tables from thirty-one to forty were cabins specially meant for guys who brought girls with them, and thirty-four was a secluded cabin with comparatively less noise made by happy high customers who Anna freed from their miseries.

The waiter escorted us through the service stairs used by hotel staff to the third floor which led to a passage that directly took us to the table discounting Neha of the embarrassment of being X-rayed by drunken eyes. She and Shashank cozied up on the sofa while I slid on the inner side of the sofa facing the floor captain.

"Will you guys care to tell me what hell is going on?" I said

"What do you mean? Nothing is on, man." Shashank said as he adjusted his arm around Neha's waist.

"I saw you wink at Raghu."

The floor captain came for the order and the suspense was beginning to kill me. Raghu gave him our orders.

"Focus guys!" I yelled.

The captain came back, "Nothing get a bottle of water," Raghu shooed him away.

"Why are you so worked up?" Neha asked.

"Didn't you guys set me up to drop her?"

"Yeah, we did, because Hrida asked me to," Neha said.

"I suck!"

"Poncho kill the drama already!" Raghu begged.

"She was trying to say something about her boyfriend but I deliberately ridiculed her so she got pissed and left without saying anything." the waiter came back with our order, and made our respective drinks.

"Why would you do that?" Shashank asked.

"Because I'm a dick," I cursed myself. "Now please can you tell me about this boyfriend?"

"*Aare*, she was seeing this guy in school who was our senior. He shifted out of town after school. He was in touch with her, but later he just disappeared. He changed his number and stopped responding to her mails and all. It's been two years now," Neha paused to take a sip.

"Continue." I said impatiently.

"Nothing ya... this guy is a ghost. He has just disappeared. It's not that she still longs for him or anything like that, she just wants to officially break-up with him before getting involved with anyone, but that hasn't happened.

Yesterday we had a night long discussion about you and the message she sent you. I asked her to simply forget him and respond to you. She just told me that she wanted to meet you alone for a while... that's it."

"Shit, shit, shit," I yelled. The waiter ran to us again.

"Nothing, repeat the order," Raghu said. "You continue."

"I'm so jinxed man. I royally fucked a potentially romantic moment with my hung up shit." I gulped the first drink as the waiter made a second one.

"Don't worry *yaar, hota hai,* and I think she loves you too. So chill," Neha said and got back to getting naughty with Shashank.

Three drinks later, I messaged her, *"I know you love me so why don't you just say it."*

It was a huge turn off, she told me years later.

For a week after that night at Pyaasa, I called Hrida once every morning and evening to which she responded either by cancelling the call or by letting the phone ring. I messaged her a couple of times a day. Depending on my mood, the content of my messages ranged from saying sorry to telling her that she was over-reacting, from begging her to forget my stupidity to telling her that I was never going to bother her again but there was no reply from her. I would have met her outside her college but it was vacation time so the colleges were closed. I tried getting to her through Neha, but she stopped taking her calls too.

"I'm telling you she is psycho. Can't you see it." Raghu said. I threw a lit cigarette at him in anger.

Neha was perhaps right in saying that it was a matter of time. Maybe Hrida was overreacting and she would be fine in a few days. Maybe Raghu was right. What if she was really a psycho. Maybe her boyfriend had come back and she was happy with him.

I crashed on my bed with all kinds of 'maybes' whirling in my mind. In the past one month, Hrida had practically turned my life upside down. I was in love, I was frustrated, I was happy, I was irritated, I was confused, I was helpless, and I was anxious. I chose the final maybe that came to my mind, "Maybe I should accept the fact that we weren't meant to be and forget her."

I bade goodbye to all the thoughts and closed my eyes to sleep, hoping to clear my mind.

2009

After Shashank's party, I went into a self-imposed exile. I couldn't accept Hrida's absence from my life. There had not been a single attempt from her to get in touch with me and that made it impossible for me to live. The riot in my head had been replaced by endless conversations between my own voices.

"Has she forgotten me?" Voice One said.

"Yes looks like it. Maybe she is already dating someone else," Voice Two replied.

"No, can't be," Voice One stressed.

"Why not?" Voice Three asked.

"Because..." Voice One had no answer. The rest of the voices began to laugh.

"See, even you know it," Voice Two continued bullying. Voice One began to weep.

"Look at this loser, it is because of him that we didn't have any life in the past seven years."

"Yes you are right. Remember how we blew that sweet seventeen-year-old horny girl at Bittu's sangeet." Voice Three said referring to a girl I met at Malini Didi's sister-in-law's wedding.

"She was Jiju's cousin, you asshole," Voice One yelled.

"What about Roxy?" Voice Four asked.

"Who Roxy? Voice Three enquired.

"That girl we met in Chandigarh for that shoot."

"Hrida was with me then, and I couldn't cheat on her." Voice One yelled again.

"Fair enough, where is Hrida now?" Voice Four asked

"Probably in bed with a guy with a Greek-god-like body," Voice Five said.

"Shut up!!! Shut up!!! Shut up!!!" Voice One wailed.

I opened my eyes, switched on my laptop, and googled *'Most painless ways to commit suicide'*

I clicked the first link that appeared, it said:

'101 foolproof and original ways to end your own existence on earth'

- Jump from an helicopter into a valley,
- Create a spark at a gas station and blow yourself up,
- Get plastered with explosives and blast yourself in parliament. In case you change you mind at the last moment, the guards will kill you; and if you succeed, at least you'll do some good to you country before you die,
- Sneak into a space shuttle and lie beneath the big-ass fire nozzles,
- Lie down on a railway track and pay someone to tie you in case you choose to run away...

There was not one thing that I could use right at that moment. Plus, I wanted something painless that would kill me instantly. The pain I was already experiencing was enough to last for next seven lives. I didn't want any more of it.

I ran into the bathroom, locked myself up, and hastily quested for it in the cabinet above the water tank for a few minutes before I finally found it. Phenol. My end. The study of organic chemistry in high school came in handy.

"Phenol is a strong neurotoxin and when mixed in the blood stream it shuts down neural transmission system and can kill a human body instantly."

I had to make sure that I gulped a nice mouthful because if I didn't die, my mother would kill me slowly with her melodramatic lectures.

I made myself comfortable on the pot and opened the cap of the bottle. I took a deep breath and put the bottle to my mouth. As soon as the contents entered my mouth I felt a horrendous burning sensation. And just as it was about to reach my epiglottis, the voices of all the people I loved screamed in my mind asking me to stop.

"Oh shit I'm actually killing myself!"

All of a sudden, I spat it all out. I panicked that I was going to die and shoved my head into bucket filled with water. My mouth was on fire. I spent the rest of the night cleansing it.

"See the gutless loser can't even kill himself," a voice mocked me, and the mental torture began all over again.

One morning, five days after my almost suicide day, I was having breakfast with my dad.

"Someone broke you heart, buddy?" Dad asked.

"Haan..." I mumbled coming out of my lost world. "No, nothing like that." I said and smiled.

"You haven't been eating," he said looking at my plate.

"I'm alright. I'm not feeling hungry," I was so hungry that I could have eaten an elephant. I hadn't eaten in days. My mouth was so sore due to the stunt I pulled off the other night that I could barely drink water.

"So what plans for the new year?" Dad asked.

"Nothing yet, but will do something."

"Cool. We are going to the City Club with Raunak Uncle's family. Tell me if you kids want to come. I'll put your name on the list," he said.

"Sure, I'll let you know."

I wasn't excited about it. Besides, Shashank and Raghu would have plans with their respective girlfriends. Then it suddenly hit me that it was the first time in the history of our friendship that Raghu, Shashank and I were single at the same time. Since school days there was someone or the other with either of us. No girl was ever good enough for Raghu so he was single most of the time. Shashank's love stories couldn't last for more than a month or two. But somehow his relationship with Neha lasted for six years while I was with Hrida for seven years. Shashank broke up with her some time after he went to the US. After my break up with Hrida, it was as if the Almighty had blessed the three of us with the ultimate era of bachelorhood. I called Raghu and asked him to meet me at the naka with Shashank.

The naka was originally a municipal corporation transport bus stop on the service lanes of eastern express highway which was encroached and transformed into a cigarette and chai stall. It had a four table seating arrangement where you could munch on *bhajiya* and other snacks with chai all day long. We had innumerous memories of this place. Raghu had discovered it back in the engineering days and it soon became the place to come to when we bunked college. We'd practically live in this shanty from morning till evening. Life was so much fun back then, I thought.

"Five milds and a lighter," I told the guy at the stall. I lit a cigarette and took our table.

I noticed the guy beside me. I thought I'd seen him somewhere, his charm was very familiar. I asked who he was.

'Narayan Kaka's son.' The stall owner said and smiled.

I smiled too.

Cut to a few years back:

The age group of friends we made at naka ranged from fifteen to eighty. But out of all of them there was this one person who touched my life. A grim looking eighty-year-old man, white hair, dark-complexioned, wrinkled face, body a bit frail but showed signs of what would once have been a hefty physique. He would come in everyday at the same time and smoke his Navy Cut and leave; he was never out of schedule, for years I saw him like that.

Then one day after his first cigarette instead of leaving he sat on a chair besides me at the stall and ordered a chai. There was something about this guy that made me smile every time I saw him. That day there was something off with him. I wanted to ask, but didn't. He smiled back when he saw me staring at him.

'Do you need anything *Aajoba?*' I asked as I saw him look for something.

'Do you have a light?' He said with his Navy Cut in mouth, I gave him my lighter. 'Call me Naaru,' he said as he lit his cigarette and took a long drag.

'OK, Naaru *kaka,*' I said.

'Just Naaru, makes me feel good.'

'OK Naaru.' I said hesitantly, trying to make a man four times my age happy by calling him by his name.

'Plus it feels friendly. At my age, you don't have too many friends you know.' He smiled, even though there was a mild sadness in it.

'You look a bit uncomfortable today. Is everything alright?' I asked.

'I lost a friend today...' though he subtly wiped it I noticed the moistness in his eyes '...we were friends for seventy years.' He smiled.

'I'm sorry, Naaru.' I said, not knowing what to say.

'Oh come on, don't be sorry. I'll be next.' This time he grinned. 'Till then be my friend, trust me, it gets horribly lonely up here at eighty.'

'I will,' I said.

'Live the friends you have, memories are all you are left with in your last days.' He patted my back lovingly and left smiling.

Months later, when me and Raghu went for his funeral, no one recognized us. Like us, there were hundred others who his family didn't know, but all of them were his friends.

Raghu's smack on my head brought me back; the five cigarettes I had bought were in ashes. I needed more; Raghu bought them for me.

"So what's up?" Shashank asked.

"Let's go out for New Year's... out of town I mean," I said.

"Wow, someone seems liberated," Raghu chuckled.

"Have you guys noticed that all of us are single?" I said.

"Ya, but where do we go?" Shashank asked.

"Any place full of girls, booze and dope," Raghu said excitedly.

"Bangkok!" Shashank said

"Bali, Bali, Bali," Raghu insisted.

"Goa," I said.

After an hour, when almost each and every country in the world had been suggested, we finally locked down on Goa.

Goa. The sight of sun setting in the sea and its yellowish orange light lighting up the white sand beach already glamorised by bare imported human bodies was enough to take away one's worries, for a while at least.

Trinity, a tent suite resort, spread over sprawling fifty acres of land shared a two-feet white compound wall with the whitest of sands of Ashwem beach. The only reason we got the last minute reservation was my dad's friendship with its owner Mr Charan Awesome. Yes his last name was *'Awesome'*. I had laughed my lungs out the first time I had heard of him. But the man by all means deserved his last name. He literally was a younger version of cricketer Imran Khan. He was six-feet-three and had neck length grey curly hair. His fair skin was tanned by all the fun and heat endowed upon him by Goa. His light blue eyes twinkled behind the rimless glasses and lean well-worked-out body was any girl's dream.

"Hi..." I said not sure if I should call him uncle.

"Hey, hi..." he said in a very cheerful voice and shook my hand. "Tell me how can I help you?"

"I'm Arjun Kulkarni," I said hoping he would remember his conversation with my dad.

"Oh yes, Arjun... how are you, buddy?" he said and whistled out to a guy and gestured him to get the keys. "Number one," he yelled, "How's Arvind?"

"He's fine," I said.

"It's the best room I have here. You are going to love it," he said as he walked us across the white sand to our tent.

"I'm really thankful to you for letting us in on such a short..."

He cut me short.

"Oh skip the formalities, buddy. Your dad and I are school time *gotis*," he said handing me the card to the room. "Just have fun, I'll be happy," he smiled.

"Thanks." Shashank said.

Anyway, boys, let me wrap a few things up then we'll have dinner together?"

"Sure, thanks," I said.

"Here, take these." He pulled a cigarette box full of joints from his pocket and handed it to me. "Have fun," he winked at me and left.

The 'tent' was a twenty by twenty room with wooden flooring. A huge round bed big enough for five people and covered by drapes suspended from the ceiling occupied the centre. A Jacuzzi in the bath with its windows facing the beach lent a view of bare bodied girls. It was paradise for single horny boys. Raghu and Shashank jumped in the tub to warm their bodies. I lit a joint and strolled on the beach, the wind blowing my hair and my feet sinking in the warm white sand. A couple of bikini-clad girls smiled at me. *Later* I said to them in my mind, for now it was the mind blowing view of the sunset. For the first time in months since my break-up, my mind was blank. I sat there feeling the warm breeze and looking at the sun go down. I took a long drag and held the smoke. A smile grew on my face as the marijuana began to kick in. *You don't need anyone to make you happy,* I told myself.

At 10.30 in the night, I was woken up by persistent knocks on the door. I sleepwalked up to the door and opened it. It was the hotel attendant who had come to tell us that dinner was served. Raghu and Shashank had disappeared so I got ready and left to meet the stud. Awesome was waiting for me in the restaurant.

"Come, have a seat."

He got up and hugged me. The happy smile and the slight sway in the walk highlighted the effects of the pot that he smelled of. "Where are Raghu and Shashank?"

"Don't know, maybe they went to the city."

"Okay, what will you drink?"

"Beer's fine."

The attendant standing beside him rushed to fetch it.

"Uncle, thanks again for squeezing a room out for us. I know how hard it must have been," I said almost mumbling the word 'uncle'.

"Are you kidding me. I'm so happy you guys are here." The waiter came back with my beer. "I would have vacated the entire property for you boys."

Two hours, a delicious dinner and nine beers later, the conversation steered to girls.

"I hear someone broke you heart."

A wave of shock cruised through my blood stream when my mind registered what he said.

"Ho... how did you know?" I asked.

"Arvind told me," he said calmly as he took a sip of his single malt on the rocks.

"Dad?"

The wave of shock hit me with twice the force this time.

"What the fuck!" It came out louder than I wanted it to.

"I'm sorry. I shouldn't have brought it up. It's none of my business," he said.

"Oh no... I didn't mean to, I just, it's just..." my mind struggled to fish out suitable words out of the riot that had broken out inside my head,

"How did dad come to know? Does that mean mom knew too? Who would tell them? Devika? Shashank? Raghu? Why would they tell them? Shit, shit shit."

"It's just painful, isn't it? I know," he paused and lit a joint. "Its been thirty years since I got my heart broken," he said and pulled in a long drag.

"But no matter how much time passes, the pain and the helplessness remains," he said as the smoke escaped out of his nose and mouth.

"I'm sorry. What happened?" I asked.

"It all began with her smile. Lata and her family were our tenants. I would go to collect the rent, and every time I went, a smile waited for me. I wanted to see more of her so I began to follow her to her college. I would wait outside for the whole day so that I could follow her back home. Eventually following her graduated to walking with her and the smile developed into holding hands. Life with her was bliss. We were seeing each other for three years," he said as he emptied the contents of his glass.

"One day her father found out about us and he decided to marry her off to a Tamilian IIT engineer. I was simply rejected for being a rich, non-Tamilian arts graduate. I tried hard to convince him but in vain. What surprised me was she said nothing and instead she quietly married the engineer," he took a gulp of the whiskey directly from the bottle.

"The picture of her marriage still makes me scream my heart out, but what's the point. For years after that, my dad tried to get me married. Every girl more beautiful and wealthier than the previous one, but my heart belonged to the dusky Tamilian girl who now belonged to someone else," he dabbed the tears that had filled his eyes.

"Did you ever meet her again?" I asked.

He smiled, "When life decides to play dirty, it does cruel things to you. I met her ten years back. She was here with her husband and son for a vacation. The pain resurfaced again. Her smile, her warmth, her eyes – nothing had changed. I could clearly tell from those eyes that the love for me still lived in her heart, but as I said, what's the point."

"Since then, she comes here every three years or so. I make her jealous by hugging and kissing younger firang girls," he giggled.

"But when I look at her, I realise I have missed out on a whole chapter called marriage. I gave up on life after she left, but she moved on. She is a wife and a mother who takes care of her family. I'm still the same twenty-four-year- old she left. Honestly, I'm very happy with my life right now, but sometimes when the crowd goes back home, and the villas and beaches are empty, I feel the need to hold on to someone." For the first time since I met him, I saw an aging man with a broken heart.

"When you are young and heartbroken, you easily decide that you'll live alone all your life. Trust me it doesn't feel good to be alone at my age, so... take your time to heal your heart, but someday, when love knocks on your door, open it!" He said as he got up from his chair.

"Okay? now enough of the storytelling. You go to sleep and I'll see you tomorrow," he said and walked away into the darkness of the silent white sand beach.

I sat between the dancing fairy lights hung all over the resort feeling the cool breeze and listening to sounds of the sea. What Awesome said made perfect sense, but at that moment, I just wanted to be alone.

Give yourself some time, you'll survive, I told myself.

The new year's eve party at Trinity was a glamorous affair. Awesome had converted the whole resort into a dance floor; six DJs that he flew down from Amsterdam created euphoria with their music while skimpily dressed sexy models serving alcohol at bar counters located at every hundred feet made sure people got drunk. A huge digital clock showed the time. Awesome kept a watch on his party with the security head from the gallery built beside the DJs' console. Either it was the party or there was something about Goa that made otherwise shy girls go wild smooching and hugging random strangers when it hit midnight. The boys and I were dancing with one such group of girls.

After three hours of dancing, we took the girls to our room for a joint session which ultimately ended up in six bodies sexually romping in pairs of two. Shashank took the huge bed with his Delhi girl, Raghu took the smaller spare bed with the Delhi girl's US return friend, and I took the couch with a little plump *Firang* friend, of the friend, of the Delhi girl. As horny teenagers we had wished for an orgy, but I never thought it would actually ever happen, at least after meeting Hrida. A while later, I realised that the firang tongue wagging inside my mouth had disappeared and I opened my eyes to see the girl kissing Raghu. I almost puked at the thought of the same tongue slobbering our mouths at the same time. Swaying and swinging, I left the room.

An hour later, Shashank and Raghu found me on the beach.

"Come hither my love, let my lips kiss you," Raghu said as he fell on me trying to hold my face. Shashank jumped on us and we began to laugh.

"Do you realise we kind of kissed each other?" I said grimacing.

"But why the fuck would you guys kiss the same girl?" Shashank said as he got up.

"Because I don't like copulating with dead bodies," Raghu yapped. "Bloody dork started snoring half-way man," he said while we guffawed. "Anyway this moron was going nowhere beyond first base, so I jumped in."

"Oh fuck you, I just gave her up for you," I said.

"My girl knew her stuff man... pure pleasure," Shashank boasted.

"Seriously speaking, I don't think I'll be ever able to sleep with anybody else," I said. "I keep seeing her every time I'm making out."

"Poncho, lose the cheesy crap, man, its freaking me out now," Raghu said slurring.

"I love her, man!"

"It's been around three months now, *and she is gone.*" The last part of Raghu's sentence hit me bitterly, but I stayed quiet.

"You are not the only guy who has been in love and has got his heart broken," Shashank said.

"Ah, this coming from you a guy who simply broke a girl's heart just because you 'thought' you were incompatible."

"Oh come on, don't you lecture me over Neha now."

"You just deserted her without trying. Very convenient; you'll be cursed."

"Cursed?? Arjun, what is wrong with you man! You seriously need to go see a shrink, there is nothing like a curse. Hrida is gone, and she is never coming back. She is probably dating somebody already or preparing to get married," Raghu's words were slitting my heart.

"Stop it!" I yelled.

"Why? What's bothering you? You claim to be so much in love with her, but within three months, even you have started making out with random girls. Why won't she be doing it? Can't you see that she has forgotten you?"

"You know what, it is probably because of this blunt attitude of yours you couldn't find anyone good to be with. You are an asshole, so obviously, you attract the same kind of girls."

As soon as I completed my sentence, Raghu landed a mighty punch on my left cheek, knocking me on the ground. I clutched the sand and got up in rage, but gave up the thought of hitting back the instant I realised whom I was about to hit.

"Just go fuck yourself, loser!" he screamed at me.

"That's exactly what I'm going to do. You two are dead for me," I screamed dabbing my bleeding lip with my sleeve. "I curse the day I met you two."

"Poncho, enough is enough!" Shashank ordered.

"Fuck you!" I said and left the beach, with Raghu still yelling and abusing me. Three hours later, I was on the flight back to Mumbai. The new year had started, and I had lost some more people I loved. But at that moment, I really didn't care.

2001

The day you admit yourself as an engineering student, you solemnly sign on the warrant of persecution and agree that you'll, without any objection, allow your mind and soul to be sodomised by the atrocious demands and treatments bestowed upon you by the professors, who feel righteous to vent their personal and professional vexations by bullying you at every possible opportunity. There are students who bear the blisters with smiles and mirthfully show it off. But since I was thrown into this black hole with my hands and legs chained to a tetra pod, my mouth occasionally blared out my frustrations at the professors.

One such incident cost me the afternoon of 31 December and I was holed up in the cementing lab that resembled a rat-infested cave. I could see orgasmic pleasure beaming from our professor Miss Mary Mathews' face when she asked me to rewrite the whole semester's experiments.

Ms Mathews looked like the ugly step sister of Cinderella. A round, grey-coloured face, her oil soaked hair tied with a rubber band while a moustache similar to that of a boy going through puberty adorned her upper lip. She had a manly voice and spoke flawless English with a heavy South Indian accent.

Whenever my phone vibrated, she looked up from her files and raised an eyebrow which almost touched her hairline. It was five in the evening and Raghu had been calling me for the past four hours. I pushed the phone in my pocket to avoid anymore stinking looks from Ms Mathews and got back to wasting ink and paper. An hour later, the phone began vibrating again; after a few minutes of enjoying the vibration in my pocket, I pulled the phone out. *Seventeen missed calls!* All of them from Hrida. I felt a sudden rush of blood in my body. I simply stuffed all my files in my sack and ran out of the lab, leaving Ms Mathews screaming behind me.

I started my bike and throttled it out of college. At a safe distance away from the college and Miss Mathews, I stopped and dialled Hrida's number. My heart began to pound.

"Hi..." she said.

"Hi... you called?" I asked adjusting the rearview mirror to see my face.

"Yes..." her voice filled with controlled eagerness.

"Why?"

"How are you?"

"I'm good..." I said resting my elbows on the fuel tank my face still visible in the mirror.

"I called to tell you that I'm done."

"Done with what?"

"Done with being pissed at you."

"Hmm..." I saw a smile grow into grin in the mirror. "I love you," I said after controlling myself for a while.

"Thank you," she said. Who the hell on this planet replies to an *I love you* with a *thank you*? But she had scared me enough in the past eleven days, so I kept my trap shut.

"When can we meet?" I asked.

"What's your plan for tonight?"

"We are going to this party at Yeoor hills." I said. "I wasn't planning on taking anyone, so I'm still a stag."

"Well now you are not... I'm coming with you," she commanded. "But I have to be back by one, max."

"You will, I promise. Be ready by nine, I'll pick you up."

"OK, bye. And hey, thank you again," she hung up.

Yeoor hills was a part of a national park which the people of our city used as a makeshift hill station. So having any party there was illegal. But as I said, in our country, no one cares, hence everything can be managed. The money provided by our parents wasn't ever enough to pay for our vices, so managing events and arranging parties were the easiest ways of making a quick buck. Raghu and a common friend of ours had arranged this party. Good music, good food, lots of girls, lots of booze – back then, it was the definition of a kickass party. But that day, none of it mattered. All I cared about was that the girl I loved was with me, smiling her heart out and dancing freely. She was happy. I began the new year smiling, dancing, and laughing with my friends and Hrida beside me.

Fifteen minutes after twelve, we left the party to keep up with Hrida's deadline. Riding down through the dark forest roads, I heard three *wows* and two *oohs* from her before I was finally asked to stop. She squeaked with joy and ran to the peepal tree which had hundreds of fireflies flying around it. It looked like it was decorated with white rice bulb string lights used during Diwali. I switched off the headlight and there was total darkness around us. The only source of light was fireflies shining on the tree. Hrida stood there mesmerized. In a few minutes, she returned and swiftly hopped onto the bike.

There was this happy silence for a while till we rode down the hill.

"I had fun today," she said looking at me in the mirror. I could clearly see the love in her eyes as she smiled.

"Me too," I smiled back, there was again a moment of silence with both of us looking at each other.

"Didn't it scare you back there in the dark?" I asked as I hit the highway.

"No, besides why would I be scared when you were with me?" she winked at me.

"Do you really have to go home right now?" I asked trying to push my luck.

"I've promised mom so she'll be waiting. I haven't been out for so long before," she said. "But we still have ten minutes."

"I love you." I said. She just blushed. "And I'm sorry for saying those mean things."

"Did you seriously think that this through-the-mirror-apology of yours will be accepted?" she said with a raised eyebrow.

"Okay, what do you want me do?" I stopped the bike a hundred metres away from her building gate.

"Scratch your head a little and get back to me with something creative," she said and got off the bike.

"I really thought I had lost you," I confessed.

"Don't worry, you never will," she said patting my head like a dog. "Can I leave, please?"

"Please stay for a while!" I said pouting.

"I don't want to go, but it's past one." I knew she really meant it when she said that.

"Fine." I said as she extended her hand towards me. Not knowing whether to kiss it, squeeze it or pull her close to me, I held it for a few seconds before she left. I stood there and watched her go. She turned back a couple of times before disappearing into the gate.

The smile, the glint in her eyes, the spring in her walk, the blush on her face – all of it was for me... because of me. Finally, for the first time in my life, the girl I was in love with loved me back. It had been just over two months that I had met this girl and I barely knew anything about her. She was yet to confess her love for me. I had no idea what I was going to do with my life but I decided that I was going to marry her. I lay down in my bed with thoughts of Hrida whirling in my mind. I went through everything she said to me, reliving every moment I spent with her that evening. I finally decided to write her a letter asking her to forgive me. I rushed to my computer and typed out a letter.

Letter of Repentance

To,

Miss Hrida Bapat,

It has come to my notice that my action of using mean words and generalising you in the category of selfish snobs who have ill treated me in past could be seen as offensive and extremely hurtful, considering my claim to love you. I never intended to hurt you and I feel terrible for being so harsh. I want you to understand that I was merely heartbroken when I got to know about your boyfriend through your message. Though I can now see that it was no fault of yours and my actions were fuelled by my anger. Please accept my heartfelt apology. Moving forward, I shall attempt to curtail my erratic behaviour. That said, I would very much appreciate it if you accept my apology and forgive me.

Sincerely, your just friend (for now),

Arjun Kulkarni.

I slept wishing that the clock would speed up by a few hours so that I could see her again. I woke up in the morning and rushed to the courier office and couriered the letter to Hrida's house.

I had been staring at her gate in the rearview mirror for twenty minutes before she emerged out of it. As she neared my bike, I turned and looked back at her. I sped off as soon as she sat on the bike. The letter that I wrote had had gargantuan effects on Hrida. The moment I hit the highway, she planted a kiss on my shoulder.

"Apology accepted," she said and wrapped her arms around my waist.

"Thank goodness," I continued smiling. "I hope it didn't create any problems for you at home." She began to laugh.

"No, not at all, in fact your packaging was so flawless that my poor mom rushed to me with a worried expression."

"I'm sorry about that."

"Its okay, you don't need to keep saying sorry," she said leaning back. "Anyway what's the plan?"

"Let's go to Raghu's place. His house is a lodge for next two weeks."

"Cool..."

Whenever Raghu's parents were out on a vacation, his house became a bunkhouse. Large-hearted Raghu would let random people come and stay over. Once he met a cyclist at the naka. This guy had ridden all the way from Delhi to protest against fuel price hike and had no place to stay. Raghu brought him home and offered him the couch to sleep for a night.

I was a bit skeptical when I rang the doorbell. A half-naked sweating Raghu opened the door.

"Wrong timing, man!" he complained.

"Why what were you up to this time?" I asked.

"I was just about to enter..." he swallowed rest of the sentence when he saw Hrida behind me.

"Hey! Hi!" He nervously faked excitement to cover up what he was up to. "Forgive my nakedness. Miss Bapat. Please have a seat. I'll be back."

Hrida giggled looking at him.

"And don't you dare disturb me for an hour," he whispered to me gritting his teeth and rushed back to his bedroom leaving Hrida and me in splits.

"You hungry?" I asked as I sat three feet away from her on the other end of the couch.

"Depends on what you have to eat."

"Nothing, was thinking of calling for a pizza."

"Hmm... *chalega*."

"What will you have?" I found the menu under the table and began to read it. "There's spicy chicken, cheese and barbecue chicken..."

"I'm a vegetarian," she said cutting me short.

"Oh, okay. Sorry."

She's a vegetarian! A voice screamed inside me.

We were halfway through eating the pizza when Raghu appeared from the room with a girl behind him. Raghu's ruffled hair and the girl's red neck told the story of what had transpired in the room.

"Hey, you want to have a bite?" I asked

"Yuck... veggies! Why are you pushing veggies down your throat?"

"Hi..." I said looking at the girl.

"Hi..." she said coyly.

"This is Rinkie my girlfriend. This is Arjun and that's Hrida."

The way Raghu introduced her, I was sure he'd break up with her in the lift on his way down.

"I'll drop her and be back in a bit. Please order something edible for me," he said grumpily and left.

I gathered the pizza boxes and dumped it in the kitchen. Hrida flipped a few channels on the TV before switching it off. I came back to the couch and sat a feet away from her. I stretched my head on the couch and stared at the ceiling. There was a long silence in the room. I slowly slid my hand on the couch and cupped Hrida's hand. I turned my head to look at her and she was looking at me with a mild smile, her eyes trying to read my mind. I smiled at her and hesitantly pulled her towards me with slight force. She shifted towards me and I put my left arm around to hug her. Her smell intoxicated me and my heart began to beat so fast that I could hear my heartbeats. I let her go and stared at her. Then after waiting for a second, I kissed her on her cheek. She closed her eyes. I slowly moved sideways and placed my lips on hers. I kissed her still lips for a couple of seconds before she reciprocated, her hands holding my face and her fingers gently whirling through my hair.

"I love you!" I said taking a moment from kissing her.

"Thank you," she smiled and bit my lower lip. Shivers ran down my body. It wasn't as if I hadn't kissed anyone before, but all those carnal pleasures didn't match up to the way Hrida made me feel.

"I have to tell you something," she whispered in my ear still hugging me.

"Oh no, what now?" I said with closed eyes.

"I won't be meeting you for a month," she said quietly.

"What?" I said looking at her. "Why?"

"I've got my finals coming up in fifteen days."

"But I can drop and pick you up during the papers, right?"

"Yes, you can, but one smile from you can toss all the data out of my brain," she jutted her lower lip. "You don't want me to flunk, do you?"

I didn't say anything. "Do you? Do you?" she pushed making faces till I smiled.

"No," I muttered under my breath putting my arm around her shoulders.

"And by the way, who gave you the right to kiss me?" she said with a straight face.

"What do you mean?" I asked in a worried tone, in spite of knowing that she was messing around with me.

"You still aren't officially my boyfriend," she continued staring at me.

"I... I am sorry." By now my mind had given these words lifetime membership on planet tongue. I began to remove my hand resting on her shoulder. She could not keep a straight face any longer and burst into laughter.

"You haven't proposed to me yet," she said as she stretched up a bit and kissed my right cheek. The remaining hours of that afternoon were spent smiling, kissing, and cuddling.

"Dev, guess what?" I screamed into the phone.

"You are in love?" Devika replied.

"You know already?"

"I've had my share of such calls from you. Shoot the details," she said.

"Hmm... her name is Hrida. She is Neha's friend..."

"Who's Neha?"

"Shashank's new girlfriend."

"Oh! Sachdev's hooked again. Man, I'm missing out on a lot of stuff."

"*Abey* listen *yaar.*"

"Sorry, continue."

"So ya, I met her four months back."

"It took you four months to tell me? She's been keeping you that busy?"

"Aww, someone's jealous!"

"Ya right!"

"But seriously, this time it's different than always."

"Looks like it, just don't waste time. Tell her how you feel."

"I have, actually... there's more..."

"There's more? I have really missed out on too many things. I'm coming there right now," she said sounding really annoyed.

Incoming message from Hrida buzzed my cell phone.

"Dev baby, I'll call you back. Bye, bye... bye." I hung up.

"Yippie, vacations" her message read. I desperately dialled her number, she cancelled the call, and messaged back – *"still in college, don't call. message me the plan."*

"Movie?" I replied.

"Works for me."

"I'll pick you up then."

"No don't bother, Neha said Shashank's coming to pick her up. I'll come with them, you get the tickets in the meantime."

"OK, See you soon. Love you!"

"Thank you."

We were twenty minutes late for the show, yet they started the movie only after we walked in. It felt like the film was being screened specially for us. The total number of people in the hall including four of us was six. There was one more couple sitting at the extreme left corner of the hall. I concluded the guy was clearly interested in something else for two reasons: One, from the looks of him, I doubted if he could recite all the alphabets in English, forget understanding the whole movie in English; two, both of them were sitting on a single couch. Shashank and Neha took the right corner and almost instantly got down to business. Hrida and I sat in the centre seats. She got lost in the adventures of the ogre and his donkey. Waiting for the right moment, for an hour I pretended I loved it too. But the stabbing thorns of the rose I had hidden in my T-shirt began to wear my patience away. I was almost about to give up my stupid juvenile plan of proposing in a movie hall when the ogre jumped to my rescue. He kissed the princess and proposed to her. I took the opportunity and pulled out the rose. *The thorns, the thorns you idiot* my mind yelled but it was too late, I had generously scratched myself.

"Princess... would you like to be this ogre's girlfriend till its time to get married?" I asked melodramatically holding the rose in my hand.

"Yes yes..." she said giggling and nodding her head vigorously. I took her hand in mine and we got back to watching the movie.

"Please don't smell that rose. It might smell a bit sweaty," I said muttering the last part under my breath.

"I don't mind," she said as she cuddled up to me.

"I love you," I said and kissed her.

"I love you too."

Proposing after hitting first base felt extraordinarily retarded, but when you fall in love, you somehow find logic in all the mindless things you do. Besides, everything with Hrida was different than the rest of the affairs I'd had. So officially, on 18 February 2002, Hrida became my sixth and the *last* girlfriend. Or so I thought.

2010

18 February, 2010. I read the date on the call sheet for the shoot as I walked in on the set. It would have been eight years had I been with her. Everyone around me was happy for it was the last day of the shoot. But I wished the work wouldn't end. It had been almost two months since my return from Goa. I had deliberately gotten myself immersed in work. It was the only thing I loved left with me. Somehow the film sets masked all my miseries and made all the hurt disappear. The larger than life houses, the lighting, the rains, the romancing actors, their emotions, their fake tears, ultra glamorous costumes, the songs, the dances – there was this honesty in the pseudo atmosphere that gave me hope like millions of other people in our country. The day ended with a lot of jubilation. A smiling director, a relieved producer and an exhausted dancing crew. When you work at a certain location twenty-four-seven, you are bound to get attached to it. I looked around the house for one last time realising that the next time I visited the floor, there would be something else in its place.

"Hey, aren't you waiting for the wrap party?" Ashwin, my first AD asked.

"I have plans, I got to meet someone." *Who?* a voice yelled inside me.

"Oh, so there *is* someone," he smiled. "Let's meet this someone someday."

"Someday, sure!"

"Okay buddy, you have fun." He hugged me and left.

As I sat on the bike, a sudden wave of emptiness hit me. After working nonstop for two months, there was nothing to do now. My next assignment wasn't due for two months. I hadn't taken a break for the past two years hence I had deliberately planned this break so that I could go on a vacation with Hrida. In the blink of an eye, however, everything had changed. I was left with sixty-one days to kill and had no clue how. I checked my watch; it was 1.30 a.m. I needed a drink and the only place in this city that could get me inebriated at that hour was Pyaasa.

Bada Anna had diligently designated Fridays as ghazal nights at Pyaasa. Since the time I met Hrida, I had hardly been there. Life had changed so much in the past seven years that switching back to my old college life wasn't going to be easy. The watchman parked the bike as I got off it. Subbu welcomed me at the gate and warmly shook my hand.

"Long time no see, boss!!" He said smiling. One of his central incisors had given way to a black hole.

"What happened to your..." I asked pointing to his teeth.

"Teeth?" he chuckled. "Time for retirement."

He shook my hand again and asked the waiter to take me up.

The whole floor was part of the huge *mehfil*, a make shift stage placed in the centre surrounded by tables that were dimly lit by red china balls hanging over it. The session was already in full form and most of the patrons were flying super high. I sat alone on the corner table and ordered my drinks. My body hadn't intercoursed with alcohol since new year's eve so as soon as the waiter brought my drink, I swilled a nice half-a-glass down my throat in a clichéd broken heart lover style. I suddenly felt a hand heavily landing on my shoulder.

"How long, has it been, my friend?" he asked me in a slurred voice, I turned to see who it was.

"For what?" I asked resentfully.

"Not too long it seems." He smiled. "Hi I'm Shekhar..." He said extending his hand. "Phadke..."

"Hi." I said shaking his hand. The singer sitting on the make shift stage switched to another song by effortlessly playing hard notes on the harmonium.

"Waah waah.. waah waah," the whole crowd screamed unanimously.

"Can I sit here?" Shekhar sat before I could say no. "Happens you know... this anger, helplessness, *hota hai...*" Trying to convince me, he began to shake is head like a cow trying to get a bug off her neck. "What's your name, by the way?"

"Dil ki choton ne kabhie.. chain se rehene na diyaa..
Jab chali sard hawa maine tujhe yaad kiyaa.."

The singer crooned.

"Waah waah.. waah waah.." The crowd said in unison.

"Arjun." I said before listening to the rest of the ghazal.

"Hum ko kiske gum ne mara, yeh kahani phir sahi...
Kisne toda dil humara, yeh kahani phir sahi.
Dil ke lootne ka sabab poocho na sabke saamne,
Naam aaega tumhara, yeh kahani phir sahi."

"What are you drinking?" Shekhar almost snatched my glass and smelled it. "Repeat...repeat..." he said snapping his fingers at the waiter standing close to us.

"So... I was saying... four years back..." He took another sip from his glass. "I was sitting where you are right now." God knows how he remembered that.

"Nafaraton ke teer khakar doston ke sheher me,
Humne kis kis ko pookara yeh kahani phir sahi,
Hum ko kiske gum ne mara, yeh kahani phir sahi...

"*Waah waah... waah waah..*" Only I screamed and some of the lesser drunk people who were still in their senses turned towards me.

"Kya bataye pyaar ki baazi wafaa ke raah me,
Kaun jeeta kaun hara yeh kahani phir sahi..."

"Do you know how it feels to see the person you love get married to someone else?" Shekhar started again and looked at me pensively. He finally managed to get my attention.

"No, I don't." I was petrified with just the idea of seeing Hrida getting married to someone else.

"Hum ko kiske gum ne mara, yeh kahani fir sahi..
Yeh kahani fir sahi... yeh kahani phir sahi.."

"What made it worse was that the someone else she married was my best friend..." he swigged his drink down yet again.

"I was in Delhi for a conference when she broke up with me onthe phone." He smiled. "I wasn't emotionally mature enough for her, she said."

"I'm sorry... I don't know what to say," I said. He began to laugh, banging his hand on the table.

"That is what he said, when I asked him how he could stab me in back like this," he continued laughing. "Anyway, it's been too long, thirteen hundred and sixty nine days, three hours and..." he stared at his watch twitching his left eye, "... sixteen minutes to be very precise."

"I know... It's hard to forget..."

"Now, I'm just waiting that this... this..." He said tapping his finger on the glass. "Makes me forget so that I can carry on with my life."

"What happened with you?" He suddenly asked.

"It is fine, there is nothing to be embarrassed about. Look around, you'll see tears in everybody's eyes.

"You see, that guy there?" he said pointing. "He got divorced six months after his wedding as his wife fell in love with her assistant at work." His voice filled with sudden elation.

"That bald guy beside him... his wife died last year and the one sitting behind us... the same story as mine." He took a sip from his glass.

"So you see, everyone here is heartbroken... you aren't an exception..."

"I broke up with her," I said.

"So *you* are the heart breaker??" He said with widened eyes.

"Yes... I broke my own heart." I said and smirked, but the dude was too drunk to understand any kind of sarcasm.

"I don't understand..." he said taking another sip of his rum. I had no intention of explaining the complications of my relationship to a drunken stranger.

"She..."

My phone rang as soon as I opened my mouth to tell him what happened. Yet again, Devika saved me from a situation I didn't want to be in.

"Just a sec," I said and walked out to the balcony to get away from the noise.

"Hey wassup?" I asked checking the time in my watch. It was quarter to three in the morning.

"Hi..."

"What's wrong, Dev?" I asked sensing the aridity in her voice

"Can you pick me up... please?"

"Yes, where are you..."

"Juhu... beach..."

"Give me thirty minutes, I'll be there." I smothered the intense urge to chide her but Devika calling for help meant there was something seriously wrong.

"Ek plate nimboo..." I told the waiter as I walked back into the hall. Now the immediate scourging task at hand was to shunt the high I had acquired from the alcohol.

"Heyyy, youuu areee backkk..." Shekhar said hanging on to the last syllable of each word.

"I'm sorry I have to go." I began to squeeze the lemons one after other in my mouth.

"Whyyy?? Whattt areee youuu doinggg..." He gave me a scandalised look.

"Sorry, buddy, got to go somewhere."

Four lemons and an extremely sour mouth later, I paid my bill. "You take care and good luck with your plan to forget her." I said in a scorned tone pointing at his glass, knowing he was too drunk to be offended.

"No matter how heartbroken you are, you are never coming back to this place ever again." I told myself. I tipped the security and left Pyaasa.

The cool breeze hitting my face helped me clear my mind. I don't remember the last time Devika had asked anything from me. If it came to it, she could kick someone's ass really bad so there was nothing to worry, but her voice sounded as if she was in pain. What could have happened?

"Maybe she got too drunk and fell off the building; she might have called before dying." Voice One said.

"Or she got knocked down by a car," Voice Two said.

"Someone might have mugged her and stabbed her," Voice Three said.

"Or shot her in the head," Voice Two said.

"Maybe she got raped or something." Voice Four said.

"What the fuck! What the fuck! What the fuck!"

I yelled my lungs out and screeched the bike to a halt right in the middle of the eastern express highway. Thank goodness it was 3.30 a.m., else the municipal sweepers would have had to scrape my body off the road the next day. I calmly got off the bike, looked around for any speeding vehicles and walked it to the side of the road. I struggled with the helmet strap for a nice fifteen seconds before I violently pulled it out and threw it away. Throwing my hands in the air and heavily stamping my legs on the ground I began to scream hysterically, eventually rolling on the road. I was seriously losing my mind. Raghu was absolutely right, I needed a psychiatrist. I had let the hell of negativity loose on me and it was sucking me in. If I didn't do something about it, I would soon be scribbling Hrida's name on the walls of some mental asylum. In the past six months of the break-up, I had only grown from bad to worse. My drama concluded in six

minutes or so when I realized I was rolling on the sides of the
eastern express highway where toilet deprived population of the
city relieved itself. Now the hysterically screaming-me became
the hysterically dusting myself, turning round and round like
dog chasing his tail and making sure I was clean. I pulled out
the headphones and plugged it in the phone. Loud music was
the only way I could block the contorted voices inside me. For
the rest of the twenty minutes that I took to reach Juhu Beach,
loud electronic sounds took care of the voices inside me.

I parked the bike and dialled Devika's phone and the
pretentiously polite recorded voice of a woman from service
provider told me that her phone was switched off. I crossed the
road and walked to the crowded food stalls. This city indeed
didn't sleep. It was past 3.00 a.m. and yet I had to push through
the crowd to the beach. There was no sign of her. With every
passing minute, my heart began to palpitate more. I dialled
her number again, in vain. There was no way I could contact
her. I wandered through the stalls with the vendors practically
hounding me as if it was my moral responsibility to buy the
food they were selling. I walked back to the bike.

"Done strolling on the beach?" she said and smiled at me
as she saw me walking towards her.

"Finally..." I hugged her.

"I'm sorry, you had to go through all this trouble."

"It's fine once in a while, but next time find someone else,"
I said and she slapped me on the shoulder.

"What were you doing here anyway?" I asked sitting on
the bike

"Office party and then got freaking drunk," she said as she jumped onto the bike. I adjusted the mirror to see her and I flipped out when I saw her face.

"Dev... show me your face!" I turned frantically and held her by her chin with my right hand *"It's a freaking cut!"* I screamed looking at the cut at the corner of her lips.

"Yes I know," she said, dabbing it with a bloodied handkerchief.

"How did it happen?"

"Let's leave this place and I'll tell you on the way."

"Dev, how the fuck did it happen...?"

"Kartik slapped me." I had already guessed that it would be him. I took a deep breath to calm my nerves.

"Where is he now?" I asked failing to mask up the fury in my voice.

"Can we please leave... I'm sleepy."

I stared at her with rage.

"On the beach, snogging with his colleague." She finally blurted.

"Get off the bike right now." She got down immediately. My tone must have scared her. I took her hand and walked towards the beach.

"Where is he?" I asked and she pointed to the far end of the beach.

When I reached the spot, the pig had already hit the third base with the chick. I tapped him on the shoulder.

"Hey... aaa..." he said turning to me trying to remember my name.

"Arjun..." I said.

"Ah Arjun." He extended his hand towards me to shake mine.

"You made a huge mistake by hitting her." I held him by his collar and threw three nasty consecutive punches at his face. The first hit his jaw, second hit his teeth, and the final one hit his nose. He began to bleed almost instantly. The girl lying beside him was totally oblivious of the fact that the guy who was groping her just a few seconds ago was getting his ass kicked. She was so drunk that she just lay there on the sand.

"You fucking whore, you called him here." Kartik said as he spotted Devika and tried to get hold of her arm. I got hold of him again and kicked him in his crotch. He fell on the ground moaning.

I got on my knees and grabbed him by his hair. "If you ever, I mean ever, come near her again, I'll make a yo-yo out of your balls," I said and pushed him away.

No matter what time of the day it is, the *janta* of our country is so hungry for entertainment that they'd instantly turn into spectators. I put my arm around Devika and pushed my way through the crowd. I saw her stop at a distance as I sat on the bike.

"Poncho..."

"What?" I asked noticing her stare at me.

"Can we please put them in a cab?"

"Are you for real, Dev?"

"Come on ya... *ladki hai!*"

"What about him?" I asked.

"Please?"

"Arrrggghhh!!!" I got off the bike. "You get the cab, I'll get them."

Ten minutes later, after struggling with two drunk and partially unconscious bodies, I simply dragged both of them and dumped them in the cab. Devika gave the driver Kartik's address and we turned to leave.

"*Aare boss...*" the cab driver called out to me, "*Paisa?*"

"*Ladka dega, nahi toh uska kapda uthar ke leke jaana.*" I chuckled and zoomed off.

The bastard's slap had delivered a pretty nasty cut on Devika's lip. I held her face and dabbed it with a wet towel. She groaned when I pressed it a bit harder, but a smile broke out a second later. It was living alone in the city that had made her emotionally strong. But unless you are a Kryptonian settled on planet earth or born with super human powers, your body tends to get hurt no matter how strong your emotional firewall is.

"I'm sorry about creating a scene back there," I said when I saw her looking at me. The earlier smile had transformed into a smile that I had never seen on her face. I had never been smart enough to decipher a girl's mind yet. I tried and failed.

"Done! You are all stitched up." I said as I applied an antiseptic cream on her lip.

"Thank you."

"How you feeling?"

"Much better."

"Good, so now I can bash you up?" I said and got up to collect the box of cigarettes.

"Sure, I'm all yours," she said, her eyes constantly following me.

I lit the cigarette and went into the balcony. Resting my elbows on the edge of the wall, I exhaled the smoke. It was six in the morning and the sun was yet to say hello. Sounds of ringing alarms coming from a distance, chirping birds, occasionally passing vehicles, splashes of water on the cars, newspaper boy's tingling cycle bells... everything set the perfect morning ambience. The view of the city in the dispersed blue light of the February morning mist felt quite soothing after all the buzz I had seen in the past twenty-four hours. I stood there feeling the cool breeze, staring at the view with a blank head. Devika slid her hands across my waist and hugged me from behind, resting her head on my back. I flicked the ash and cupped her hands on my stomach with mine.

"I feel so heartbroken right now."

"Don't worry, I've broken his jaw, teeth and nose." I exhaled the smoke out. "Three things for breaking your heart."

"Forget him, he was a prick anyway," she tapped my hand asking for the cigarette. "I feel bad that yet another relationship of mine got flushed down the drain." She loosened her grip, "Something is seriously wrong with me."

"Nothing is wrong with you, baba." I turned to put my arm around her, "You just fall for all the wrong guys." I squeezed her with my arm and kissed her on her head. She nuzzled on my shoulder for a bit and shifted her hands from my waist to my neck and began to gaze into my eyes. I couldn't read her mind, but behind that smile, the pain in her eyes was visible.

Devika had always been a total *bindaas* chick and that is probably why in last few years she had been fooled by a couple of guys. Guys would charm her thinking she was an easy lay, but when their hopes were shattered they would run away. For her good, I hoped that whoever she chose to be with next never hurt her again. I opened my eyes as I felt the warm air of her breath on my lips. Before I could say anything, she placed her lips on mine. It took me a while to realise what was happening. She slowly began to suck my lower lip. I slid my hand around her waist, pulled her close and kissed her back. A minute later, she took a moment to look at me and gave me a blank stare. When I couldn't figure out what that stare meant, I decided to apologise. But she kissed me back before I could open my mouth. As I reciprocated, she groaned with pain. She began to bite my neck, breathing heavily. Holding her gently, I carried her to the bedroom while she continued to kiss me. I had no idea where it was going, but for the first time I did not see Hrida when I closed my eyes to kiss. I could not recognise the feeling inside me. It wasn't love, I assumed. It was probably lust that had been buried inside me. Sliding my arm on her back, I held her by the neck and placed her on the bed. I began to unbutton her shirt while she desperately peeled my t-shirt off and threw it away. Lying on top of her, I began to kiss her wildly. It was some kind of a trance and my body refused to listen to any of the rules set by my mind.

"Are you sure about this?" I asked her as she tussled with the buckle of my belt.

"No," she said and smiled at me, there was a sudden rush of lust in my blood as she said it. All I remember after that was: what had started as friendly comforting hugs and kisses ended up in a sensual animal wanting.

It was the suppressed lust inside that blasted out of me and I had no regrets about it. We spent the rest of the day under the sheets, sleeping in each other's arms and making love whenever we woke up. Both of us had no intention of discussing the whats and whys of what had happened. We were happy and were getting what we wanted. There was no room for compromises, pain, love or any other complications.

2012

"Too busy, boss?" I asked peeping through the gap of his cabin door.

"Buddy!" Rakesh said in his roaring Gerard Butler like voice and embraced me in a bear hug as I walked to him.

"You got some timing, buddy," he put his arm around me and walked me to the couch opposite his desk.

Rakesh Kapur, Mr India 1974, was a bespectacled six feet-five inches cave man with fair skin, blue eyes and a grey bushy beard. The hair on the rest of his body made up for his half-bald head. His Mr India title got Rakesh lead roles in three films, but of all them tanked at the box office. So after failing to create magic with his acting skills, he joined Subodh Banerjee, the legendary film producer-director as a production assistant. Due to his killer business sense and eye for good scripts, he quickly climbed up the rungs in Subodhda's company and soon became his right hand man. Rocky, as the industry began to know him, was a fierce fighter. Once when one of Subodhda's mega budget multi-starrer failed to pull the audience to the theatres, he personally travelled all over the country to find out what went wrong. He was so convinced that the film would work that he quite literally begged all the theatre owners to hold the film for another week. That film till date holds the record to be the longest running film in the history of Indian cinema. After that day, people in the industry began to swear by his judgment about the scripts, so much that even if he casually mentioned he didn't like the script, producers would shelve the project. The biggest film companies in the country offered him jaw-dropping amounts to work for them, but his loyalty to Subodhda was unshakable. After Subodhda's death, differences cropped up between him and Subodhda's sons so he broke out and founded Big Fish Entertainment. Now twenty-six years and thirty blockbuster films later, BFE was the number one production house in the country. He was the most lovable and warm film producer I had met in my career. Years of experience had seasoned him. People would kill to just assist in his films and he had signed *me* to direct three films for him. I couldn't have asked for anything more.

"What do you think?" he asked stretching a life size poster of his latest film.

"Haan? haan? haan?"

A huge grin emerged from behind the grey bushy beard. "Isn't it a smash hit already?"

I covered my mouth with my fist in excitement and blushed behind it. The poster of *Heer* in-fucking-deed was mind blowing. Neera Dutta sitting on white sand beach of Cape Town in a blue two piece bikini with a tag line that said *"Her quest for love ends this summer..."*

"I'm speechless..." I said.

"This film will create mass hysteria, mark my words," he almost jumped with excitement as he said that.

"Neera will triple her price. Oh, that reminds me I have to get her papers signed for your film," he said sinking into a huge fluffy black Italian leather king's chair.

"Neera Dutta is going to be your first heroine," a voice screamed inside me. I felt a sudden rush of blood in my body.

"Baby, will you please get me Neera's contract for Arjun's film?" he spoke to his assistant on the phone.

"Did you like the latest draft I sent you?" I asked.

"Loved it..." he picked up the phone again. "You'll eat anything or just coffee is fine?" he asked me resting the receiver on his chin.

"Just coffee is fine."

"Okay, ya baby, also, send me two super hot coffees, just like you..." he smiled and hung up. "Except for a few things, the script is flawless."

The 'baby' who had an elephantine body came in with the contract he had asked for.

"Thank you, baby," he said and blew a kiss at her.

"If it wasn't for Neera's dates, I would've asked you to start shooting right away." He pulled something out from his drawer and began to write.

"But if life gave me what I wished, I would have been a superstar today," he smiled and tore a cheque and handed it over to me. The amount left me breathless.

"Rupees ten lakhs only." It read.

"Boss?" I looked at him in shock.

"A promise is a promise. We had a deal. You give me the final draft and I pay you your signing amount." I read the cheque two more times.

"Thank you," I said.

Incoming BBM messages from Aditi began to ting my phone.

"hEy.. arE yoU homE??" I tried hard but could never understand the logic behind typing capital letters at random places in the word.

"mE jUzz came bCk hOm.." and three Dancing smilies.

"*whAT yO UptO..*"

"*mUm's oUt oF toWn.*" and five Sad smilies.

"*sO ill b alOnE tOnitE.*" and three Eyelashes and three Hearts.

"waNNa dO sUmThinG??" and two Grins.

Her typing speed was so fast that before I could complete my reply, I would get another message, there was no point in competeing with her.

"*Dinner tonight??*" and a plain smile, I asked quitting my attempt to reply.

"*yiPPie!!!!*" followed by a row of smilies.

"*yeS Yes yES!!!!*" and three Hearts.

She immediately updated her BBM status to "*diNNer with ARjun*" followed by a hug, a kiss and a heart.

"*whErE?*" and two thinkings and three confused smilies.

"*You decide.. I'll pay.. be ready by 9,*" I replied.

"*woGAY!!!!*"

"Someone's brought a smile to your face!" Rocky said looking at me from the gap of his specs. "Who's the girl?"

I laughed. "No one actually. Just my neighbour."

"Ooow!! Getting naughty with the neighbour's wifey, haan buddy?"

"Daughter..."

"Suuweeeeeet..."

"She's a kid, boss."

"Oh god... what's wrong with you buddy, aren't you supposed to have fun at this age and go honka-bonking as many bom-boms you can. What are you doing with kids?"

I smiled.

"Did no one tell you, you are supposed to make hay while the sun shines?"

"Okay boss, as you say, I shall make the hay." I winked at him as I got up to leave.

"Go get lost and have some fun!" He walked up to me and gave me a hug. "I forgot to ask you, how is the new house?"

"Good, really good."

It took me a little less than two hours to reach Bandra from Rocky's office in Lokhandwala. Aditi had already called me four times. It was quarter to nine when I parked the car and checked my watch as I hung up on Aditi's call. As soon as I opened the door and stepped out, five boys popped up in front of me and surrounded me like they do in South Indian movies. Oily dark brown faces, hairstyles that looked like experiments by hairstyling interns, knee length t-shirts with prints of demons and monsters, jeans that fitted tightly like ladies' leggings, shoes in unexplainable colours, pierced eyebrows, lips and noses, and arms tattooed with one of the most clichéd designs.

"Arjun?"

One of the boys said stepping forward. "Ad's boyfriend!!" He introduced himself in a god-knows-where-it-belonged-to accent. "Renzil."

"Huh?"

"My name is Renzil!" he said raising his pierced eyebrow in attitude.

"Ya, I heard that."

"Then what didn't you get?"

"Who are you?"

"Bro have you lost it? I just told you I'm Renzil," he said while rest of the dodos laughed.

"Seriously? Or am I just imagining things?" I muttered looking up in the sky. "Yes I got that, Renzil. I meant what do you want?" I asked.

"Stay away from Ad," one of the boys with golden rebonded hair spoke for him.

"And who's that?"

"Quit playing games with me; Aditi is mine."

"Good for you."

"So you are not taking her out for dinner today."

The authority with which he said that amused me so much that I chuckled out loud, irking the rest of the roaches. Renzil stopped them as they began to close in on me.

"Look bro..." He said trying to patronize me by putting his arm around my shoulder. "I'll make it very simple for you to understand." Suddenly maturity replaced authority in his voice.

"Okay!" I said in a mocking tone.

"I have stopped *ma* boys cuz I don't want to hurt you."

"Hmm."

"But it won't be good for you if you take Aditi out for dinner. In fact, I don't want you to see her anymore."

"Thanks for that, *Aditi's boyfriend,* but I suggest you don't stop *your boys* the next time." I endearingly patted his cheek and walked away.

Though sushi is visually very enticing, I could never figure out a thing when it came to eating it. Everyone in Bombay Wasabi seemed to know Aditi, so I assumed she was a regular. She waved at the girl at the reservation desk and pulled me in the restaurant. The restaurant looked like a lavish film set. A Japanese village replica built on a high roofed floor. Cozy woody looking shacks built over a huge artificial water body and were connected to each other by bridges. Red lanterns with traditional Japanese signs, life size statues of Buddha, a huge fountain in the centre of the restaurant, Tibetan staff dressed in traditional Japanese costumes, colourful food highlighted with spot lights on large sushi bars spread on the sides of the floor looked spectacular. This was all on the thirty-fourth floor so each shack had a breathtaking view of the city below. I didn't even know places like these existed in Mumbai.

"You like this one?" Aditi asked pointing at a shack, I shrugged.

Aditi turned and told the girl, "Send someone fast, I need something to drink."

"You seem to have some muscle out here," I said.

"Ya sort of... happens when your dad owns the place," she winked at me.

"Oh, nice." I was pretty stunned, so that was the only reply I could think of.

"Listen, I want to booze but these people won't let me. Will you please order some whiskey for me? Please, please please?" she said as she saw the waiter walking towards us.

"Okay, but just one, alright?"

She jutted her lower lip out to show her sadness. "Wokay." The waiter came to our shack.

"Hi, get me a large JD with coke, and..." I turned to Aditi.

"Virgin mojito," she said.

"Okay, anything else, sir?"

"Well that's all for now."

"Perfect," the waiter said and left.

"So what triggered the generosity of spending time with me today, huh?" she said folding her legs on the sofa.

"Nothing, was happy and I didn't want to be alone." I smiled. "Besides I owed you a treat for my birthday."

"Thanks, come let's take a walk around the sushi bar. Aren't you hungry?"

"I am but, you'll have to find me something to eat. I cannot tell what's what." She laughed on hearing that.

The sushi bar was an amazing colourful sight with all sorts of rice rolls, buns, shrimps, mushrooms, different types of raw fish and meat, red, green and yellow sauces, and the villain, the *wasabi*. I had burnt my mouth by eating a spoonful of it the first time I had been to a sushi place. I couldn't understand how something so beautiful could taste that fiery. I rejected one thing after the other as I walked past the platters. I looked at Aditi who had swiftly filled her plate with all the exotic stuff. I was supremely flustered looking at the alien looking food. I turned to Aditi for help and she bit her lower lip to control her laughter. I held her neck in an attempt to mock strangulate her.

"Cruel girl!!!" I said, "Couldn't your dad own an Indian restaurant." I began to laugh with her.

"Poor baby, let me help."

My plate was full in a matter of seconds. Aditi kept tossing one thing after another on my plate. We returned to our shack with our plates piled high with food. I prayed and skeptically put a piece in my mouth. This time, surprisingly, whatever I ate tasted good.

"Nice?" Aditi asked.

"You saved me!"

"Cool... now order me another drink."

"You finished it already?" I said as she fluttered her eyelashes at me.

"Is that enough for you to call for another drink for me?"

"*Bevdi!*" I smiled and signalled the waiter to repeat the order.

"What's with you today? You've been smiling throughout." Her curious eyes bore into me.

"I had a sudden epiphany of sorts that I have a life and am allowed to be happy in it."

The waiter brought the drinks.

"And who was stopping you all this while."

"Me."

"Okay. Why?" she asked taking a sip from my glass.

"Long story."

"How long?"

"Really long."

"Well, the evening's just started and we have a lot of time, so start."

"Hmm, there was a girl and I loved her. She loved me too and life was bliss. Years passed and she fell out of love. I found out and thought it was as phase. Months passed but nothing changed. I was hurt and she was not happy. I couldn't bear it, so I broke up with her, end of story." I said and took a deep breath.

It wasn't as if I was being secretive or anything, but for years after my break up with Hrida, I was looking for closure. After a really long time, I was happy. I had lost unaccountable number of things and people after the break up and I had no intention of ruining the happy space I was in by going through all of it again. So I zoomed through seven years in a single breath.

"You did the right thing. I wish my parents had realised it before I was born. I would have been spared of misery of being divided between both of them," she said and for the first time since I met her, I saw sadness in her eyes.

"It took them thirteen years of a bad marriage to realise that they were misfits."

I had no words to console her.

"Nothing could match up to the pain of seeing your parents behave like strangers with each other. Pasting notes on the refrigerator to talk to each other, sleeping in different rooms, going separately to the family functions, waiting for the other to finish the dinner to avoid sitting at the dinner table at the same time, bringing you different cakes on your birthday and finally moving out of the house," she subtly dabbed her watered eyes.

"I still remember the day when dad shifted out of the house. I cuddled up to myself on the couch and watched him pack his bags. My mom left the house without even looking at him. I simply don't understand how people who claim to be in love suddenly choose to disregard each others' existence. I will never forget the look on my dad's face when he left.

"For almost a year after my dad left, I would pray that somehow my mom and dad would fall in love with each other again. I wanted to be back with both of them, but none of the prayers worked. Mom filed for divorce. I felt intense bitterness towards god when their divorce came through, but I guess god has no jurisdiction over things like love. It's been four years since then and a lot has changed. Mom's got a boyfriend and she is all set to marry him. Dad is already married with a child, yet sometimes that twelve-year-old me wants my parents to be back together," she smiled and shook her head.

Sometimes you are so taken over by your pain that you curse God for being unfair to you, but then you realise that there are people with far more heartbreaking stories.

"You want another drink?" I asked, and she began to laugh.

Bandra to Marine Drive and back in fifty-three minutes. I wish that could happen in the day. At midnight it was rather pleasant without honking cabs, unruly bus drivers and red lights. I looked at Aditi. All the way, she rested her chin on the door looking outside. I could see her smiling in the left rear view mirror of the car. The cold midnight air blew through her hair. The tears had spread the eyeliner but her face was beaming with happiness. In spite of all the bitter things happening around her, she somehow found a way to be happy. I smiled to myself. As we neared our complex, she closed the window and sat stiff in her seat. She was visibly disturbed.

"Hey, is everything alright?" I asked.

"Ya, I'm fine. Just don't stop the car," she said in a scared voice.

"What's wrong?"

"Nothing, let's just go home fast."

I noticed a couple of bikes trailing us. One of them overtook us and skid the bike to halt in front of the car. One of the three guys jumped off the bike and walked towards the door where Aditi was sitting. When the attempt to open it failed, he began shout at the top of his voice.

"How long are you going to sit in there?" Renzil screamed.

"Stay in the car; do not come out!" Aditi said to me and before I could say anything, she unlocked the door and got out of the car."

"So finally I caught you red-handed, you bloody whore. What the fuck are you doing with him?"

"Who the hell are you to ask me that?"

"I am your boyfriend, you understand? I am your boyfriend..."

"You were... I told you six months ago that it's over. Why don't you just leave me alone?"

"It will be over when I say so, you bitch," he said and pushed her on the car. That was my cue to get out. As soon as I got out, the rest of the roaches surrounded me. I tried to make way, but one of them pushed me back.

"What does he have that I don't? Car, money, great body? Huh?"

"It has nothing to do with him. You are a fucking loser." Renzil slapped her.

I got agitated and slammed two of the boys on the road. I ran to Renzil and held him by his neck and pinned him on the car. Hearing the commotion, two beat marshals on patrol whistled from a distance. The rest of the boys ran away, leaving Renzil behind.

"Let go of me, you asshole," Renzil said struggling to escape from my grip.

"What's the hurry? Let the cops see your machogiri."

As the cops neared us, tears began to flow out of his eyes and all the machismo suddenly disappeared. I loosened my grip.

"Get in the car." I told Aditi as I saw the beat marshals stop near us.

"Is everything alright?" One of the officers asked. "What are you doing out so late?"

"Yes kaka, no problem. We were just leaving."

"Leave right now," the other officer thundered.

"Right away," I said and turned to Renzil and menacingly whispered, "If you ever come near Aditi again, I'll squeeze all the masculinity out of your crotch, do you understand?"

"Yes." He said obediently and walked away.

I sat in the car and drove Aditi straight home. The incident had shaken her so much that she was trembling. I put my arm around her to console her.

"Don't worry, everything is fine now," I said as we walked out of the lift. "He won't bother you anymore." I opened my door.

"Can I sleep at your place? I'm scared to be alone."

"Alright!"

That night, after I put her to bed, I sat alone at the window thinking about all the miseries people are in. I wondered who writes such cruel fates for people. Does anyone on earth have a perfect life? Would my life have been perfect had I been with Hrida today? Was there any guarantee? As always, I had no answers, but finally I had accepted the change in my life.

I don't remember at what I had been staring since my mind had transported me to la-la land and placed me on the well manicured lawns under the soothing orange light of setting sun in the sea. I was talking to Hrida with my eyes closed. She was right next to me, her head resting sideways on my arm. She was playing with petals of a flower, giggling at my inanest of jokes.

"I love you baby," she said and gently kissed my cheek.

"I love you too," I replied. And as soon as I said that, there was a thud leaving me in excruciating pain.

Eight months back, when I first saw this four-feet-five-inches gnome-like professor, I felt bad for the man. His round brown face, grey hair pasted on the scalp with oil, reddish brown teeth as result of excessive chewing of gutka, extra small shirt that stank of horse shit, twenty-two inch waist trousers, and size four shoes were totally pitiful.

'Surveying I & II, Prof Santosh Singh' He wrote on the board standing on a stool the first day he came to class. God shouldn't be so cruel to anyone, I had thought. To add to his misery, someone saw his ding dong while peeing in the loo. The boy who saw it said it resembled an eraser; the news spread like wild fire. Since then, the students all over campus began calling him Eraser.

I tried to figure out how such a short man had managed to smack my head when I was sitting on a three-feet bench. However he had done it; it inflicted so much pain that out of anger, I considered picking him up and throwing him out of the window. I suppressed my wrath realising submissions' season was about to start and any act of vengeance would cost me my whole term's work.

"Is anyone up for a bet? I say this dreamy head won't make it across sem four to third year," he looked at the class, brazenly excavating leftover food from his teeth with a match stick.

"No one? really?" He began to laugh. "See, even your classmates know you won't make it."

In a normal case scenario, I would have gotten back with something equally 'ass-holish', but at that moment I had become thick-skinned. I buried my head in the drawing sheet and went back to Hrida and her thoughts. Thankfully, the lecture ended in a minute's time but there was one more painful session left towards the end of the day and if I wanted to make my attendance for the first lecture count, I would have had to stay back.

"The gods must be really pleased with me today to have gifted me with your presence in both my lectures," Prof Singh said acrimoniously as I walked into his classroom for the last lecture. I went to my desk without acknowledging his presence, further inviting his tartness. For the next two hours, the prick unleashed his bitterness at me by asking random questions and calling me names.

"So is this dumbness hereditary or have you painstakingly developed it?" he said and laughed. "What! Don't you find it funny?" He began to point at the students.

"Yes you, it is funny, isn't?" he asked one of the medal bearers.

"Yes, yes sir," he said smiling reluctantly.

"Then why don't you laugh?" He said forcing him to laugh.

Then asking one student after another, he made the whole class laugh at me. My patience was wearing thin. I was just a millimeter away from splattering him like a bug on the board. I cursed Raghu for pulling me to college. I would have happily waited for Hrida outside her college rather than getting verbally raped by the Lilliputian bastard.

Raghu rode the bike back from college. There was complete silence on the bike. A feeling of total worthlessness deluged me after the lecture. The bastard had quite literally fucked my mind sore. It felt like I had been run over by a speeding road train. I don't know what these professors intend to achieve by applying mincing-the-morale-of-the-students technique. For me it only bred hatred for engineering. With each passing semester's tormenting syllabus and professors, my resolve to run away became stronger. But I had to make a move, and fast. The rancidness of the course was forcing me to question my own credibility. *Soon,* I promised myself. I sorely needed Hrida so that my life loathing feelings could be anesthetised.

"You go, I'll get a smoke," Raghu said as he braked outside the naka.

It began to rain behind me as I walked in. I tapped Hrida's shoulder and before she could turn to me, I sat on a chair next to her.

"What's wrong baby?" she said looking at me carefully.

"Why what happened?" my tone gave away the abjection within me.

"Your face looks flushed."

"Oh that, no nothing happened, I'm just too tired," I said as I caught the cigarette packet that Raghu threw at me.

"Really?" She paused, her eyes on me. "Is that how you are going to dodge it?" she asked raising an eyebrow.

"Poncho got raped by a baby penis-ed professor today." Raghu said lighting a match stick for me.

"Why? What did you do?" Hrida asked surprised.

"I didn't do anything, the guy is a prick," I said as I took a long drag and exhaled the smoke.

'The monster ravaged my poor girl's innocence,' Raghu mock wept as he stroked my hair and began to laugh.

'You dished me out to him bitch. I'm never listening to you again,' I jabbered.

Hrida softly pinched my cheek. A smile propped on my face.

And just like that, all the irritation disappeared. Hrida's charm worked yet again. Maybe it was really Hrida's charm and love for me or maybe I had started believing that she could make all my miseries and hurt disappear. Either way, it worked for me.

"I just wish I had enough guts to tell dad that I want to quit," I said.

"Quitting is fine and if you decide to do it, your father will understand. The question is what you will do after that."

"I don't know." I said putting another cigarette in my mouth, "What will it take for you to pick it up?" I snapped at Raghu getting annoyed by the whirring of his phone vibrating on the table.

"Then, till you know it, hang in there," she said and pulled the cigarette out of my mouth and crushed it.

"Hey, are you here?" Raghu asked.

"Who are you talking to?" I asked Raghu.

"Okay, wait I'll come," he said and hung up. "Give me some change."

"Who's coming?" I asked, handing him my wallet.

"Kintu!" Raghu said with an evil grin. He took some money out of my wallet and left.

"What?"

Cut to 1995:

First day of the school, standard seven.

I was more than happy to return to school. In my first year of the new school, I had become friends with Shashank and Devika, and this year Raghu too was shuffled to my class so I was looking forward to it. I sat beside Devika, while Shashank and Raghu sat at the desk behind us. The class teacher walked in with a bunch of new students – three boys and a girl. She introduced them to the whole class and asked us to welcome them. As I looked at all of them, my eyes got stuck on the girl, Kintu.

She had fair skin, a freckled face, small eyes and a cute smile. Her hair was tied up in a single pony tail. I fell in love with her almost instantly. My heart began to jump when the teacher asked me to sit beside her. She didn't speak to me until the recess. I passed a note to Devika saying *"I think I have fallen in love with her, you have to help me."*

So, as always, my knight in shining armour jumped to help me and broke the ice with Kintu. I froze and kept staring at her as Devika introduced us to each other. As the days passed, her cuteness began to grow on me so much that whenever I spoke to her I began to stammer. I would simply follow her all over the school and blindly obey her.

"Arjun baby I feel like eating a chocolate," and zwoop! A chocolate would come out of my pocket.

"You know baby, the school bus was so crowded in the evening that I hurt my knee yesterday," Kintu said.

That night I cried to my dad about how the bus was crowded and how *I* had hurt my knee. My poor dad sent his driver to drop me to school. I made sure I picked and dropped Kintu every day so that she never hurt her knee or anything else again.

I knew that she had a crush on me, so I was itching to ask her out, but could never muster enough courage to tell her how I felt.

"I don't know what happens to me when I'm around her. I forget what I have to say when I look at her," I told Devika.

"It's good that you can't because she is using you."

"Don't say that, Dev. I think she loves me too."

"Hah! Loves you!" she mocked.

Three years later, one day after fighting off Devika's disapproval and the heebie-jeebies in my stomach, I finally asked Kintu out on Valentine's Day. I borrowed some money from Radhika and the car and driver from dad and took her shopping. I bought her clothes, sandals, and accessories. I felt like a grown man buying stuff and carrying the bags for his wife. When she was finally satisfied with all the stuff she bought, I took her to her favourite restaurant. I had carried a note with me telling her how I feel about her just in case the words didn't come out of my mouth. It never got used.

"I had so much fun today baby. I like being with you," she stretched across the table and kissed my cheek.

"Wait I have to show you something," she said and pulled out a leather wallet and handed it to me. "Do you like it?"

"This... this is awesome, I really like it... thank..." More than the wallet I liked the fact that she bought a gift for me.

"Really? Aww... you think he'll like it?" she said holding my hand.

"He? Who?"

"Atul ya, my boyfriend? Oh... didn't I tell you about him the other day?

"No, you didn't!"

I never saw her after that day.

My last words to her echoed in my head as I saw her walk towards us. Nothing except her height had changed and that too because of the heels she wore.

"Hiee Arjie, where had my baby been for so long?" Kintu said and hugged me. *"Arjie? Since when did you start calling me that?"* a voice yelled inside me.

"Hhhh-Hi..." I stammered, I didn't understand why. Hrida was a zillion times better looking and a better person than her. Perhaps it had something to do with my past with Kintu that turned me into the same fifteen-year-old-boy who lost all power of speech in front of her.

"Kintu, Hrida, Arjun's girlfriend. Hrida, Kintu, my girlfriend," Raghu said pulling out a chair for her. His words kept ricocheting in my head. *My girlfriend? How? When? Why?"* I gave Raghu one of our patented WTF looks and he winked at me.

"So you are the buyer of all the things she is wearing right now," I tried to say to him telepathically.

But when I thought of it, I wasn't really pissed at him. I was indifferent about Raghu dating Kintu. I was with Hrida, 'The Hrida' so I didn't really care about Kintu, or any other girl for that matter.

"Ooooo...So Arjie finally found himself a girlfriend..." Kintu said poking her index finger into my stomach. "I never thought he'd ever have enough guts to propose to a girl."

"You know, I'm sorry what's your name?" Kintu said.

"Hrida!"

"Oh ya, Hrida, you know this boy here spent three-and-a-half years following me like a puppy, but never told me that he loved me."

"Why the fuck did you call her here?" I tried to ask Raghu telepathically again.

"Oh really?" Hrida said and from the looks of it she seemed to be thoroughly enjoying Kintu's bragging. "That's odd, he didn't take that long with me."

"Ya?" I saw a hint of jealousy on Kintu's face. "You won't believe, but he would spend hours staring at me in class. I found it really sweet."

"I'd freak out if you try anything like that with me." Hrida said grimacing.

"I felt really bad that I broke his heart, but back then, he was so emotionally immature, I wasn't ready for someone like that."

"Bitch, you should have realised it before you brought those clothes with my money..." The intensity with which I yelled in my head, she could have actually heard it.

"No, thank you that you did." Hrida said and held my hand below the table. "Else I would have had to fight you off at some point."

Hrida had thwarted all of Kintu's attempts to belittle my relationship with Hrida, so she finally came up with what she did the best – patronise.

"If ever he breaks up with you or bothers you in any way, come to me, I'll tell you how to control him," Kintu said like a school teacher.

"Where *else* would I go, sister? God knows what I would have done without you, thank you Kintu thank you so so much." Hrida got up and dramatically hugged her making sure she embarrassed her enough to shut her up for the rest of the time.

The encounter with Kintu had brought out the 'protective girlfriend' side of Hrida which I had never seen before. Every time she looked at me, there was this unexplainable force that pulled me towards her. Everything about Hrida made me feel wanted – the way she held my hand, the warmth with which she spoke to me, her smiles, and her hugs. Waking up to her calls and messages, dropping her to college, bunking lectures, checking the phone a hundred times after she was gone, waiting for her outside her college, evening jogs together, coffee at cafes, and never-ending conversations on the phone at night had all become part of my daily life. I had gotten completely addicted to her. No matter how much time I spent around her, I wanted more of her. I had turned into such a sissy that I couldn't stop thinking about her. The world around me seemed pink with red heart-shaped balloons floating in the air around me. I knew I had to snap out of it before my own cheesiness choked me.

It had been a week since I attended any lectures, so one morning after much deliberation, I finally dragged myself to college. I checked the time while parking the bike. It was eleven thirty and I had to wait for half-an-hour for the next lecture to begin. I pulled the phone out and there was a scheduled morning message from Hrida.

"Good morning.. just woke up.. hope your day in college is going good.. No college for me today.. meeting my school friends later so got to get ready.. call me in the break."

"Morning baby, just reached college missed second lecture but will attend the rest of them. I'll see you in the evening?" I replied.

There was a message from Raghu too.

"The word around is.. it's out.. they'll be putting it up by recess.. so you better ride your ass up here immediately.."

"I'm here.. buzz me when the lecture ends.." I replied.

Shit! Result day! I walked out of the college and spent the next thirty minutes smoking back to back cigarettes. It was one of those times when my numb mind turned itself into a time machine and transported me to the future showing me every tiny detail of the impending gory situations I was going to get into. I was so piss scared thinking of the aftermath of the results that everything around me – from honking vehicles to chirping birds, from amplified droning noise of the tea stall vendor's kerosene stove to the continuously barking dog sitting right beside me, that occasionally mimicked a roaring tiger looking at another relatively weaker dog – everything simply got muted.

"Boss, it's official... they are putting up the *'resluts'* in an hour," Raghu said, and as if he read my mind, he scared the growling dog away.

"Sixty more minutes? Shit man... I so hate engineering. This pressure is too much for me..." I said sipping tea. "I cannot handle it anymore."

"Raunak will hang me if I drop a year," Raghu said and my mind immediately provided me visuals of Raunak Uncle tightening the noose around Raghu's neck.

"Screw it man... let's go get a beer," I said.

"I veto it." Raghu grinned.

"Vetoing mean refusal by the way."

"Oh, okay," he said scratching his head, "Let's go".

Eight strong beers and two hours and fifty minutes later, when our brains were unable to control the swinging in our walk and spinning of our heads, I made the call.

"One, two, three..." I counted the number of times phone rang, and before four, he picked up.

"Sachdev *man*, how are *you*?"

"Not bad, Poncho, boozed up at three in the afternoon."

"Ya man, we were too sacred."

"We? Raghu's there too?"

"Yessss..." I said exhaling my breath heavily.

"Okay and what exactly has scared my bitches?"

"Resss... *Reslut*sssss..." Raghu guffawed as I said it.

"Oh they are out? So what does your slut say?"

"Call him... call him here..." Raghu said.

"Actually we want you to see her for us..." I said, Raghu snatched the phone from me.

"You be the go between for usssss," Raghu said in a hissing voice and hung up, the guffawing continued.

In the next twenty minutes that Shashank took to reach our college, we gulped three more beers between the two of us. He dumped us in the car and went to check our fates on the resluts board while Raghu and I slept in the back seat of his car. Sometime later, I heard blurred voices of Raghu and Shashank speaking.

"You got six man," Shashank's voice said.

"Shit man.. shit man.. shit man.. I"m so screwed." It was Raghu's blur voice. "What about Poncho?"

"Ten. Four for first year and six for second."

"Ten? Are you sure?"

"Ya, I checked it twice."

"Yippie!" I tried to yell waking up, but couldn't, so I hugged Raghu and went back to sleep on his shoulder.

A painful sprained back woke me up. My legs were still on the backseat of Shashank's car, but the rest of my body was on the floor, left hand stuck between the driver's seat and the gear box, and head resting face down on the dirty mats. Besides the sprained neck, the hangover was killing me, so it took me a while to restart the brain and untangle myself. It had gotten dark outside. I checked the time. I had slept a nice five hours.

"Are you okay?" Neha asked as I walked out of the car trying to tidy myself up.

"Ya I'm fine." I croaked. Ruffled hair, crumpled clothes, red eyes, a swollen disoriented face and killer headaches. It was the classic 'hung-over' me. "Has anyone seen my phone?"

"Here, take it." Shashank said pulling the phone out from his pocket, "*Maushi* called twice, but I didn't pick up."

"Thanks. Where is Hrida man? She hasn't messaged since morning? Did *she* call?"

"No, Poncho your result..." Shashank brought up the topic which I was trying not to think about. I had flunked ten subjects out of the sixteen I had appeared.

"Ya I know, where's Raghu?"

"He went to get your bike." Shashank said, "So what next?"

"What next? Nothing," I said trying to sound as unfazed as I could.

"Will you please stop pretending that you don't care. You've just dropped a year."

"Fuck you man, Shashank! Yes I've flunked ten subjects and I know I've dropped a year, so what? Do you want me to weep over it?"

"And why is her phone switched off?" I said after I heard the pre-recorded pretentious switched off message from the service provider for the tenth time.

"I need a coffee... can't fight this sleep anymore," I said breaking the silence as I snatched Shashank's cigarette.

You've lost a year! Shit! A voice screamed inside me.

"Sir? Sir?" I heard the waiter at the cafe counter saying.

"Hi, get me a double shot of espresso."

"Sure sir, I'll send it to your table."

"No... I'll take it away, what table?" I turned to where he pointed. "Hrida!"

"Ma'am's sitting there."

My heart literally stopped for a couple of seconds when I saw her, and an immediate second later began to jump in its place looking at her smile. It felt like someone drilled a hole in me and drained all the obnoxiousness that was fuming inside me all day. A whole minute after my brain started sending it signals to walk, my legs began to move towards her.

"Hey, why is your phone switched off?" I asked tapping her shoulder.

"Arjun? Hi..." She gave me a why-are-you-stalking-me look. "Its battery died," she said in a rather bland tone.

"What's wrong baby?" I asked concerned.

"Arjun, this is Abhimanyu..." she turned to a guy sitting beside her. "Arjun..." she said pointing towards me.

"How you doing, man?" Abhimanyu said extending his one feet long palm to shake my hand.

The man must have been the outcome of some kind of a genetic experiment. Even though he was sitting on the couch, I could tell that he was seven feet tall, had thirty inch biceps, George Clooney's voice with Tom Cruise's smile and Brad Pitt's charm.

"Hi..." I mumbled trying to recollect the name. "Abhimanyu? "The Abhimanyu"?" I asked Hrida, I recollected where I had heard the name, *"Abhimanyu... is a ghost man, he just disappeared..."* Neha's voice was saying in my mind.

Hrida just nodded a yes.

"Meeting some friends, haan?" She kept quiet.

"You gotta be kidding me!"

A wave of rage swept me from head to toe snapping a few cables without which you only have your voice to scream out loud and no words to talk, so before I began screaming, I stormed out of the cafe with my soiled face, ruffled hair and crumpled clothes. Leaving the love of my life around everestine charm of "The Abhimanyu".

"What the fuck... What the fuck... What the fuck..." Voice One yelled.

"Bloody moron, I had told you there was something wrong," Voice Two yelled.

"What were you fucking thinking?" Voice Three said,

"Did you see that guy? Voice Four said. "No wonder she ran back to him."

"Why do you have to say that?" Voice One asked.

"Look you fucking cunt, this is why." Voice Five said, providing visuals of me and the monster standing against the X & Y axis of the graph. He was so tall that he almost touched the infinity mark. I looked like a tiny pebble in front of the Everest plus my mind made every possible effort to make me look like a rag picker in front of the designer-clothes-clad dude.

"God knows if he was ever gone," Voice Two jumped back. "She was possibly two timing you all this while."

"That can't be. Hrida would never do that." Voice One returned back trying to dominate.

"You are so thick-headed! She flatly lied to you, don't you get it?" Voice Three said.

"There has to be a reason. She has never lied." Voice One was defensive.

"Arjun! Wait!" I turned and stopped as I heard Hrida call my name just before I got into Shashank's car.

"I was going to tell you," she said breathing heavily as she came close.

"Tell me what? That the love of your life that you waited for so many years is back and you want to get back with him?" I was so pissed that rest of the voices took over my mind.

"You are getting it all wrong, Arjun."

"Oh really? Then why were you so scared back there? Or was I imagining that too?"

"I was scared because I didn't tell you earlier."

Shashank and Neha got out of the car.

"What's happening guys?" Neha asked.

"Why?" I asked ignoring Neha.

"Because Abhi has wanted to meet me for the past month, and I knew it would bother you if I had told you. I didn't want that."

My anger totally looked through her genuineness.

"Abhi? Wow." I said as she referred to him by his nickname.

"You knew about this?" I asked Neha.

"Abhi is back?" Neha asked Hrida.

"'Couldn't you have told him that that your boyfriend wouldn't like it?"

"I wanted to meet him too." She said and paused. "I had to clear a few things with him."

"Oh ya, I know the big closure and all," I smirked.

"There is no need to be rude."

"He wants to get back with you, doesn't he?" I almost screamed.

"Poncho, don't create a scene here," Shashank said pulling me back.

"Yes," Hrida replied.

"Wait a minute... does he know you are with me now? Have you even broken up with him, Hrida?"

She kept quiet.

"This is amazing, you stay away from me." I took a deep breath and began to walk away from Shashank's car.

"Arjun please wait ya," Hrida whined.

"Don't scream... don't scream... don't scream..." Voice One repeated.

"Scream! Scream! Scream!" the rest of the voices cheered.

"Rickshaw!" I screamed at the top of my voice.

2010

I was desperately swimming across the sea, my hands fiercely cutting through the dark choppy waters but the container vessel stacked with billions of containers tied to my shoulders was slowing me down. I turned to look back when I heard the thundering sound of the lightning bolt strike the conducting rod of the ship, and saw the eye of the storm forming just a few metres behind me. The load was too much to pull. I was exhausted but I knew I had to make it fast or the storm would have me and my containers for dinner and I wasn't going to let it happen. I took a deep breath and fired up all the energy I had and began to pull my containers to safety. The lightening thundered again and it began to rain. The winds grew gusty, the water started freezing. The spine chilling temperature of the water was forcing my brain to give up the resolve to save my world I had locked in the containers, but my heart was determined not to give up. I turned on my back and wound the rope around my hands for better grip and got back to pulling it. The rains blinded me and I couldn't see anything. Suddenly I felt land below my legs. I smiled and my heart began to race.

"Almost there... no giving up now," I told my mind.

But then, as if some evil power heard me speaking to my mind, all hell broke loose upon me. The lightning struck the bolt again and lit up the night like a day. The winds began to whirl around me, dragging me to the eye of the storm. I tried to hold on to it by anchoring my heels on the rocks. My bleeding heels turned the dark waters below me red. I was slipping away. I could feel the warmth of my tears rolling down my face.

"No!" I wailed, "Please stop!"

"What you want isn't happening," a growling voice said followed by thunder.

And in a fraction of a second, I was right in the vortex of the storm with all my containers flying in circles around me. I looked at all of them for the last time before the water gulped me down. I felt the agonising salinity inside my throat as the cold, freezing sea water entered my lungs. Finally, I saw the last air bubble escape out of my body. Everything went silent and 'the white light' appeared.

I opened my eyes desperately, gasping and snorting.

"You planning to come out of that bed anytime soon?" Devika asked pulling the curtains aside.

"That explains the white light!" I whispered to myself, "What a nightmare," I said to her. She smiled back.

My eyes kept following her all over the bedroom while my naked body lazed on the bed. She dropped the bathrobe revealing her black boyshorts and stretched her hands behind to hook the bra up. Her still wet hair dripped water on her bare back which slid down her spine to her hips. I could see her face in the mirror as she applied the moisturizer on her neck and chest. A wave of lust shuddered through me. I got out of the bed and slid my hands over her waist to her belly. From the goose bumps that sprouted on her body the instant I touched her, I could clearly tell that her body reciprocated with the same intensity. The scent of her body combined with the smell of the cosmetics was fatally intoxicating. She rolled her eyes and dropped her head back on my shoulder as I began to nibble her neck.

"Shhhhhhhhhh..." she turned and pushed me away placing her hands on my chest, "Away you go from me!" She said. "You are going to get me fired."

"Yippie!" I said resting my bare body on the window wall and draping myself with the curtain.

I looked at her. The morning sunlight that bounced off her face made her skin glow.

"Dev, what's this?" I said as I stretched to pull out an envelope lying on the parapet of the window. She began to laugh.

"God!! its been *there* all this time. I've been looking for it all over."

"What is it?"

"Offer letter."

"For what?"

"A post opened in ANZ last month. They are offering a good package but it's in Delhi, so ..."

"I think you should take it," I said trying to mess with her.

"Really? *Chalo* I'll mail them then." She played along.

I stood there looking at her through the mirror drying her hair with the dryer, her eyes too locked on to me.

"Shit..." She said noticing the hickeys I had left on her neck the earlier night. "Were you planning to have me for dinner? Pass me the concealer."

"Why?" I asked.

"Because..." she turned to me, "I don't want the bitches in my office to know that I am hiding a *Kratos* in my house who does atrocious things to me." I passed her the concealer.

"The next thing I know is my house is full of corporate suit-clad sluts." She sucked her lower lip in to control her laughter and began to nod her head. I just gazed at her jutting my lips out in sadness as her eyes fixed themselves on me again.

"Oh god..." She did a classic Devika-eye-roll and walked up to me stomping her legs on the floor. "Okay, but let's please make it quick." She whispered putting her arms around my neck. "I can't bunk office today," she said, her eyes eyeing my lips.

I held her face and began to suck her lower lip. She pulled me closer holding my hand and placed it over her hips. Fingers of her right hand running through my hair while the left hand held them fiercely for grip. I let go of the curtains to lift her up and in the bargain my legs got tangled in the bathrobe that was still on the floor. So with her in my arms, I tumbled onto the bed. A few seconds of guffawing later, gnawing at each other's bodies began, leaving a few more hickeys behind. I slid my hand up her back and clicked the bra open, mentioning that is of importance because I find it a gargantuan achievement. After tossing her bra away, she repeated the same action with the boyshorts she wore. Then the sheets covered us up to keep the act a secret from the ceiling fan, the wardrobe, the rest of the furniture and the pigeons in the window.

Devika and I, apart from each other's bodies and the bed, shared one more thing – a similar state of mind. It was amazing how I had no absolute thoughts in my head. For the first time in years, there were no debates over what was right or wrong. The contentment of being together had brought the animals out of two empty and emotionally drained souls who wanted each other's bodies and bodies only, or so we thought then.

It took us four hours and a wake-up call from Devika's father to get done with the let's-please-make-it-quick thing. The phone rang three rounds before Devika picked it up. Since I was sleeping, she began to sneak out of the bed to talk, but I pulled her back and snuggled up to her.

"Shut up it's Pa." She whispered gritting her teeth.

"Hi Pa," she said groggily

"No I'm fine, was sleeping."

"Ya it's an off today."

"I mean I didn't go."

"I know I said I'm fine."

"Because I didn't want to go."

"Pa, why have you called?"

"Yes I know. I'm booked on 5th night, so I'll be late, but I'll be there."

"Isn't it enough that I'm going to be there for the wedding?"

(Long silence and excessive noodling of hair.)

"What guy?"

"And why wasn't I told about this?"

"What do you mean why?"

"Who is gonna marry him?"

"Me? right?"

(Long silence)

"Because, I want you to meet someone."

"Yes, there is someone."

"Pa, stop yelling or I'm hanging up."

"Stop yelling."

"Pa?"

"I'm hanging up."

"You are still yelling Pa."

"No, Ma didn't know. I was planning to surprise you guys."

"I'm bringing him along with me."

"No."

"Okay."

"Fine."

"Yes."

"Bye."

"Bye."

"I'm hanging up."

"Phew!" She chucked her phone away and pulled her hair. "Arrrggghhh..."

"Dev?" I said and turned her towards me as she calmed down after three punches on the pillow. She wrapped her leg around my waist and upped her chin with closed eyes asking me to kiss her. I did.

"What happened?" I asked kissing her cheek a minute later.

"I told Pa I'm seeing someone and that I'll bring him to Nishi bhaiya's wedding."

"I heard that, but why?

"Because he wanted me to meet some US-based big money IT guy," she picked up the packet of grass and began to roll up.

"What's the harm in meeting him?"

"Harm? If I agree to meet, they'll conveniently assume I've said yes for the wedding and push me off their chest in fifteen days," she slurred licking the Rizla to tape it. "You remember last time na?"

"Ooow, that got out of hand."

"Right?" She lit the joint and took a long drag.

"So what's the problem now?"

"I am *not* seeing anyone!" She said raising her eyebrow and held the joint between her fingers for me to drag it.

"I can play the part if you want," I said and pulled in a hard one.

"You will? Really?"

"Ya, but on one condition." I took the joint away from her.

"What?"

"For a month, you'll roll up spliffs for me." I smiled

"No way!"

"Then forget it." I shrugged. She rushed to climb up on me and pinned both my hands with hers on the bed and kissed me.

Seven days later, I was on a flight to Gwalior with Devika.

Nishi bhaiya was Devika's first cousin. I found it amazingly silly to call a guy year younger than you *'bhaiya'*, but since Devika called him that I blindly followed. The guy was a walking flesh shop. He was five-feet-one-inch tall with a round face, round body, moobs for a chest, a triple chin, permed-curly hair, scary L-shaped locks, bunny teeth and thick-glassed Gandhi specs. Years back, I had met him at Devika's birthday party, He was a chubby kid then but now it seemed like someone had pumped air into him.

"Debucho, aye Debucho!" He yelled in his ultra rugged voice making himself the centre of attention at the airport.

"I didn't know they called you that. What a cool name!" I goofed.

"Oh come on, your Poncho wins hands down."

"Debucho, here!" He came running towards us. I moved away from his line of run as the thought of what if he couldn't stop himself petrified me.

"Nishi bhaiya!!" Devika waved and jumped.

"Debuchooooo!!" He skidded twice before he could bring his sweaty body to a halt.

"I'm so happy to see you kiddo. You've gotten so thin."

"Ya and you look like you've put on a tonne."

"What do I do ya, this mouth doesn't stop eating," he whined.

"Aww!" She pinched his cheek and they hugged again.

"Wait I'll take the bags," he enthusiastically leaned to pick up her bags lending me a full view of his hairy butt crack.

"Nishi bhaiya, this is Arjun." Devika said as he picked up the bags.

"Hi, Arjun..." I extended my hand.

"Hi, hi Arjun..." He said putting the bags down. "Oh he is 'the guy'?" Devika just nodded. "Oh man, 'to be jijaji' I am so happy." He said and engulfed me in a bear hug, his sweat now wetting my clothes too. "I'm so happy man, I"m so happy," he said to himself nodding his head and yet again leaned for the bags, What luck I was in to have gotten to see a three inch hairy butt crack of my 'to be brother-in-law' twice in a day.

"Hey Nishi bhaiya, I'll take it," I said trying to take my bag from him.

"No!" The look he gave me after the no scared me significantly, so I let him be.

Devika's ancestors were high ranking Sardars in the palace of the Maharaja of Gwalior and that explained her family's ownership over this palatial property right in the centre of the city with sprawling well-manicured lawns, perfectly cobbled roads, and grand lady statued fountains. The area was so huge that after we crossed the elephantine arch gates, it took nearly thirty seconds for us to reach the royal porch. I had heard stories about the house from Devika, but had pictured it more like a bungalow, but this place was behemothic.

"Must have twenty rooms at least?" I asked Devika pulling the luggage out of the car.

"Twenty-two," Nishi bhaiya said as he snatched the bags away from my hand. "But every single one of them is buzzing with people right now, so you'll be sleeping with me. Debucho, we've put you in Tittu's room unless you want to share your room with Rakhi bua."

"No, I'll manage with Tittu." Both of them giggled.

"I still think I should have stayed in a hotel," I whispered to Devika.

"No!!" came instantly followed by the scary look. I surrendered and obediently followed my 'to be brother-in-law' to his room. Walking down the corridors propped with framed swords, daggers and the portraits of heavily-moustached fierce looking warrior ancestors of Devika, the thought of what would happen to me if these people found out what Devika and I were up to made my stomach cramp.

"Haven't you seen those swords? Stay away from me," I said and brisk walked away from Devika as she came close to kiss me. I caught her flying kiss before entering my room, though.

The tinkling sound of ghungroos skittering all round me woke me up. But since my eyes were still glutted with the sleep fairy's magic sleep potion, I could only see five or six multi-coloured lehenga-clad female figures hopping all around the room.

"Good morning!" one of the girls said waving her hand to me while rest of them giggled. I waved back and buried my head in the pillow. By the time I woke up, the warrior family had almost completely painted the groom yellow with haldi. Hundreds of ladies surrounded him while the lucky few who made it across the crowd smothered his flabby body with the turmeric paste. I stayed in the room for most part of the day, trying to avoid a rendezvous with Devika's father. And since I was put up in the groom's room, it was always crowded with aunties who didn't want to miss the chance to bathe their dear nephew, or over-enthusiastic cousins who accompanied an extremely effeminate tailor for the final fittings of the groom's wedding costume or the totally psyched out groom himself who, every thirty minutes, gulped a mouthful of rum to keep the pressure off. So I kind of didn't miss much of the action. By the time it was evening, Nishi bhaiya was three bottles of rum drunk and was sleeping in the bathroom hugging the pot making noises like the possessed Emily Rose. The sangeet party was an hour away and the bride was on her way. Devika assigned me the task of getting Nishi bhaiya ready. So with the help of a few other guys, I pinned the yellow stained drunk body of the groom under the cold shower. An hour of tussling with clothes, eleven lemons, eight redbulls and five puke fountains later, Nishi bhaiya was ready for his sangeet party just in time before the bride arrived. The joint mission to sober up the groom introduced me to Devika's cousins, who like Nishi bhaiya shared the same excitement to meet their 'to be jijaji'.

The bride's entourage consisted of another hundred expensively dressed people. From the greetings and touching-of-the-feet that took place, I could easily tell that it was the girl's father. He looked like one of the men from the framed photographs in the corridors so I assumed he too belonged to some warrior family. But it was difficult to spot the bride in the crowd since every girl was decked up as if it was her sangeet. Then in the crowd of unknown faces, my eyes fixed themselves on the face they knew forever – Devika. I imagined her walking down the stairs in a classic Madhuri Dixit from *Hum Aapke Hai Kaun* style. The only difference was the golden and red lehenga. Her eyes were fixed on me and just when I was about to go on my lust trip, Nishi bhaiya squeezed the living hell out of my hand.

"There she is," he said.

"She, who?" I asked, words barely making out of my mouth.

"Nishi-ta." He said, while his body went cold.

"Nishi!"

A man in the crowd yelled in a voice ten times rugged than Nishi bhaiya's. He forgot he had my hand and pulled me with him to meet her. The bride as compared to Nishi bhaiya was quite a babe. I somehow managed to loosen Nishi bhaiya's grip on my hand before he could reach the storm's eye and found my way out of the crowd to the bar counter.

"Do you not like my face?" I asked as Devika slipped her fingers between mine. "Just look at them; they'll batter me to death if they find out."

"You deserve it, bloody Dracula!" She further clung to me by my arm as the lights dimmed for the show to start.

The programme started with the speeches by the heavily moustached jubilant fathers of the bride and the groom telling the stories of their great grandfathers who stood by each other's side in the battlefield some hundred years ago and how proud they felt that their kids chose each other to spend the rest of their lives with. They then proudly announced the performance by a certain Meera bai who was a descendant of a royal courtesan. I let Devika navigate my body through the narrow steep staircase of the house to her room. I wasn't quite comfortable with the idea of making out in the house. Questions like what if all those fierce looking men downstairs barged through the door? What if there were spirits of Devika's ancestors watching us? The thought of flying daggers and swords spooked me. But the big daredevil that Devika was, she didn't bother a tiny bit and zonked my mind out with her antics. Suddenly a familiar rugged voice announced the special performance by the children of the family for their beloved brother.

"Shit, shit, shit I have to go," Devika said. "But this will be continued," she ordered and ran out of the room.

I followed her a few minutes later, scanned for any staring eyes and climbed down the stairs. I found an inconspicuous spot besides the bar to drink peacefully and got down to business immediately. The performance by the *children* of the family was a synopsis of Nishi bhaiya's life and his love story with Nishita. After all the performances were finished, the dance floor was thrown open for the drunken crowd. The groom, the bride, their parents, the cousins – everyone began shaking their leg to the latest item numbers. I was significantly drunk too, so before the courtesan inside me erupted, I decided to leave after I was through with the drink in my hand. No matter how hot a girl looks in the western outfits, it cannot beat the oomph that a traditional lehenga brings out of her. Plus the moves that broke out of Devika, only got me hornier.

"But this will be continued." Devika's words ringing in my mind brought a smile.

"Isn't she something?" he said. I gulped the last sip, looking at him, and semi-banged the glass on the bar.

"Excuse me?" I asked, alcohol adhered extra sharpness to the tone than I intended.

"Her?" He pointed towards Devika with his nose before taking a sip from his glass.

"I know who you meant by she. Who are you is what I'm trying to understand."

"Oh I am so sorry. Avinash," he said extending his hand towards me. I stood there, my hands tucked in my pockets till his next sentence. "I'm the father you are here to meet."

In a fraction of a second, my face lost its attitude, shoulders slouched, throat dried, legs stiffened, body went cold, and alcohol began to evaporate through my ears. My hands sprung out of the pockets to shake the hand of 'to be father-in-law'.

"Hh-hi, Uncle, I mean Sir," I said uncomfortably. I mean if it was Hrida's father, the obvious reference to him would be sir, but here I was just pretending, so calling him sir felt really weird.

"Uncle is fine."

He smiled, "What are you drinking?"

"No, no more, Uncle, I'm through." I chose to refuse, though I could have well used a bottle to relieve myself of the stress. If I was really dating Devika, I probably wouldn't have fretted much, but pretending was draining me.

"Oh come on, I insist, please." He turned to the bartender, waiting for me to name my drink.

"Whiskey... On the rocks..." I mumbled the last part. He gestured the bartender with his head.

I couldn't believe my luck. I hid sober myself in the room all day to avoid coming face to face with him and when the time came, I was drunk, eyeing his daughter and spewing unnecessary attitude on him. But then he nowhere looked a father of a twenty-seven-year-old girl. He barely looked forty with a slim well toned body, clean shaven face, and a bald head. I had pictured him as a bushy moustached guy with hefty paunchy physique like the rest of the warriors around.

"Here." He handed me the glass and got back to enjoying his daughter's dance. I kept whirling the whiskey to death, occasionally looking at him. Then my luck chose to strike again. Devika zoomed up to me and without noticing her father, swigged my drink down.

"I so want to eat you right now," she said grabbing my shirt lustfully and pecked a kiss on my lips. I stared at her father in horror. His face stiffened but he calmly looked on.

"What's wrong?" she asked, then following the line of my sight she finally noticed her father. "Oh hi, Pa," she pecked him on his cheek and disappeared in the crowd.

The guy went unusually silent. I mean anyone would in the given situation. I began to mentally prepare myself for a royal thrashing by the supposed father-in-law and his warrior family.

"You see that guy in the brown blazer?" he said in a stern tone.

"Advait, and that's his father sitting beside him." I saw what he wanted me to see and got back to intently listening to him.

"Do you like him?" He asked.

"Sorry sir I'm not into boys." I thought of saying but thankfully he didn't give me much time to respond.

"He specially flew down from San Francisco to meet Devika, but she refuses to meet him." I readied my right arm to cover my face in case he decided to slap me.

"You know why?" My eyes twitched and body froze as he raised his hand, *"here comes a slap, here comes a slap"* a voice yelled in me, but he held my shoulder.

"Because she thinks she loves you, bloody fool!" he said poking his index finger into my chest.

"You know he is an American citizen, reaps around four hundred thousand dollars a year, owns a Jaguar and a bungalow back in SF."

"Wow uncle, can you put in a word for me? I'll meet him if Devika isn't ready." What do I care how much he earns or what he drives or where he lives.

"Honestly, I'm not a huge fan of the work you do," the way he said, it I felt like I picked pockets for a living.

"But if being with you is what makes her happy, I'll have to make do with you." His eyes were on me. "You better be good, son. We warriors don't take messing around with our daughters too kindly." I pasted a very innocent smile and nodded my head vigorously to agree with him.

"I'll see you around." He patted my shoulder and joined the crowd.

Devika's father's subtle threat made me push a few more drinks down my throat. I climbed up to the roof and collapsed on the charpoy. The winters weren't far gone so the cold was enough to shrink my ball sack and send shivers up and down my body. A few rounds of heavily inhaling and exhaling the air later, I felt warm air on my lips. The familiar scent of a body brought a smile on my lips.

"Thank you," she whispered taking a break from kissing.

"Hmm." I responded and moved to make room for her to sleep besides me.

"Your 'the talk' with 'the father' really saved my ass," she said now resting her chin on my chest. "Did you see that guy?"

"Who? Mr Francisco? Yup, your dad even gave me a guided tour of his assets."

"Bozo was staring at me throughout."

"I don't blame him." I opened my eyes to look at her. She grinned and nuzzled on my chest. "But I wonder what he does with all that money. No booze, no smoking!"

"Spends it on flight tickets to meet girls who don't want to see him."

"Ouch! That's mean. You know, I think my dad likes you."

"Really?"

"Ya."

"He said that?"

"No, but I can tell from the body language and the way he looked at you. He even referred to you by your name while talking to me."

"So?"

"I mean, he generally refers to my boyfriends as *that guy, that loafer, loser, joker* or whatever, but never by his name."

"*Aacha!*" I pulled her close and wrapped my arm around her. "I see that all the warriors have a liking for this Brahmin."

"Hmm." She wrapped her hands around my body and held me close.

You can never tell what life has planned for you. I mean a year ago, I was sitting in some cafe talking to Devika about my wedding plans with Hrida. All of a sudden, I am in Gwalior to convince *Devika's* father to let her marry me. I opened my eyes and grazed at the stars as they had stopped spinning around me. Visuals of happy faces of people flashed in front of me – the whole warrior clan, the father, the cousins, Nishi bhaiya, Devika. For a change it was nice to have people around. Coming here wasn't a bad idea after all, I thought.

"I have to tell you something." She said still hugging me.

"What?"

"I'm late."

"For?"

(Long silence)

"I missed my period."

"Are you saying you are pregnant?" I asked and a while later I looked at her as what I asked her sunk in me.

"Yes, I think I am."

All I contributed was dead silence.

"Don't worry, I'll deal with it when we get back." She said and hugged me tight.

The words "*Yes* (then a pause) *I think I am*" ricocheted inside me for a billion times. The miasmic clouds of guilt began to accumulate in my head. The memories of all my blunders in my life began to ooze out of the plugged dark hole. I messed up my relationship with Hrida, then broke up with her, hurt my parents with my stuck-up shit, dumped Raghu and Shashank, and now I had slept with my best friend and got her pregnant. I was such fabulous selfish fuck up that I screwed my relationship with the only person left in my life who stood by me, no matter how much I sucked. The guilt inside me muted me around Devika. I hardly spoke to her on the wedding day but there were barbarous riots inside me which were ripping me apart.

"What the hell have I done!" Voice One mumbled looking at Devika as she fastened her seat belt in the flight.

"We asked you to get laid, not knock up Devika," Voice Two said.

"How different are you from the rest of the jerks she has dated?" Voice Three said.

"Ya at least they don't pretend to be her best friend to use her," Voice Four said.

"Look how heartbroken and shattered she was and what you did to her," Voice Two said.

"Stop it, stop it, stop it, stop it." I whispered as the visuals grossed me out.

"Hey, what's wrong?" Devika asked, and I realised my blunder.

"Nothing, it's the flight, take offs make me jittery." I said and tightened my seat belt. Devika wasn't clearly convinced, but she simply smiled and held my hand throughout the two hour long flight back.

"Bloody pile of poop, all you can do is stink," Voice Two continued.

"Look it isn't entirely my fault." Voice One said.

"Classic Arjun Kulkarni, he'll always find someone to blame," Voice Three said.

"Go ahead; blame her. Say she seduced you into giving up your innocence," Voice Two said.

"You disgust me man. If you have empty sex with someone, at least have the balls to own up to it," Voice Four said.

"It wasn't empty sex," Voice One shrieked back.

"Oh great so now you love her too." Voice Two said.

"No, I don't, I just..." Voice One said shrieked back.

"Arjun, your bag!" Devika squeaked and ran behind it as the conveyor belt at Mumbai airport began to drag it.

"Freak, it broke my nail," she said sucking her finger.

"I'm, I'm, I was just, just...I'm really sorry."

"It's okay, let's go now," she said pushing the trolley away.

My patience was wearing off and the self-belittling voices within had left me disoriented. I closed my eyes and began to breathe heavily. A few minutes later, I saw Devika staring at me as the cab stopped outside my house.

"You want to get down or you coming home with me?" She asked.

"No, I think should go home." I got off the cab and pulled my bags out.

And the cab zoomed away, the look in her eyes stayed back.

Ten days later, when I was busy holed up out of guilt, an e-mail from Devika tinged on my Blackberry.

Hi,

I am not pregnant anymore. I took care of it. Sorry to have spooked you with the news. You know me, I don't think much before I talk. Besides that, I told Pa that, it was all a hoax so you don't need to pretend anymore. Arjun, I am yet to understand the nature of our relationship in the past month. What happened was ought to end, but for that I don't want to trash the years we spent together. I know you love Hrida and will always do. And another thing I know is that I'm not Hrida, so it's all cool. You don't need to worry about anything. ANZ made an offer that I couldn't resist, so I took up the job. Just boarded the flight for Delhi so will call you when I land. Take care.

Love, Dev.

PS: I've left box full of joints back home. They should last a month. Have fun.

2003

When life fucks you, it is advisable to not resist, because your resistance will only leave you feeling raped. So after the fight at the café, I let my life drag me by my leg. Weddings didn't exactly evoke the feeling of excitement in me but there was nothing to do here in Mumbai other than have endless nerve wracking conversations with myself which could happen irrespective of location. In addition, Voice One came up with reasons to convince me:

One, I *had* to go away from Hrida or anything that would remind me of her.

Two, I needed something so buzzy that it would annihilate all the psychological aftereffects of my result of 10-flunked-subjects.

Three, I would get to meet the newly-born offspring of my cousin Malini and,

Four, with a year to kill, Raghu was ready to go with me.

So when Mom asked me to pack my bags for Jammu, I quietly agreed.

Billions of images of Hrida and the everestine Abhimanyu cozying and snuggling up to each other brought out best of my mind's preposterously outrageous comments, abnormally amplifying the

level of frustration in the thirty-six-hour-long train journey from Mumbai to Jammu. I was so exhausted by the internal contorted noises of the voices speaking to themselves that I muted myself externally. All the conversations happening around me were a montage of sequences that I wasn't interested in.

"Radzzz!" Malini didi screamed and hugged Radhika as she unlocked the netted door of her house. A minute after screaming, hugging, kissing and jumping with her, she squeezed me and then Raghu after screaming our names out loud. Touching of the feet of my parents by jiju, Bittu and other younger members in the house took place followed by me, Radhika and Raghu repeating the same with didi's in-laws and other senior members. Thanks to Radhika and Raghu's excessive chattering, I got away with only a smile which I had to force my face to display. But then when my facial muscles refused to fake the smile threatening to blow my cover, something happened and I no longer had to force a smile.

"Here, bug your Mamu now." Malini di said handing Rishi to me.

My first nephew. A five-month-old with balloon-like pink cheeks, dark brown glinted eyes, scanty hair, red drool-dripping lips, four frontal teeth and tiny fingers with cuspated nails that clawed my face at the first opportunity. I could only look at him and smile, and smile. No matter how good you are with words, it is impossible to explain the feeling that holding a baby that belongs to your bloodline generates inside you.

"Hello baby!!" I said and shook his hand.

"Phhrrrrrrrrrrr..." came the reply with a spray of drool, followed by "Kheerrrk, kheerrrk, kheerrrk kheerrrkhhh," some hearty laughter.

Never in my life had I thought I'd enjoy being spat upon by someone. Conversations with him were simple. Everything was phrrrrrrrrrr, kheerrrk, ghrrruup, yaaayaamm, oowwhuuoohh. The best part was the giggle he attached to his vocab. In just a few minutes, the baby unleashed its charm on all the Mumbaikars and got them gyrating to his clowning.

Three hours later, when the superstar got drowsy and everyone finally got saturated with the greetings and jubilation, Raghu and I exchanged a look. It had been close to forty hours that both of us had let cigarette smoke inside us. The house was so crowded that it would get extremely challenging to notice two missing boys for a few minutes. So at the first opportunity, both of us ran to the nearest cigarette shop and burnt the hell out of our lungs.

Raghu instantly befriended the convenience store owner. Since we were going to be here for fifteen days, it was extremely necessary to gather information on location of nearby cigarette shops.

"Can you believe it? This guy delivers suttas at home." Raghu said almost jumping at the news. I found it oddly comforting. Since we were not in Mumbai, there was no reason for us to step out of the house frequently.

"Did you get it?" Bittu asked Raghu.

"Hmm." Raghu responded.

"Quick, light it." She ordered Raghu.

"Do you want one?" she asked the girl who was with her. She shrugged a *yes*, so Raghu lit three cigarettes and handed one each to Bittu, me, and the girl.

"Poncho, you guys haven't met before right?" Bittu asked as the smoke escaped out of her nose and mouth.

"No," the girl said and I shook my head.

"She is Smiley, my cousin." She said, "Arjun, bhabi's cousin, and this is Raghu, her almost cousin." Everyone laughed.

"Bittu!" Radhika barged in banging the door open. *Crap!* I dropped my cigarette in fright, Smiley hid hers behind her while Bittu continued smoking,

"I saw that," she said glaring at me.

"You smoke too?" she asked Bittu in a scandalised tone. "Yuck!"

"And you two... imagine what jiju will do to you when he finds out you are supplying cigarettes to his sister."

"Ya, but he won't find out na." Bittu pulled Radhika close, "Will he? Will he? Will he?" she said kissing her after every 'will he?'.

"You smell of smoke. Go away!" Radhika said disgusted. "Your hubby to be is here and is asking for you so come down fast."

"And you... you are dead," she left piercing her nails into my arm.

I know, I said in my mind.

Angad, the hubby to be, was an IIT-D, IIM-A pass out. He now helped his dad in his apple export business. Why do people waste time, money and effort to do something that they know they'll abandon eventually. But why blame him, even I was somewhat of the same brand.

"Poncho!" Dad called me. "Ravi Uncle, Bittu's father-in-law," he said and I bent to touch his feet.

"So, civil engineering haan?" he said placing his hand on my shoulder. "Which year?"

"Third year starts when we return," my dad said. *Crap, I still have to tell him about the results.* I felt a huge thud in my stomach.

"Uncle is a civil engineer as well," he continued.

"From IIT, not to miss." Bittu"s father-in-law boasted.

"Oh so it's you from whom Angad gets his stupidity?" I thought of asking.

"But you know, Arvind, Angad after IIM-A has made me proud. I mean, even I got a degree from IIT, but it felt good that my son surpassed me."

Dad gave me a hopeful look. Maybe he wanted to shoot the same line someday. What he clearly missed was the familial stupidity of exporting apples instead of using the degree that they obviously slogged their asses to earn. But my dad was so awestruck by the fool's bragging that it was pointless to say anything against him. As for the highly literate moron, it's useless to inject sense into such great souls. They are so happy boasting of how they chose their family business over a hotshot job the degree offered that they'll never see logic in anything said against it. Coming from a guy who planned to drop out of engineering, let alone surpassing his father, would in all possibility fuse him. I would have any day preferred to listen to Rishi speak in his stress relieving ununderstandable language than get caught in a hareheaded conversation that reminded me of the things I had run away from. Since the supply of words from my brain was scarce, I glided out of the IIT-IIM-bragging crowd with a smile.

I spent the rest of my days in Jammu ferrying the bride to costume fittings or Smiley and other cousins to parlours, accompanying jiju and his family to random relatives for dinners where there was awesome Punjabi food, expensive alcohol which I couldn't drink or sitting in corner through painful discussions on colours and patterns of saris by the overcritical ladies who were yet to shop for Bittu's wedding or going vegetable shopping with didi's father-in-law or babysitting Rishi. But I didn't mind the inanity of any of the activities as long as it kept the obnoxious memories of my results or Hrida's 'cheating on me' away. It had been sixteen days since doomsday, but the noxiousness of that day refused to stop harrowing me. The moment I stepped away from the high pitched exultant buzz, the wicked voices took over.

"You coming?" I asked Raghu to avoid being alone.

"No, I am fine, don't feel like it," Raghu whispered stretching a sari as he stood in the centre surrounded by ladies.

"At least give me company," I gritted.

"Raghu hold it properly ya..." Malini di scolded. "Poncho, shoo, go play outside."

"Like this?" Raghu slouched looking at me in helplessness and began to drape the sari around him.

I grabbed the cigarette box and timidly began to walk up the stairs to the roof.

"At last you are alone. I thought you'd never leave," Voice Two said.

"Stop bothering me," Voice One said.

"Thank goodness," I said under my breath when I saw Smiley on the roof.

"Hey!" I said, startling her. The pouch in her hand dropped on the floor.

"Shit, I didn't bolt the door?" she said hurriedly collecting the contents of the pouch.

"Were you just rolling up a joint in the house?" I borrowed Radhika's scandalised tone.

"You are smart," she mocked.

"How old are you? Thirteen? Fourteen?"

"And, you are funny too!"

"What else do you do?"

"Pretty much all the things that a seventeen-year-old girl isn't expected to do," she winked and clamped the joint with her lips and pulled in a long drag.

"Come on now, stop being such a chacha. Pull one."

"No, I'm fine," I cringed.

"Wait a minute, you've never gotten stoned before, have you?" she almost condescended.

"Well, not exactly, but I've felt the buzz passively," I said quietly as her face began to light up to laugh. She laughed at me for the next three minutes... non-stop.

"I-I'm sorry but that was incredibly funny," she continued laughing.

"You want to try one?" she offered. I shrugged.

The first three drags felt like a normal cigarette, but when it began to kick in, my face went numb, throat dried, lips stretched and my body went into slow motion. I paused significantly after every word I spoke. Everything around started appearing in the sets of three. A few puffs had craned the huge load off my chest and it felt feather-light. My mind was experiencing the blissful silence it had craved for, like centuries.

"This... is... so... awesome," I said.

"I knowww!" she paused, and stared straight into my eyes.

"Come, let's go up there," she said extending her hand. I held one of the three cold hands I was seeing and let her guide me up the ladder to the water tank. Both of us rested our backs on the tank and gazed at the sky, still holding hands.

"I wish it would always feel like this – weightless, boundless, painless," I heard her breathe heavily.

"Hmm." I let her hand go and ran my fingers through my hair and pulled them.

"Tell me something." She sat up folding her legs. "If you were a girl, a hot one, who never deprives her boyfriend of anything, yet 'the dog' strays around just for a kick," she said counting the conditions on her fingers, "What would you do?"

"Ah, umm, that's heavy."

"And you love him so much that you can't leave him..."

"Hmm." I closed my eyes.

"What? Tell me now."

"I'm thinking."

"Bugger! Give me your arm." I did and she rested her head on it.

"Are *you* in the situation we are talking about here?"

"Yuck! No!"

"Good, because it's too much to think about," I said as she began to laugh.

"Arjun!"

"Hmm."

"I wanna kiss you," she said. I turned my head to her to find her face uncomfortably close to mine.

"Can I?" She asked after I stared at her for don't know how long.

"I don't know," I said looking at her lips, thinking if I should.

"No, no." I said, last *no* a little louder more of telling myself than her.

"Why? Do you have a girlfriend or something?"

"Yes, I mean no. I just haven't officially broken up with her yet," I said.

"So this is how it feels, when you don't officially break up!" Voice One said.

"Smiley said what?" Raghu screamed, when I told him about Smiley wanting to kiss me.

"Let me get this straight, *Smiley* said she wanted to kiss *you* and you said *no*? Right?"

"Ya, right."

"Because?" He stared at me, "You thought it wasn't right since you hadn't officially broken up with Hrida?" He said himself when I didn't reply.

"Yes."

"Can I please slap you?" He waited for an answer.

"Get lost, Raghuvir." Shashank pushed him away. "You did right, kiddo."

"What is wrong with you guys?" Raghu sounded like a disheartened kid in the toy store whose parents refused to buy him toys. "Refusing to have sex and be a touch-me-not is a girl's job not ours."

"She didn't want to have sex," I said.

"I know genius, I'm just saying."

"Yes Mr. Randy, but when you are in a relationship, it doesn't feel right to stray," Shashank said.

"Oh come on, don't patronise me. I've dated girls too *and* strayed at the same time. It's normal."

"You have dated girls, but you've never been in a relationship with anyone."

"And you guys think there is a difference between the two." Raghu said. Both of us shrugged and he began to laugh. "You guys are panties, pure silk panties. I better leave before I throw up." He left laughing.

Both of us began to laugh.

"It's 5.30, let's go pick the girls," Shashank said stubbing his cigarette.

"I don't want to meet anyone."

"By anyone you mean Hrida."

"Yes." I lit a cigarette.

"Poncho, you've got to give her a chance to explain."

"There is nothing to explain, Shashank. You too saw what happened that day."

"There is, trust me."

In the fifteen minutes that it took from the naka to Hrida's college, I thought of all sorts of venomous words to spew on Hrida to vent my anger. But a cigarette and an Aarey lassi later when I saw her walk out of the college gate, my heart began to jump in the rib cage and the rush of the blood evaporated the loathsome feelings inside me. My feet went cold as she came close.

"Hi," she said to me and smiled. I turned to Neha without responding.

"When did you guys come back?" Neha asked slapping my hand.

"Yesterday," I tried to sound as bland as I could.

"OK. What's the plan now?"

"Nothing, let's meet at the café," Shashank said to me.

Neha hopped onto his bike and he zoomed away. Hrida stood there looking at me. I kicked the bike to start, and waited. My ego had clogged the words in my throat, so as a gesture of asking her to sit I looked at her. She hopped on the bike. I looked at her face in the mirror. What's worse than the agony of being in love is the pain that accompanies as a consolation price which is always ready to suck you in. And then follows the generation of countless contrasting emotions that leave your innards in total chaos. One part of me was dying to look at her, hold her, talk to her; while there arose an anguish out of the memories of the past in another. I hated every bit of Hrida for what she had done to me. I however wished all my hatred could somehow disappear and life reset itself to normalcy.

"How have you been?" she asked with a lovelorn look in her eyes, but I chose to glue my eyes on the road.

"I tried calling you a thousand times, you know, but couldn't reach you so messaged you. Didn't you get them?"

I had read each and every one of the hundred and thirty-eight messages she had sent more than once, most of them saying sorry and begging me to respond.

"I was worried. You should have at least told me before you left. I missed you baby," she said and pecked a kiss on my shoulder and I cringed to show my resentment. A wave of sadistic pleasure swept through me seeing her face flush the smile, she gave up looking at me. Though my rudeness was beginning to annoy me, my ego refused to give up.

"How long won't you be talking to me?" She stared at me through the mirror.

"Would saying *never* do the trick for you?" Her tone irked me so I snapped back.

"I have been saying sorry for almost a month now. What more do you expect out of me? And for no fault of mine."

"Classic! So you've already decided it wasn't your fault."

"Well since you haven't given me a chance to explain, I had to."

"Oh yes, the explanation. I am so sorry to have ceased you from doing it for so long. Please enlighten me." I geared down and pulled the throttle in anger. Now I stared at her while she huffed away.

"I said sorry, so please get on with your explanation, let's just end this disaster today itself. I don't want to see you again."

She looked at me jarred. "When I said I'm meeting my school friends, I didn't lie. I did meet them. I didn't know Abhimanyu would also be there with everybody else. He had been constantly pushing me to meet; when I didn't heed, he got Tanya to get me to meet him. So we weren't alone that evening, nor was I cooing with him. It was my bad luck that everybody just left before you came. I could have left with everybody else but this guy has been an asshole and I simply couldn't leave without settling my score with him. He means nothing to me. What happened in the past is the past. No matter how much he implores, what he wants is never happening. I love you Arjun and you know that. I can't keep assuring it to you all the time. If you don't want me, I'll leave...." the rest of the words that came out of her mouth got silenced by a huge thud.

The state transport bus driver had made his trademark we-own-the-roads erratic turn and the rear bumper of the bus clasped my mirror and dragged the bike along with us for a nice ten feet before the bike slumped on the road. Right from the moment that douche made the turn, to the moment where I felt the heavy weight of my bike falling on my leg, I saw everything in slow motion. It took me a couple of seconds to regain my senses. I got up in a fit of rage and limping, ran behind the bus hurling abuses. Halfway through I stopped and turned to look at Hrida. I saw a crowd surrounding my bike. *Shit.* When I returned to the spot, Hrida was lying on the road motionless. My heart sank in horror.

"Hey Hrida... Hrida..." I said trying to wake her up, I had never been so scared in my life, I helplessly looked around at the staring faces in the crowd. "Oye, get up, please, Hrida!" I said trying again. The ten whole seconds that she took to open her eyes were the longest ten seconds of my life. I took multiple deep breaths, while my body perspired to cool itself. I walked her to the footpath and sat her down. Someone from the crowd brought my battered bike. A few people had caught the driver and pulled him down from the bus for a handsome thrashing. The traffic constables patiently waited for the crowd to vent their frustration. Suddenly Hrida began to laugh at the whole scene.

"You should have seen your face," she said trying to get over her hilarity.

"I almost shat in my pants." I could still feel thumping of my heart.

"Eww... gross!"

"Are you alright?" I asked. She nodded a yes, "Bloody asshole ruined my bike. *Maar bhenchod Ko!* I yelled looking at the crowd and sat beside her.

"So, can we get done with the break-up you wanted or have you changed your mind?"

"Ummm... not now... let's do it maybe a hundred years later."

"Rascal!" she punched my arm. "You wait and watch what I do to you now."

"You really scared me." Making sure no one noticed my public display of affection I held her hand tightly.

"You too," she said, and bit my shoulder.

2010

It took me six kilometres of drunken driving and one thousand eight hundred and sixty-two footsteps to reach the door of my house. I held the frame of the door and replayed the whole journey from Pyaasa to my complex in my mind and tried to think if anyone had seen me walking with my trademark drunken sway or if I had bumped anyone off with the car. The blurred visuals of me speeding in the narrow lanes, the sound of the car screeching at sharp turns and thuds of overshooting a speed breaker sent chills down my spine. I rested my head on the door and ballooned my cheeks to heave a sigh of relief. I should stop drinking, or at least driving after drinking, I warned myself.

One litre of alcohol had done a magnificent job on me. My eyes closed themselves and the body drifted to sleep. A few minutes later the brain restarted itself and woke the body up. The bed was inside the house and I was still outside it. I stuffed my hands in the pocket to find the keys.

"Crap!" I had forgotten to take them when I left home that morning. I virtually smacked my head but it was a little too late for the happy realisation. I twitched my eye to look at the time in the watch. I would rather sleep at Pyaasa than wake Mom and Dad at 4.13 a.m., but I wasn't ready to go through all the foolhardiness again. I took multiple deep breaths to pump oxygen in the body to revive itself from the drunken daze and

pressed the doorbell. As I heard the chiming of the doorbell, I prayed that mom wouldn't open the door.

"Good morning, Baba," I said to Dad fixing a grin on my face.

"What happened to your keys?"

"I forgot to take them. Sorry had to wake you up," I said entering the house trying to not slur my words.

Dad went to his room without responding. I held the handle of the door to maintain my balance. I carefully leaned to untie the left shoelace, but as soon as I loosened the grip on the door handle, I fell sideways, bringing the shoe rack down on me, making enough noise to wake the neighbours. So before I could do anything to save the situation, the lights went on. I was lying in a heap of shoes and sandals. From the corner of my eye, I saw 'the Mother' standing a few feet away from me. I got up and tussled to remove the shoes, trying to avoid direct eye contact with her.

"Hi Aai," I said looking into her raging eyes. She scared me so much that I gave up on removing the other shoe and began to sway-walk towards my room with one shoe still on.

"Will you care to explain yourself or you don't feel the need to?" she said.

"I'm sorry I forgot the keys."

"So you're only sorry for forgetting the keys?" There was no good way to answer that question so I chose to go mute.

"Do you realise how horribly you've ruined your life?" There hadn't been a how-to-handle-your-life lecture from Mom for a while so it was only fair that I gave her a chance to stuff my ears with all the clichés available in the 'lecturing your child' handbook. I slowly walked myself to the couch and rested my ass on it.

"Have you looked at what you have turned into? You can't even handle yourself." I was so drunk that I needed a support for my head; so I buried my face in my palms.

"You are an exact definition of what civil society calls an alcoholic; a drinking, falling, throwing up piece of food, doing nothing other than being a nuisance to people. Life isn't a movie, Arjun. That a girl leaves a guy and he drinks his life down the gutter. You have to accept that God didn't want you and Hrida to be together." Mom spoke as if god himself had hissed his plans into her ears.

"Your filmy career is influencing you too much. Quitting engineering was the biggest mistake of your life. You should have listened to us, but you chose to trust a random girl over your parents and look where she got you." After the break-up, Hrida had suddenly become a stone in a shoe for everyone around me.

"You are almost twenty-eight years old, still an undergrad, working for peanuts with no future."

My mother in described my present and predicted my future in one sentence.

"That is why you are supposed to listen to your parents and not strangers. We had plans for you but you chose to ruin them for your juvenile schemes. When I look at kids your age, it shames me. You've disappointed me, Arjun..."

"Yes Aai, I am a huge disappointment to you, to Baba, to Radhika and to everyone I've ever known. Thank you, you guys provided me with everything I wanted. I'm sorry I didn't turn out to be the ideal son. Sorry I didn't suffocate myself in the rotten atmosphere of engineering and chose to follow my selfish dreams. I'm sorry that I don't have an eight figure pay package. I'm sorry that I'm a complete failure, a classic drunkard and a hopeless loser." The uncivilty in my voice notched up with every sorry.

"There, I apologised for everything. Wait a minute, did I miss anything?" I said hopping on one leg fighting with my shoelaces.

"Oh and yes, sorry I fell in love. I should have sought approval from my control freak of a mother before I did. Can I please go to sleep?" I said and threw the shoe away. She didn't respond.

"Is that a yes? Haan? Can I go to sleep?" As soon as I said, that my face felt a mighty slap from Dad.

"I hate you both!" I screamed in a rage.

Mom's eyes finally welled up, ultimately satisfying me.

I stormed off to my room and crashed on the bed.Demonic faces began to laugh at me as I closed my eyes. The ranting had blown up most of the alcohol in my body leaving behind a scanty amount, barely enough to flare up the laughing faces and doze me off. I had to make sure I slept before the daze faded and the voices took over.

"One... two... three..." I began counting numbers, my best weapon against the voices.

"Twenty-one... twenty-two... twenty-three..." Visuals of Hrida getting married flooded my mind.

"Thirty-nine... forty... forty-one..." I saw Devika's teary-eyed face as the cab zoomed off.

"Just go fuck yourself loser!!!" Raghu's voice screamed.

"Seventy-five... seventy-six... seventy-seven..."

"You are just somebody that I am ashamed to say I loved." Hrida's voice said.

"Hundred...hundred and one... hundred and...." I slept.

I woke up to two voices – a screaming girl and a begging guy. The velocity at which my life was changing had stunned me. After the fight, I moved out of my parents' house and started sharing a house with three extremely opposite characters. My senior at work Ashwin, a highly sexual character who needed to get laid every night. His girlfriend-worshiping surd cousin Humpy who was petrified of her, and his almost bi-polar background dancer girlfriend Tamsin. Sleeping to Tamsin's thunderous moaning in the next room and waking up to her violent screams was a daily occurrence. Their topics of fight would range from as trivial reasons as Humpy forgetting to wash their left over dishes to leaving his stinking sock in Tamsin's clutch to some grave ones like Humpy objecting to Tamsin spending time with random guys from work late at nights to Humpy's father disapproving of her religion. The volume of their voices would depend on the seriousness of the fight. Going by Tamsin's hysteric screams that day, it was clearly a serious one. Usually I got to hear just screams and a few muffled sentences, but that day I was sleeping in the living room since Ashwin had had a 'friend' to stay over the night before so I was witnessing the fight between these two half-naked people from two feet away. Humpy had forgotten to wear a condom while having sex with Tamsin and now she had missed her period.

"...you know how high we'd gotten that night. I thought I wore it but I wasn't sure." Humpy whined as he followed her everywhere around the house with morning wood in his underwear and socks on his feet.

"So if you weren't sure, you should have fucking told me!" Tamsin in her translucent lavender panties and a white ganji screamed and threw an ash tray at him. It hit him right on his head. Thank god for his turban else he would have had to flaunt groovy stitches on his forehead for the rest of his life. I covered my face with the quilt and turned the other way to give them some privacy.

"I am sorry baby, let's go take care of it," Humpy said meekly.

"Right! This is the third time you have done it. Do you know what your fucking 'taking care of it' does to my body? I look like a pale panda with those dark circles, I can barely move my body at the rehearsals and to make things worse, I bleed all day long..."

The information was getting a little too much for me. I got off my make-shift bed and walked past them to the kitchen, pretending I wasn't listening.

"Morning, pretty boy!" The tone and volume of Tamsin's voice suddenly turned civil and endearing which quite baffled me.

"Morning Tam, Humpy," I said, trying to sound unfazed by the ongoing riot and their nakedness. "I'm gonna go make some coffee. You guys want some?"

"I'll have, I'll have." Humpy said raising his hand like a school boy eager to answer his teacher. Tam stared at him in rage.

"You are a sweetheart, I'd love some." She said and blew a kiss towards me. I smiled and left while the yelling continued behind me.

"So what do we do now?' Humpy whined, 'Should we keep it?"

"Have you lost your mind completely? Let's keep it? And what?..." their voices faded as I entered the kitchen.

I wondered what had kept them together all this while. If

it was the love, then sanity was too steep a price they paid to maintain it.

Why can't there be a perfect relationship where there is no conflict between the couple? Why can't God just blow some magic dust and say, "Here this is the person for you to spend rest of the life with. Go live happily ever after." Why does love always have to be mixed with complications, tears, sadness, war of wills, heartbreaks? I guess happily ever after comes with an expiry date, may be that is why the romantic movies do such good business world over. I plugged the morning psychobabble as I walked back in the living room with coffee.

"...you got some timing to screw things up. This had to happen when my parents were gonna come." Tam yelled again looking around for something to throw.

"Here you go," I handed her her mug before Humpy got hit by something else.

"Ahh, how I needed the coffee." Tam said smelling it, her tone flipped again.

"I'm sorry, but when are they coming?" I asked.

"You didn't tell him, didn't you?" she turned to Humpy in anger.

"Hey no, my mistake, I forgot." I quickly covered up and saw Humpy's relieved face.

Tamsin had lied to her parents that Humpy owned the house and she lived alone with him, so whenever they came to visit her, the roommates had to bunk outside the house till they were in town.

"They are coming tonight, but they'll be gone by tomorrow," she said apologetically.

"Oh come on, its no big deal, I'll manage." I said.

Office that day felt like a fish market, crowded with girls parroting lines of the lead heroine's sister's part that we were auditioning for. These lines will haunt your dreams tonight, I told myself as I walked past a girl rehearsing the dialogues. Sleeping on the couch had gifted me a sprained back. I opened the door to the audition room and hoped that we found our girl soon, else the pain in the back shaken with terrible acting skills of the rejectables would make a lethal cocktail towards the end of the day.

The lighting was done, and the camera was ready to roll.

"Aroga Singh!!" Shilpi, my colleague called out a name peeping out of the room in the corridor. "Did you see that? It's a freaking gaggle outside man, it's going to be a loooooong day," she said and blew out air making a whistling sound as the girl walked in.

"Hi, write your name and number on the board." Shilpi instructed the girl, she did as told.

"Thanks, now give your profiles please." I adjusted the camera focus, the girl obeyed with a smile. "Thanks, I'll give you the cues if you want."

"Okay, thanks." The girl said dabbing her under eyes with a puff.

"It's okay, Aroga, the character you are auditioning for is a dying leukemia patient, so it's fine if you flaunt your dark circles," Shilpi said impatiently as the puffing extended beyond permissible time.

"I'm ready, so let's roll."

"Action!" Shilpi ordered. The girl took a deep breath and began.

"So it's official, isn't it? There is no cure for me?" she hurriedly blabbed and blanked out. "I'm sorry, give me a second please." She grabbed her dialogue sheet.

"Okay, I'm ready." She chucked the script.

"And action!!!"

"So it's official, isn't it? There is no cure for me?" Her tone bland, with no sign of pain of a dying person, "I know I'm gonna die, but I'm fine with it. I don't have any regrets about my life..." and she blanked out again.

The same process repeated with most of the girls that followed her. Some went blank after the first two lines, some flawlessly zwooped through the lines but gave acting a miss, one of the girls began to cry even before she started, some failed to match the role so argued over length and pretended to refuse it. Then there were these two girls who almost cracked the scene right and gave decent performances. Shilpi and I switched sides with every alternate girl, with the hope that the next one who walked in would be our girl, but the tapes kept exhausting, faces kept changing, mugs of coffee kept coming in, but the one we were looking for eluded us. The back pain had worn my patience out, so I crashed on the couch. Shilpi's cordiality too had evaporated out of her body making her a degree thornier with every next girl.

"Tell me when you are ready," Shilpi said curtly.

"I'm ready."

"Action!"

As the girl said the lines, her voice seemed unbelievably familiar as if I was almost sure of who it was. I opened my eyes to confirm.

"What I'm worried about is you, Pooja," Kintu continued.

"I know that after mom died, you've felt responsible for me, you've been there for me every time I needed you. Not once have I missed mom or dad; you gave me everything I've wanted." I stared at her fair freckled face in the display screen of the camera as she delivered her lines effortlessly.

"I've seen you not having a life because of me, and that is not a good feeling to die with. So promise me, you'll be happy after I'm gone," her eyes watered.

It had been more than seven years that I had seen her. So much had changed about her, the short ponytail had given way to shoulder length hair. The blue denims and lemon yellow tee she wore revealed less of her body than before. There was no trace of the patented bitchiness.

"For once let someone else take care of you. Akash... I mean, yes, I know how you feel about him, and you probably don't know this, but he loves you too. Promise me you'll give him a chance, this is the one last thing I ask of you before I die." Kintu sobbingly concluded and there was a long silence. Shilpi and I exchanged the we-might-have-gotten-the-girl look. It took a while for Kintu to recover.

"Hi, are you alright?" Shilpi warmly asked Kintu as she opened the door to see if there were any girls left.

"I'm fine. It'll just take a while," Kintu said and chuckled as the tears kept coming.

"Please take your time." Shilpi said, "Can you believe it? She was the last one!" She returned to me and whispered, I nodded my head in disbelief. "Will you stay with her while I run her tape through boss?"

"Oh ya, come soon."

Shilpi rushed out to show Kintu's audition tape to our director; I stayed back in the darkness behind the camera, contemplating whether to show myself or not, while Kintu decked herself up.

"Hey bye... say bye to Shilpi from me, will you?" Kintu said as she gathered her stuff.

"Ya, I'll do that."

"I'm sorry I don't know your name."

"Arjun!" Ashwin banged the door open and barged in before I could open my mouth. "Are you done?" he asked me.

"Yes, give me a minute, I'll wrap up," I said as Kintu stared at me.

"Hi, Ashwin, I'm the 1st AD," he said extending his hand towards Kintu.

"Hi, Kintu."

"Just saw your tape, it's brilliant." Shilpi entered behind him. "You'll hear from us soon."

"Thanks."

"What did boss say?" he asked Shilpi.

"He'll get back." Shilpi said.

"You chuck it man. Shilpi will take care of it." Ashwin said pulling me by my hand.

"Where are you guys going? Can I come please?" Shilpi begged.

"It's a boys' night out, sorry," he said rushing out of the room, dragging me with him. Kintu smiled at me before I got out of the room.

"What is this place?" I asked Ashwin as he parked his car below a building.

"It's a bar." He stretched and pulled out a whiskey bottle from the seat pocket. "Here, swig a couple of pegs," he said after gulping a few millilitres himself.

"Aren't we going in?" I took a sip from the bottle.

"Yes, but it's better to enter in a daze."

"I don't understand."

"You will, give it some time." He took another long sip and dumped the bottle in the back of the car. "How do I look?" He asked as we got out of the car.

"Complete Shah Rukh..." I said.

He hurriedly entered the narrow staircase. I followed him. We climbed the dark staircase, before entering a brightly lit room with a reservation desk and a brawny bouncer behind it. He gave Ashwin a jubilant smile the instant he saw him. From the sound of the type of music that played behind the leather cushioned door, I figured where Ashwin had brought me. It was a dance bar. Before I could say anything, the bouncer opened the door and a sonic wave of music, cigarette smoke, and smell of varied perfumes and alcohol hit me.

It was a huge forty by forty hall with couches lined by the sides of the walls, leaving a large area for the patrons and the bar girls to dance on, the multicolored lights gyrated on the floor while the air conditioner granted it a subzero temperature. Around fifty girls clad in multicoloured flashy saris and lehengas swayed mildly to the music while their faces shot naughty expressions at their respective customers. The customers then showered bundles of money on them. There would be so much of our country's currency straying on the floor that the waiter every fifteen minutes broomed it in gunny bags as if it was trash. Customers ranged from gangster-like heavily bearded dark guys wearing gold chains and rings to nerdy corporate professionals whose wives were probably under the illusion that their husbands were busy slogging their asses at work.

The bouncer guided us to a table which I assumed was Ashwin's regular one. Ashwin tipped the guy and he left. As soon as we sat, the manager walked to us with a smile and shook Ashwin's hand. The sound of music was so deafening that it was impossible for anyone to have a conversation. Ashwin raised his index finger gesturing the manager to get one quantity of something.

"Why did you bring me here?" I typed on my cell to talk to Ashwin.

"To have fun, now shush."

The manager returned with a bundle of notes and handed it over to Ashwin. As the waiter made our drinks, Ashwin scribbled something on a piece of paper and handed it over to the manager with two hundred rupee notes. Minutes later, the girl in the orchestra began to sing the latest item number and Ashwin's face lit up with excitement. Then out of nowhere, a fair-skinned girl appeared and did a whole three sixty degree turn in front of our table while her red navel revealing lehenga floated in air. Ashwin picked up his currency bundle and began to drop one note after another on her head in quick succession. Then as if to compete with him, Mr. White Pants at the table next to us got up and began to dance around her in an attempt to get her attention. when that didn't work, he threw a whole twenty rupee note bundle on her in one go, but that just bought him a smile and she continued her pelvic thrusts around Ashwin while his hundred rupee notes lay below her feet. She pulled Ashwin deeper into the crowd on the floor. The scenario everywhere around the bar was more or less the same. The good looking customers easily got the girls' attention while the ugly looking guys had to empty their pockets to get a mere smile from them.

Ashwin returned to the table and gestured me to come with him. I followed him out of the hall into the corridors of the lodging area of the hotel. I saw the two girls waiting outside the room, so it wasn't rocket science to guess that he had struck some kind of package-sex deal with his girl and her friend.

"Make me proud," he said and slapped my behind before going into his room.

I felt an unrecognised hollowness as I entered my room. The girl was a dusky babe with a great body, streaked hair, and an expressionless face. The white glittering low waist saree she wore gave a mind blowing view of her navel. Without wasting any time, the girl began to undress herself. After stripping every piece of clothing on her body she walked up to me and began to undo the buckle of my belt. Her deadpanned attitude made me freeze in my place. Ever since I'd hit puberty, nude women and thoughts of having sex had only evoked blissful feelings within me; but looking at her nude body made me feel disgusted about myself. Her hands began to feel me as she pulled my denim down. She closed in further and began to kiss me, as soon as I felt her lips on mine, I cringed. She immediately backed off, sensing my reluctance. I hurriedly pulled my denim up and buttoned it. There was a completely naked girl standing in front of me, and I felt more embarrassed about my pants being down in front of her.

"Do you have a girlfriend?" she asked

"No," I said, and half smiled at her.

"You love someone?"

"No."

"Find yourself a girl, you don't seem like one of those guys who can pull a girl's pants down and start."

"I'm sorry, about all this," I said and left.

I had no reply to the girl's statement. Maybe I really needed a girlfriend or maybe I didn't. I learned one thing about myself that day. No matter how soul-sucking my loneliness was, I wasn't meant for junk sex.

Since I had abandoned Ashwin's alternative accommodation plan, I had no option but to find shelter in our office where again a couch waited for my sprained back. I cursed myself for leaving the motel.

The reality of moving out of the Mom and Dad's protective cocoon had begun to bite me. Life was no longer a cake walk. The comforts of the air-conditioned bedroom in my parents' house was replaced by a hot room with a snoring roommate. Dinner was no longer ready on the platter, unless I cooked it. Traveling in the city meant running to catch a government attention deprived local trains and fighting to breath in its overcrowded compartments. In spite of living in the city for so many years, it suddenly had started feeling alien. I had a new house and new friends and I had chosen this independent life, but the only regret was the unaccounted emptiness that came along with it. I had spent all my life in a comfort zone of people who cared for me, people who knew me, so I was struggling to adapt myself. There was no one around me who I could emotionally attach myself to. The only person who came to my mind at that point was her, and the only place to find her number right then and there was on the board she held. I sprang out of the couch and fished for Kintu's audition tape in the cupboard.

"Hi..." I typed hurriedly and not knowing what else to say, sent just that word. It was almost midnight, so waiting for her reply was stupidity. The sleep fairy's magic potion had gotten me sleepy enough so I crashed on the couch and closed my eyes. I was half asleep when my phone tinged.

"*Arjun?*" Her message read.

"*Yes. How did you know?*"

"*I didn't, I guessed it. I wanted it to be you.*"

"*It was nice to see you today.*"

"*I know. Howz you and your girlfriend, Hrida right?*"

"*We are not together anymore.*"

"*Oh, I'm sorry.*"

"*It's fine. Listen, do you wanna go out for a coffee some time?*"

"*Would love to.*"

I replied with just a smiley.

In the following week, 'the coffee sometime' happened once every day after office. Kintu began spending time at my place, sometimes staying over. It felt like I was meeting an altogether different person. There was no trace of the snobbish Kintu I knew seven years back. Now she spoke of her career and independence and fortitude instead of expensive brands, cars or money. She had taken over the maternal and girlfriendial responsibilities towards me by force-feeding food, doing up my room, scolding me for not attending to my back pain, and turning Tam into her BFF. Even though the whole change was too sudden for me, I didn't really mind because I was liking it. Meanwhile, since the day at the bar Ashwin hadn't spoken a word to me. He had shot down all my attempts to make a conversation with him. He left for office without taking me with him, and that meant I had to travel by public transport to office. I concluded that my under-performance with the sex-working professional that night would have been the reason for his sulking housewifely behaviour. The ever-warring couple living in the next room too had called a truce, so the house for a change had been in total silence. But sharing the same room, same bed, even the same office desk and not speaking a word to each other made me feel weird. I had to do something before it got any weirder than it was. With his birthday just around the corner, I decided to throw him a sweet sixteen party on his thirty-third birthday.

Kintu and Tam helped me decorate the house with pink and red balloons and drapes. One of our costume designer friends designed a slutty purple frock and tiara for Ashwin. Humpy procured premium quality charas and Tam rolled the joints. Kintu locked the menu and I ordered it. Tam and her friends choreographed a medley of mujras for the birthday boy.

Everyone close to Ashwin was going to be there at the party but there was a high risk that birthday boy himself would go to celebrate the birthday with his friends at the dance bar so I entrusted the task of delivering him home on time to Agent Shilpi, who very efficiently played the part of a seducing colleague and brought him straight home from office. The poor guy got the shock of his life as the light went on just when he was about to make his move on her. There were screams wishing him. When everyone in the party hugged, kissed and wished him, I tried my luck. I held a joint for him to pull a drag. He hugged me and finally gave up his annoyance over me.

"Swift move with the starlet." He whispered in my ear, "I'm proud of you." I smiled and hugged him back.

Tam pulled him in the crowd and made him wear the frock and the tiara for the cake cutting. From the happy faces of people dancing, yelling, swaying to the music, I could tell the party was a hit. It reminded me of the party pimp I was once a friend of. Even though it had been close to a year since I had chosen to stay away from Raghu and Shashank, I hadn't fully accepted the reality of them not being in my life anymore. I stood there in the corner and looked around if there was anyone who could be my new best friends. From Ashwin's Delhi based cousin Raj who would pull everyone in the corner of the room and speak to them in hushed tone as if he was some kind of spy, to his sexed up best friend who took the first opportunity to jump on Tam's *firang* friends; from a couple of struggling actor friends who after a few drinks spoke of heavy stuff like depth in the character and lack of substance in content of contemporary cinema, to a certain guitar strumming Pandey who entertained the girls surrounding him with his latest compositions; from a couple of lone drinking women who occupied the corner of the room and stared at the dancing crowd with straight face, to a bunch of guys that only drank and danced, and drank, and danced. Tam, Humpy, Shilpi. I tried pasting the faces of Raghu, Shashank, Devika over everyone in the party but my imaginary mask fit no one. There was no one out there who could replace the friends I had lost.

The alcohol and the black clay joints had done a good job on me, but the music and the drunken babble of the crowd was spoiling the fun, so I decided to take the party over to my bed. I chucked the remaining whiskey in my glass and dragged my feet to the bedroom. I banged the door open alarming a furiously snogging couple.

"Oh, I'm so sorry." I slurred and turned around. Nano-seconds later when my baked brain registered their faces a smile swept my face. Ashwin and Kintu. With no intention of embarrassing them, I left the room. Kintu followed me trying to zip herself up.

"Arjun, I'm sorry," she said catching up with me in the lobby while I waited for the lift.

"It's okay."

"It's not what it looks like." Her genuine begging amused me. She was indeed a good actor, I thought to myself.

"I desperately needed the part, I was just making sure I get it."

"Why are you explaining yourself?"

"Because I care for you. I really needed the part Arjun, please understand."

"Kintu," I said placing both my hand on her shoulders, "I understand, you are a climber and there is nothing wrong in it. You don't need to apologise for that."

"Baby, I'm sorry."

"Hah! Just accept what you are, you'll feel better," I said and left.

What I saw in my bedroom honestly had no effect on me. Firstly because Kintu wasn't my girlfriend, nor did I feel anything for her, and secondly, Kintu was always a reaper and Ashwin was being the hornithologist that he was. What happened was just bound to. I didn't care about the hows and whys of the situation because the people involved weren't that important to me. Contrarily, it magnified my inner want of running away from Mumbai. I was pure misfit for this city and the people in it. In past ten months, I had lost Raghu, Shashank, Devika, Mom and Dad to my fate. So before I found new people and lost them again, I admitted myself in a film school in Los Angeles.

"Hey Arjun, I'm sorry if I screwed anything for you." Ashwin said as I pulled my bags out of his car at the airport. "I didn't mean to spite you."

"Don't say sorry, there is nothing wrong you did," I said and hugged him. "It's all cool."

"You take care, man. Wish you luck." He hugged me again before leaving.

Teary eyed mothers, fathers, brothers, sisters, wives waved to their loved ones standing outside the gate with a heavy heart. Even though there was no one standing to wave to me, I turned one last time to look at everything I was leaving behind in Mumbai. The moment I walked in through the departure gate, the fact that I was surely not going to see Hrida anymore sank in. Ever since the day she walked out of the cafe that night, I had hoped with all my heart that she would come back some day, and when she did, I would be there waiting for her. Now I had to curb all my futile hopes of patching up with her and literally move on. Throughout the formalities at the airport counters, memories of Hrida hounded me. So before my mind's poise bolted on me and I made any attempts to escape out of the airport, I switched on the heavy metal music on my phone and rushed through the boarding gates, into the plane to my seat and buckled the seat belt tightly till the flight took off from my beloved city.

2005

"*B*e at James'... right now... I'm shitting my pants." A message from Raghu read.

"*I'll be there in 10.*" I replied.

Every suburb in Mumbai has a cycle coffeewala who provides amazing coffee, tea and almost all brands of cigarettes to the insomniacs all night long. James, our coffee guy, was a veteran out of rest of the city's cycle boys. Even though he operated between midnight to six in the morning, the spot where he stood had somewhat became a landmark for the city people. Raghu had discovered it for us. Apart form late night yummy coffee and unlimited supply of cigarettes, unlike other cycle boys, James had ample of hot girls coming to him. Shashank had scored 'the dangling Deepa' there. Thanks to a year long drop, we had had a hundred percent attendance at James'. That night, out of the fright of the re-exams results, Raghu had summoned me to James'. To be honest, I too to fretted at nights, but a message or a call from Hrida would annihilate the fear. For some reason, she was so sure that I was going to make it big someday that she would literally fight me for my apprehensions.

Hrida! I thought of her and tiny pink heart shaped balloons appeared in the background while her smiling face blew kisses at me. I parked my bike and walked towards Shashank.

"James ek coffee," I said snatching Shashank's cigarette.

"Who is he talking to at 3.00 a.m.?" I asked him looking at Raghu who in course of the phone call had walked quite far away from James."

"Kanya, but obviously."

"Oh God!" I said and whistled out to call him.

Kanya was Raghu's latest muse, but unlike every time, he declared that he had fallen madly in love with her. "You guys were right. Being in a relationship is so different from dating," he said to me earnestly on one of our late night calls. At first I ignored his mush thinking it was all a hoax and she would disappear once the fizz flatted, but when he crossed his standard two month break up mark with her, I sat up to take notice. He even started bringing her for group outings. We were happy that Raghu had finally found someone who interested him beyond physical intimacy. However, the girl was a boyfriendaholic. She would cling to Raghu all day long and make him cling to the phone after she went home. It had been around four months that Raghu was with her and not once in all that time had I seen him without her around him or his phone to his ear.

"What do you talk about for so many hours?" I said as he hugged me. "Weren't you with her like two hours back?"

"Shhhh..." he said pointing his phone.

"Hang up, Hang up!" I slapped his hand.

"Honey bun, I'll call you back in two minutes," Raghu said before hanging up.

"Call you in two minutes? You guys still have things to talk about?" I asked.

"She is worried man. She thinks her younger sister is having an affair."

"So what's your play in all that?" Shashank asked.

"Nothing, she is worried and I am just being there for her."

"And what about your results?" I asked.

"Ah that, shit I forgot. I am so scared yaar Poncho." He lit a cigarette. "But I have you guys."

"Ya right, we are there for you, while you are on a call a mile away from us." As soon as Shashank snapped, Raghu's phone rang.

"I'm sorry guys, I'll be back in a minute," he said and disappeared.

Raghu's minute equalled an hour-and-a-half. So while he walked back and forth on the footpath talking to her, Shashank and I smoked and drank coffee in unlimited quantities and eyeballed the girls that came to James'.

"You sure you are done?" I asked Raghu when he came back.

"What's gotten into you man?" Shashank said "You've turned into a complete pansy."

"Sachdev, out of all the people at least you should understand. I love her man."

"Love shove is fine, just don't choke each other to death with your joined at the hips behaviour."

"Come on now, don't bug me, I've already had too much of brain drilling all day," Raghu whined.

"Life is gotten so slow man. All I do in the day is eat and sleep. I feel like a retired man already," I said.

"I badly need a change." Raghu said pulling his hair.

"Let's go camping. Just us boys," Shashank said.

"Ya." I agreed.

Raghu's face flushed knowing Kanya would never let him go alone.

"Or may be we can ask the girls to come," Shashank said.

"Yippie!" Raghu jumped. The smile on his face disappeared as his phone rang again. Shashank and I started our bikes and left.

The thought of spending the whole night with Hrida made my heart jump.

"Camping?" and three smiling smileys I messaged her as I lazed on my bed that night.

Nilshi campsite was a major part of my growing up years. I had spent most of my summer vacations there swimming, trekking, rock climbing, kayaking, fishing, acting in plays. Brigadier Shrikant Pandit had started this place after he retired from the army. The man was a widower and lived alone at the campsite with his Rottweiler Rosco. He would spend hours with us kids teaching us simple self defence techniques, telling us stories of his guerrilla combat days when as a major he led a small unit against the reds in north eastern part of the country. During the treasure hunts at night, he helped us track the clues and taught us how to identify poisonous snakes and insects. I used to be so awe-struck by him that months after my return from summer camps, I would want to join the army. There were so many childhood memories about the campsite that a smile propped my face as we entered its gates.

"Did you see that?" Hrida squeaked with joy as a kingfisher whooshed past us.

"It's just a bird. What's the big deal about it?" Kanya said grouchily as she got off the bike.

The two-and-a-half hour dusty bike ride form Mumbai had superlatively cranked Kanya up. She at first had completely dismissed the idea of going camping, but after Raghu's determined begging her to come or at least let him go, she agreed to come. But the Barbie had no idea it was a no-frills trip. She huffed away to her tent the moment she got off the bike and Raghu ran behind her with her bags. Hrida on the other hand was merrily jumping around. I mean come on, what's not to like about a place surrounded by mountains on three sides, chirping birds, the gushing sound of waterfalls, cool breeze from the dense forest on the mountains, the smell of burning firewood and meticulously planned colourful tents in the valley around a huge dark water lake. Only an idiot would hate it. So as long as there was smile on Hrida's face, I didn't care about the frown on the boyfriendaholic's face.

It was just past four in the afternoon and the sun had begun its descent, so the valley had started to become dark. If we were fast enough to reach the top of the hill, we could just be in time for the sunset. My love for sunsets also was a result of my stay in Nilshi. I took Hrida's hand and rushed her uphill. The temperature dipped a degree as we crossed Brigadier's vegetable and fruit plantations into the dense forest. The chirping birds fluttered away as the dried leaves lazying below our feet made a crackling sound. The lush green pathways of the hills began to turn dark as the sun made its rapid travel behind the Sahyadri range. I heard Hrida's giggling voice behind me when my walking transcended to running.

"Run run run, I don't want you to miss it," I said turning back.

The uphill road began to get steeper as we neared the top. I smiled seeing the orange light dispersed in the misty atmosphere. Nothing about the place had changed in all these years. The same old black rock plateau which wore thorny dried weeds with pride, the same old dry warm-cold breeze that brought the wild floral smell from the forest along with it, the sound of waterfall in the valley below, and at last, Mr Sun, the sole administrator of the incredible lighting and the warmth of the place. The only colours visible were shades of orange, black and gray. Darker shades of orange near the horizon, the black hues of the silhouetted mountain range and the bluish gray sky. Hrida slid her fingers between mine as I wrapped my hand around her. The feeling of the cool breeze on my sweaty-partly-exhausted body was blissful.

For a moment we sat there in silence looking at the sunset.

"I love you..." I said looking into her eyes, and leaned forward to kiss her, but before I could, she burst out laughing.

"What?" I asked irritated.

"Couldn't you find any better cliche than this?" She now rolled on the rock holding her stomach. "Kissing your girlfriend while watching a sunset. Real original, bro!"

"Yuck!" I muttered under my breath, as the silhouetted banal visuals of a couple kissing while the sun sets in the background grossed me out.

"I'm sorry," I said.

"But that doesn't mean I don't want you to kiss me," she said mischievously stiffing her lips to control her smile. Hrida had a peculiar sense of humor which irked me more than amused me. Now here I was in a situation where I was hankering majorly to make out with my girlfriend, and she filled me with visuals of cheesy lovelorn couples who I loathed all my life. When she is successful at draining the lust out of me, she naughtily invites me. I smiled slowly. I couldn't deny the fact that I was in love with this girl beyond tolerable limits. I slowly descended towards her face. I ran my thumb across her moist lower lip. It had been two years with Hrida, yet every time I got close to her, my heart raced crazily. She clasped her hand around my neck as I pecked a kiss on her lips. Then a few seconds into the kiss, my luck decided to strike. I heard Rosco's whoofing sound at a distance. The Brigadier must be on his evening walk. Shit!

"What timing, Brig!" I muttered. Hrida grinned and pecked me back before pushing me away. Rosco came close to us and straight away jumped on my girlfriend. The avid dog lover that Hrida was, she instantly became friends with the dog. I never thought my luck would outrun me so much that even a dog could cock block me. Since there was no way to save the situation, I went back to my sunset and listenting to Rosco huffing and puffing with my girlfriend in the background.

"I need a smoke, waiting in your tent, make it quick, don't have much time." Raghu's message read. I passed it to Shashank.

"Bloody pansy!" Shashank said grumpily.

"You coming?" I asked him as I got up to leave.

"Nah! I have a girlfriend too you know... can't leave her alone," he responded and I laughed.

Raghu almost jumped on me as I entered the tent.

"Light, light, light, fast," he said agitatedly. "She doesn't know I'm out." I could totally understand his desperation. He had been holed up in his tent all day without a smoke.

"Where is she?" I asked clamping two cigarettes between my lips to light.

"Loo," he said and snatched the half-lit cigarette.

"What if she comes out and doesn't find you."

"She won't. She takes exactly eleven minutes to deep cleanse her face."

"You timed it?? How many times has she been inside?"

"Nine, counting this one," he said as he peacefully exhaled the smoke.

"Whaaaat?? Dude, is she crazy?"

"Works for me, as long as I get to fag. I dare not ask her about it. As it is she is mad at me over the bike ride."

"She is still pissed about it?"

"Don't ask." He lite another cigarette, "Camping was a bad idea."

"What did you do all day?"

"Nothing, watched her read a book, then heard her blast my balls out for bringing her on a bike and screwing her complexion. Then she started with the chronicles of her family which ended just a while back, so ya that's about it." The poor guy was clearly rotting inside his tent.

"Bring her out, we'll have fun. The night's just beginning."

"Raghu!" Kanya screamed. Poor Raghu dropped his cigarette in fright and ran out of my tent.

After dinner that night, everyone except Raghu and his pricey Barbie had gathered around the campfire. I had always thought a person who can play a guitar always has the privilege of being the centre of attention. But when I started playing, I had everyone's complete attention, except Hrida's. Even my trademark songs failed to grab her complete attention. Reason? Rosco the dog. It had been more than six hours since our little trek uphill but Hrida was still glued to the dog. At one end there was Kanya who refused to let her boyfriend go away even for a couple of minutes, and then there was my girlfriend who was showering all her attention on a dog instead of her *lover*. My misery was that I couldn't even kick or hit the mutt, it was a bloody Rottweiler; it would have shredded me like confetti.

"Get lost, you dog!" I said in a low voice to make sure I didn't upset him much, and chucked the guitar before sitting besides Hrida. The dog gave me a stink eye and left in a huff.

"Rosco, come back!" Hrida whined as he left. "What did he do to you?" She almost grabbed me by my collar in anger, "Go say sorry to him."

"What? Are you mad! I'm not appologising to a dog!!!" My human ego flooded my mind instantly at the thought of apologising to a mutt.

"Then I'm not talking to you," she declared and turned away from me.

"You are kidding, right? There is no way I'm saying sorry to a dog."

"Up to you. I've made myself clear."

"You are being ridiculous now."

"Why did you do it?"

"Because he was pissing me off."

"By doing what?"

"Oh come on, he is just a dog."

"Yes, that's what he is. A dog and a very sweet one. You had no right to hurt him like that." There was dead seriousness in Hrida's voice. I learned a new thing about her that day. She loved dogs more than she loved me. "So until you go and say sorry to him, I'm not talking to you." I saw Shashank and Neha in splits listening to our conversation.

"Oh what the hell, just go and get done with it," a voice inside me said.

The mutt was having his dinner straight out of Brigadier's plate, my ego crumbled piece by piece with every step I took towards him. And finally the historic moment that would be henceforth remembered by me as the 'Sorry Dog Day' came.

"Sorry Rosco, I didn't mean to hurt you." I felt like strangulating him when I said that. The dog didn't even look at me.

"Happy?" I asked Hrida as I returned to sit beside her.

"Good boy," she said and patted my head.

"Woof woof."

"I'll be your dream, I'll be your wish, I'll be your fantasy,
I'll be your hope, I'll be your love be everything that you
need,
I'll love you more with every breath truly madly deeply
do,
I will be strong, I will be faithful 'cause I'm counting on
a new beginning..."

Hrida sang groggily while she randomly strummed open chords on my guitar. I gaped at the hypnotic visuals of her glowing face in the dim light of the kerosene lantern, her lips pouting and stiffing alternatively to sing, and her head cocking to the rhythm of the song.

"A reason for living, a deeper meaning,
I want to stand with you on a mountain,
I want to bathe with you in the sea,
I want to lay like this forever,
Until the sky falls down on me..."

Being a classic desi, pop music to me meant songs by Daler Mehendi, Baba Sehgal and Alisha Chinoi or Apache Indian, so I had no idea what she was singing. All that aside, Hrida singing a song for me had glued an ear-to-ear grin on my face.

"And when the stars are shining brightly in the velvet
sky,
I'll make wish send it to heaven then make you want
to cry..."

The E-string of the guitar couldn't handle Hrida's aggressive strumming anymore and gave up its resistance and broke. She stopped singing and my smile gave way to a straight face. There was dead silence, all we could hear was a cricket chirping in the background. Both of us stared at each other for nice thirty seconds before our guffawing choke-slammed us on the bed. The laughing continued till our stomachs hurt and eyes watered uncontrollably. I extended my arm to tuck her hair behind her ear and ran my thumb below her eye to wipe the tear. She turned to me with a mild smile. I aimlessly brushed her eyebrow back and forth with my thumb. Then as if sensing my confusion, she smiled and blew a kiss at me. That I guessed was my cue. I gently pulled her towards me and hugged her. The intoxicating smell of her body shot my pulse. Going by her heavy breathing, I could tell that I too had the same effect on her. I loosened her from my hug to look at her. There was innocence in her eyes as she ran her fingers in my hair.

"Dog!" she said tightly clenching my hair.

"But I thought you loved dogs," I semi whispered smiling at her.

"I do..." She said and pulled me towards her, "That *is* why you are here..." She whispered in my ear before biting it. I felt like a few cables up in my brain snapped and it had no control over the rest of the body anymore. I pumped a few deep breaths as I began to kiss her. I had no idea what I was up to. My hands felt the goose-bumps on her body so I assumed that even Hrida shared the same intensity. As I slid my hand inside her t-shirt, up her bare back, it struck me that it had been over two years that I was in relationship with Hrida but I had never gone beyond the first base. I didn't feel the need or maybe I was waiting for the right moment, I had no idea. I pulled my hand out of the shirt and before my mind's ethical authority took over, I peeled her tee off her body. It felt unfair that I was wearing a shirt when she lay topless in my arms, so with her in one arm, I tussled with my shirt and tossed it away. The lust wave struck me from head to toe as she bit my upper lip. I held her by her face and began to kiss her riotously. It wasn't as if I had never kissed anyone else before, but the way Hrida made me feel, none of my previous experiences stood any chance. My mind went numb every time we kissed.

"You are gonna lose it today," Voice Two merrily said, as our bodies began to rub violently against each other.

"I'm not sure," Voice One said.

In spite of not being sure, my hand traveled all the way down to unbutton her denims while I continued kissing her.

"Stop!" She whispered gasping for breath as the button finally opened. I didn't and went ahead and unzipped her denims.

"No!" she said and pushed me away.

I blankly stared at her as she got up and put on her clothes. I was still in a trance so it took me a while for Hrida's reaction to sink in. She got off the bed and sat on the chair opposite it. I had no idea what I did wrong. A moment later I picked my shirt from the floor and wore it as I walked up to her.

"Hey..." I said going down on my knees to level with her line of sight. "What's wrong?"

"Nothing..." she said and from her shaking leg I could clearly tell she was restless and that made me uncomfortable.

She was obviously not alright, there was something wrong. In some corner of my mind, I knew I was the reason behind it.

"Buck up, you moron!" Voice One yelled.

"Hey... I'm sorry... I shouldn't have..." I cut my sentence short as she cringed at my touch, which kind of offended me so I got up and leaned against the dresser beside her. I had a terrible itch to smoke a cigarette but I stubbed the urge and for the next eighteen minutes, I watched her shake her leg, crack her fingers, and occasionally nod her head as if she was having a conversation with herself. Then she heavily exhaled a breath and looked at me with a smile.

"I'm sorry I freaked out, I thought..." She stiffed her lips and cringed to suggest the obvious, "...it might seem utterly silly to you but..." she began to shake her leg again. The mere thought of losing her virginity had made Hrida horribly uncomfortable. "...in my mind I'm just not ready for it..." she said in a choked voice.

"Hey..." I went back on my knees as before, "Don't worry, nothing happened and nothing will happen unless you want it to..." I said and skeptically took her hand in mine, "There is nothing more important to me than you. I can live without sex but not you."

"Really, pig? For how long?" Voice Two screamed as soon as the last sentence came out of my mouth,

"You know I'd never do anything that would hurt you in any way, right?"

She vigorously nodded her head in a yes.

"Then trust me, blindly..." I said and she slid her fingers between mine. I took the piercing of her fingernails in the back of my palm as her agreement to blindly trusting me.

Even though I wasn't the skirt-wearer, I knew what not being ready meant. Most of the girls I had met in the past had no qualms about having sex or losing their virginity, so back then it was me who was saving myself for the perfect one. Now when I was ready, life had flipped sides.

2011

It being a fresh student intake season, LAX in Los Angeles was so crowded that it looked like Kurla station in Mumbai. But even in that crowd, it wasn't easy to miss Viren, my six-feet-four-inches tall brother-in-law. Like a hawk he had spotted me the moment I stepped out of arrivals, and from that moment on, he waved at me excessively till I hugged him. It had been five years that he had been married to Radhika and like all typical married guys who get negligent about their physical appearance after scoring a hot wife, he too had ballooned up. So the guy who once had a body like Achilles now looked like giant version of Homer Simpson. It broke my heart to see him like that. I mean this guy was my idol of sorts. In spite of having no homosexual traces whatsoever, I had had a crush on him the day Radhika had introduced him to us. He had floppy hair, fair clean shaved face with a smile like Sean Connery's, dark eyes, and a lean soccer player physique. What got me even more interested was his story of engineering which was the same as mine. The only difference was that he gave up on his dream of becoming a soccer player instead of engineering and got sucked into a corporate software firm in LA. Radhika would tell stories of his binging sprees but then I didn't think it was so bad. In a forty-minute ride from the airport to Artesia, he stopped twice: once to buy cheese loaded hamburgers, though

I have to confess they were ridiculously delicious, and once to refill his cola.

"Hey... no telling Didi about this alright?" he said as he parked the car in front of the house.

"I promise... I won't tell her that you are cheating on her with a bagful of cheese burgers, but that stain of mayo on your shirt might." I said pointing at his paunch.

"You bloody mayo... I'll kill you," he frantically began to wipe it off his shirt.

Radhika hugged me as soon as she opened the door. In nearly a year, no one had really hugged me and meant it. Besides, it had been quite a long time since I had seen her, so tears flooded my eyes, while she semi broke down hugging me tightly. In my anger, I had swiftly snapped ties with everyone who loved me, but what I failed to realise was that even I needed them as badly as they needed me. No matter how many new friends you make, their affection will never match up to the warmth of the people you grew up with. I had horribly missed Radhika in the past few months, especially after Devika left. I needed someone to complain to about my life. And now, after she was pregnant, I had all the more reasons to be with her. I was happy I chose to come to LA.

"You realise we are standing outside your house, right?" I said trying to lighten her mood. "These goras aren't huge fans of melodrama."

"I don't care and I'll kick them if anyone complains," she giggled wiping her tears.

"You look great mamma!" I said holding her at an arm's distance. "Glowing and all..." I kissed her. "But why is the baby bump so small? Isn't it supposed to be very big in the sixth month?"

"Hah! My hubby makes up for the baby bump with his paunch."

"Don't worry baby, I won't let anything happen to you..." I said to Hrida as I carried her on my back and ran wildly through the dark rain forest. I ignored the pain that the thorns on the forest floor inflicted on my feet. I felt a lump in my throat as I heard the growling of the wolves chasing me. I turned to looked at them and saw a pair of red blazing eyes fast approaching me. I tightened my grip on her arms and began to run faster, jumping over the rocks, dodging branches, fighting with the rain to keep my eyes open. The growling behind me sounded closer. I picked up a piece of rock and hurled it at the wolf but it was too late. Before the rock could do any harm, it pounced on me. I felt excruciating pain in my ribs as the red-eyed beast pushed his weight on me and brutally slammed me on the rocky ground. His bloodthirsty fangs got hold of Hrida's feet and blood sprayed out of it.

"No!" I wailed in rage. I picked up a branch and stabbed the wolf again and again in his neck till every square inch of life bled out of him. I tore my shirt and wrapped it tightly around Hrida's wound and began to run again.

"Just some more time baby, everything will be alright then," I said to her.

"You don't have to worry about anything, Arjun. I've taken care of it," Devika said,

"Dev, where is Hrida?" I asked turning my head one eighty degrees to look at her.

"She is long gone, Poncho," I saw Raghu saying it.

"Where is Hrida? What happened to her?" I asked.

"She is dead, She is dead, She is dead." Multiple voices hissed from the woods around me. The growling of the beasts was getting closer. I began to run fiercely holding tightly to the hands of the body I was carrying on my back. Then suddenly the body I was carrying began to stink offensively. Shivers ran through me as I realised I was carrying a human carcass. I dropped it on the ground and looked at it. It was Hrida. I stood there staring at her, feeling warmth of tears coming out of my eyes. Few minutes later, a couple of wolves with 'break-up' written all over their bodies surrounded me. While one of them dragged Hrida's body into the dark woods, the others pounced on me and pinned me down on the rocky floor. The last thing I saw before I closed my eyes was the blood-stained pointed fangs of the beasts closing in on my face.

"Aaaaarrrrhhhhhhh!" I cried out loud as I opened my eyes, my heart beating insanely, my eyes watering and body shaking in fear.

I was dreaming again! Shit!

I got out of the bed and followed the delicious aroma coming from the kitchen downstairs.

"Babu, slept well?" Radhika said as I nuzzled on the back of her shoulder.

"Ummm." It felt so good to be around someone who shared the same blood line. I closed my eyes and rested my forehead on her shoulder.

"You want some coffee?" Radhika asked stroking my head.

"Haan!" I said and sauntered to the dinner table. "Where's Viren bhai?"

"Gym... should be back in a while," she said looking at the wall clock. "Poncho?"

"Ya?"

"Why didn't you tell Aai-Baba that you were coming here?"

My ego had clogged my mind so I didn't, I thought of saying. Instead I kept quiet.

"I hope you know you are turning out into a complete prick."

"Ya I have been telling that to myself for a while now," I murmured. She turned and looked at me with the stare she'd inherited from our mother.

"You keep you smart assery to yourself."

"Didi, I don't want to fight."

"You better not dare..." she said pointing the ladle at me, the chicken gravy dribbling from it. "I am not Mom, I'll thrash you left, right, and centre, understand?" her voice gave up her fake anger.

"Aye aye, captain," I said and jutted my tongue out to tease her but she had turned and got back to stirring the chicken.

"So... how's Shashank's bride?" she asked as she handed me a mug of coffee.

"Bride?"

"You know Shashank's getting married, right?"

A wave of rage and hurt swept me as I replayed her question in my mind.

"What the fuck, Sachdev's getting married? He didn't think it was important to tell me." Voice One said.

"Why do you care anyway?" Voice Two said.

"Ya exactly. To hell with him man, you don't need him anymore," Voice Three said.

"Poncho?" Radhika yelled. I stared at her blankly. "Don't tell me you fought with him too?"

I continued staring.

"Raghu? Him too?" I coyly shrugged. Radhika had a killer knack of sensing things out of me, so I prayed she wouldn't ask me about Devika next. I was too ashamed of what I had done. And if she found out what I did to her, she would slay me with the ladle.

"What's gotten into you, Arjun?"

"I wish I knew."

"And what happened with Hrida?"

"Di, I don't want to talk about it."

"Why?"

"Why? Why, because I still love her, why because even after all this while it still hurts, why because I ran away from India to get away from all that pain and commotion inside me, why because I don't want to relive everything that went worng. That is why."

Radhika stared at me as I snapped back.

"Muffin! Is the dinner ready? I'm famished!" Viren said as he opened the door.

Thank god for Viren, he saved me from another fight.

The only exhausting part of my daily routine in LA was the one hour fifteen minutes of travelling from Radhika's house to college. Even though Viren would drop me most of the time, the peak hour traffic in LA would squeeze the patience out of me. But the irritation was nothing against the contentment that spurted through me while calling shots on the monitor. The moment since I set foot on campus of Los Angeles Film Academy six months back, life had turned into a total roller coaster ride. Situated in the heart of universal studios, the school to me felt like the Mecca of film making. I was finally happy. From the huge make believe sets to beautiful actors portraying larger than life characters, nothing about the place was real. Yet it inspired billions of people all over the world to dream. I had always thought film sets were intensely honest places which never hid the reality behind pseudo pictures they created on celluloid. What I liked about film making was that the director could play god to the characters and make them do whatever he wished, without any intervention from the real god upstairs. First semester in school zwooped making films, playing crew on films, acting, directing, and producing. There was so much buzz around me for the past six months that all the hurt I brought with me from my motherland got anaesthetised.

"Poncho!" Radhika called me as I was about to leave for college. "Shashank called twice, he said he couldn't reach you. He's left his number... call him."

"OK, I'll do it in the day."

"Why haven't you combed your hair?"

"Bye Didi, see you in the evening." I kissed her and rushed out of the house.

December 16 was his wedding day, and no matter how emotionally colourblind I had gotten, I couldn't digest the fact that I was going to miss Shashank's wedding. I wondered how I ended up in such a morbid place in life. I had been quite successful in the past six months in earning some sanity for my mind and I wasn't willing to flush it. So before the visuals of all those years of loafing around with him and Raghu opened the door behind which I had locked all the rancid memories,

I plugged the earphones and let the chaos of electronic music take over.

"It's all about dreaming..." Jane Brandy, Professor for Advanced Screen Writing was saying. "The more you paint your dreams, the more you train your brain to imagine..."

"Painting dreams, I do that quite brilliantly. The only difference is they just remain dreams," I said and laughed to myself.

"... When you write a story, you actually write the fates of the characters. There will be billions of permutations and combinations to take your story forward, but what makes you a good writer is making the correct choices of combinations."

"Whoever wrote the story of my life would definitely be a highly paid writer up there..." Thanks to Radhika, my mind's gibbering had officially resumed.

"Psst... R-jun..." Leo my classmate elbowed me to get my attention. "We are going to Gordon's after class. It's Gina's birthday, you coming?"

"Only if you let me crash at your place..."

"For that you'll have to sleep with me." He winked, I laughed.

There is no better way than dousing your bleak mind with a gallon of alcohol, I thought.

The welcoming vibe at Gordon's reminded me of Pyaasa. There was a twenty feet long bar in the centre of the floor serving alcohol of all brands and types. There was an elevated stage for live music in the corner. The music was playing at a deafening volume and the amply-spaced dance floor was open for the drunken souls to swing. After the first celebratory shot, Gina began pushing drinks down anyone and everyone within her reach. The drawback of being the odd man out is that you are always the centre of attention, and I being the only desi in the group, garnered all of Gina's attention. In just thirty minutes, she'd forced four tequila shots down my throat. It put me into a substantial daze so all I could see was revolving images and feel random hands sliding right-left through my waist. I watched the rest of the group joggling their heads to the music. An hour of country music later, the band packed up and the stage was thrown open for singing enthusiasts. I was in the loo relieving myself when I heard a commotion outside in the bar.

"Abey kitna pakaoge yaaar... bas karo tumhari... Aaa Aaa, Ooo Ooo..." a female voice was yelling at someone who was yodelling on stage. I wasn't the only one around who was buggered by the annoying yodelling.

"Listen to this now..." she said.

"Inhi logon ne... inhi logon ne... hey hey... inhi logon ne le leena dupatta mera..."

The yelling female was singing now. Whoever it was, was really drunk and a very bad singer. A few minutes later the commotion began again.

"Give it to me... give it..." I saw her tussling for the mike with the bouncer as he dragged her out of the place.

"Gayatri?" I said to myself.

Cut to 2001:

It had been seven months since my father had gagged and thrown me into engineering's hell hole. It was past 8.30 that night when I walked out of college. The place was indeed a hell hole with no lights and no public transport. Usually Raghu's bike took care of our transportation, but that day he had disappeared after lunch, leaving me in that deserted place. After fourteen minutes of waiting for the public transport bus and begging the pricey rickshawalas to stop, I heard a two wheeler stop by me.

"Bitches won't stop?" the girl riding it asked.

"Ah! Don't ask."

"I can drop you if you want."

"Thank you so much, you saved my life. I've heard rapists live around here."

She began to laugh.

"Hop on!"

She pulled out a long scarf out of her sack and wrapped it all around her face and took off with a jerk, pushing me to the back of the seat. It was the first time that I sat pillion while a girl rode. It wasn't as if I was one of those male chauvinists who don't trust girls when it comes to driving, in fact I thought they did it even better than us guys, but rashness scares anyone. I was so scared that I clenched both my hands on the shaft behind and clamped my knees to the seat.

"What's your name?" her muffled voice from behind the scarf reached me.

"Arjun!" I yelled back to reply.

"They call me Gay..." Gayatri said turning back one thirty five degree and extending her hand to shake. I gave her a panic-stricken smile. Swaying and swinging between the trucks and overtaking them at a speed that would make anyone piss their pants, she turned back again.

"Which year?"

"FE Civil." I said.

"Final year, Tronics." She began honking at another truck.

"I don't want to die." I said and closed my eyes as she prepared to make her way between two trucks.

"You won't. Hang on."

For the rest of the ride, I kept my eyes tightly closed. She had officially replaced Raghu as the scariest rider I had ridden with. With short streaked hair and a thin braid emerging from the back of her neck, a slightly dusky complexion, a toothy smile that had to be looked at again and again, a large cupid's bow above her upper lip that made her lips looks irresistible, three colorful tattoos – a panda paw on the back of her right shoulder, flying pigeon on the wrist and a butterfly on the ankle – and a perfectly worked out body which made most of the male hearts in college beat out of their body, she was a classic eight on ten. So given my then single status and extreme affinity towards bunking lectures, in the following days I found myself hanging out with her more often than I intended to. It's funny how mind changes its perceptions when you grow up. I mean as a child I'd brand any girl even a year older than me as 'didi', but now the grown up me had no intention of celebrating *Raksha Bandhan* with Gayatri who was three years senior to me. Her waiting for me every day after college to drop me indicated that even she shared the same emotions. Soon the scooter rides extended to spending time till late at night. The canteen binges developed into terrace and classroom makeout sessions and before we could identify any feelings for each other, we were already dating. In the five months that we were together, all we did was bunk lectures, eat in the canteen, snog in every possible corner of the college, watch movies, drink cheap beer and party at every possible opportunity. We were so busy running around having fun that not once in all that time did we discuss our future together or our feelings for each other. In fact, now when

I come to think of it, neither of us really proposed so we weren't exactly an official couple ever. That is probably why when we went our separate ways, there was no drama. A month after we 'broke up', she passed out of college and I met Hrida. Gayatri was out of sight, out of mind. But then you can never beat life's sense of humour. So here I was, ten years later, in Los Angeles, watching her being thrown out of a bar.

"Can I walk you somewhere?" I asked catching up with her.

"Bad pick-up line, moron, buzz off!" she said without looking at me,

"Desi saale, ladki dekhi nai ke chaabi lagna shuru..." I said mockingly.

She turned to me with a disgusted look, "Holy shit..." She stared. "Arjun?"

"Yep... what are the odds..." I said before she squeaked and hugged me.

"One to a trillion. Oh my god, it is really you, fuckkkk!" She jumped with joy, "What are you doing here in LA?"

"Came to see you get thrown out of a bar," I said.

She punched me, "Smart ass!"

"You are still Stallone strong, I must say," I said. She giggled.

We walked in silence for a while.

"You wanna grab a drink?" she asked, as we walked past another bar.

"I don't mind, but promise you won't get into a brawl again."

"I promise, now shall we?"

"Whiskey on the rocks..." she said to the bartender tapping the fingernail of her index finger on the bar, "Same for you?"

"Ya..."

"So?"

"So..."

After a few moments of silence, she asked me the inevitable.

"How's the girlfriend?"

The bartender served us the drinks.

"I'm single if that is what you want to know," I said, my eyes twitched as the spirity warmth of alcohol travelled down my throat.

"Ah! Same old self flattering pig." I laughed, but not for too long, for she asked, "But why did you break up with her?"

"Why do you think I broke up with her?"

"Because you are a guy?" she said with the glass to her mouth. "And because you broke up with me?"

"I never broke up with you."

"You didn't call back after the fight."

"You could have called too?"

"I am a girl."

"Is it now?"

"Yes."

"So?"

"So?" she said and let out a huge laugh. "Bitch, you haven't changed a grain bit. Can I please hug you, please?" Not that there was any need to ask for my permission, but before I said yes she slid down her bar stool and wrapped her arms around my waist. I hugged her back.

"Veritably speaking, I broke up with her but not in the patented D-bag way." The level of casualness in my voice while speaking about the break-up surprised me. I guess I was beginning to move on.

"Excuse me buddy, I think I'm going to need the whole bottle of this..." she said to the bartender. I smiled at him.

"You seeing someone?" I asked. She nodded a yes, as she took another sip.

"Yep, Aneesh. We went to the B-school together here. He now lives in New York."

"Ouch!! Long distance relationship..."

"It's not that bad once you get used to it."

"Ya, but isn't it painful?"

"You can't crib about pain when you are clingy about your careers. Both of us slogged hard, so after college when he got placed out of LA, it was hard to give up our jobs for our relationship."

I could never understand how a relationship works when two people involved in it live miles away from each other, in this case practically on opposite coasts of America. But there was no sign of despair or discontent in her voice so I guessed she was happy.

"You look different..." I said pointing at her straightened hair.

"Good different or bad different?"

"Good, good. Just wondering how it happened"

"You'll know when you have a corporate job." She smiled and poured us drinks. "What are you doing in LA?"

"Film school..." I said.

In the next three hours, the first bottle we called for gave way to another and that to another as conversations veered from LA to India, to engineering, to my career, to her career, to Hrida, to Aneesh, to Raghu, Shashank, Radhika, and to the time we spent together in college. I realised nothing had changed between us in spite of all the time that had passed. We took off exactly from where we had left things ten years ago.

"You know, I waited for your call after the evening we fought," she said swinging my hand back and forth holding it by its pinky finger as we walked towards her home through the quaint deserted alleys of LA.

"I kind of did too."

"Shit... I should have called you..." she smiled.

"We were fun together... I mean guys are usually bitches, especially to hot babes like me. All they want is get into your pants and once that happens, all the excitement disappears and all that is left are the whys and whos and other ridiculous questions which fuck you sore. It was different with you, *tu mast tha...*"

"Ya, I know," I said and wrapped my hand around her, as we walked in silence.

"Just so you know, I never cursed you." I began to laugh, "So your heartbreak is not on my head."

"Oh... like that!"

"Here we are, home boring home. You wanna stay over tonight?" she said fishing for keys in her purse. "It's too late to travel back to Artesia, plus you are too drunk and it's not safe."

She slurred.

"Won't your boyfriend mind your ex-boyfriend staying over?"

"He has his fair share of fun in NY, so this would pass. Don't worry, stay!"

She opened the door.

I stayed.

2012

I was home. The real one. Two years of staying away from it, I had forgotten how it felt to come back home to people who had brought you to this planet.

"Baba?" I said as I opened the door with my key, "Aai?" No one responded.

I should have called before coming, I thought.

Then suddenly, I heard a man scream his lungs out. I rushed to the living room where the voice had come from.

"Thank goodness!" I muttered when I realised it was Sunny Deol screaming on the television.

I saw Dad sitting on the couch in a get-set-go position gritting his teeth and miming Sunny's dialogues. Minutes later, when Sunny started punching holes in the goon's body with his *'dhaai kilo ka haath'* my dad began mimicking his action by throwing punches in air. A few kicks followed. Dad had a penchant for Sunny Deol and Dharmendra movies, so whenever the television channels played them, me and Radhika would get to see our father transform into an action hero. He would get so involved in the fights that he'd practically have ferocious expressions on his face.

I stood there leaning on the wall, enjoying the show while my Dad bit his lower lip and moved his body in sync with Sunny Deol as he kicked the shit out of the villains. By the end of the sequence, tens of goons were left limping and whimpering in pain as Sunny Deol left wiping his bloodied lip.

"Why did you beat them up so badly?" I asked. Dad's face flushed the angry look, his fists still in fighting position.

"What did they do?" I said as I sat beside him. He took a sip of whiskey from his glass.

Silence...

"Aai's not home?"

"No, she's at the club."

"That explains."

"You saw all of it?" he said.

"No no, just some of it." Both of us began laughing.

"You have to agree... no one fights better than the Deols."

"Totally agree."

"How are you, Dad?" I asked as the laughing subsided.

"How do I look?"

"Really fit," I said, pressing his biceps.

"Your mom is to be thanked for this," he said and walked to his liquor cabinet to make a drink. "With you and Radhika gone, I was the only one left to be harrowed with her rules."

"Scary!"

"You bet. Should I make you a drink?" he asked before capping the bottle.

"No, I'm good."

"Cool, I'm going to get wasted, it's my drinking day. I'm just allowed to drink once a week."

"No!"

"Yes, beat that." I began to laugh.

"She's getting worse by the day."

"Radhika is no different. Does the same to Viren."

"I know, the poor guy was whining on Skype the other day."

"Dad, six months I lived with her in LA, I felt like strangulating myself. Always finicky about what I wear, what I eat, matching clothes, combed hair, constant nagging. Arrrggghhh!" I said, fake-pulling my hair. Dad got up to fetch some ice.

"I pity her kid, there is no escape for her."

"How is the baby? These video chats don't do justice!"

"She is out of this planet. I've never seen anything more beautiful than her."

"I'm glad at least you were with Radhika." I heard the door shut as soon as he said it.

"Are you done wasting yourself?" Mom said as she entered the living room.

"Hi Aai!"

"Poncho... Hi..." she stared at me for a while and left the room. I could clearly see the sadness in her eyes.

"Run before she starts crying." Dad nudged me. I rushed to the kitchen behind her.

"Aai..."

"You want to wait for dinner, or you're leaving?" she asked pulling bowls out of the refrigerator.

"I'd love to wait. I'm starving."

Silence...

"How are you?" I asked.

"Good."

Silence and the sound of chopping carrots.

"Did you miss me?"

"No..."

Silence again.

"Ask Baba to wrap up. Dinner is ready."

"How was film school?" Dad asked breaking the silence at the dinner table.

"Hectic, but really good. Learnt a lot, plus now I'm not an undergrad anymore," I said the last part looking at mom.

"I'm proud of you," Dad said.

"How did you manage the fees?" Mom asked.

"I had saved some money and Radhika sponsored the loan for the rest of the amount."

"Big you kids have gotten... don't need your parents anymore," Mom mumbled.

"Heard about Raghu's wedding?" Dad said ignoring Mom.

"Ya I met him a couple of days back for lunch. He seems really happy."

"Happens when you let your parents choose the girl for you," Mom said and Dad gave her a foul look.

"I know Aai... that is why I am here..."

"What do you mean?" I finally got her attention.

"I mean that I am done with all the stupid and immature behaviour. I've been upset at life for being unfair to me, but it took me a while to realise that while doing it, I was being unfair to the people around me. I'm sorry Aai, Baba." I looked at both of them, "I know nothing I say or do will make the hurt I caused you both to disappear, but I'm sorry, really sorry." Mom stared at her plate. I looked towards Dad for help.

"You cannot just say sorry and expect us to simply forgive you. You have to pay the price," Dad said faking a frown.

"Fair enough, so will saying you too can choose a girl for me to get married to be enough price?" Both of them looked at me incredulously.

"I'm serious, I want to get married." It finally did the trick; Mom smiled.

I might have been a bit hasty about opening my mouth about getting married, but if that meant winning 'the Mother' back, I was ready for it. Besides, even though I had no plans of saying what I said, somewhere deep inside I meant it.

"Poncho, what's your height in centimeters?" Mom asked as I snuggled between her and Dad that night.

"Why?"

"They need all sort of details on those matrimonial websites. I'll start enrolling you on them first thing tomorrow morning."

"You are so doomed, buddy!" Dad whispered to me.

"And also give me your latest pictures. You look fit now compared to your earlier pictures."

Shit, I'm doomed indeed! I thought.

"And..." she continued.

I fell asleep.

It was Nth time that day that I had cancelled Hrida's call, but there was no way I could take it. I was already two minutes late. Any more delay in delivering his cappuccino meant getting verbally whipped by him. Him who? My Director, my boss, my master, my pharaoh or whatever that means the owner of slaves. Rizwan Qureshi, the seven time national award winner, highest paid and most sought after film director in the country. I was the happiest person the day I landed a job of his DA. Two years of begging and scraping my shoe soles finally bore some fruit. I was going to be an assistant of the biggest director in the country. Being so closely associated to him meant getting to learn the craft from the master himself. But all my happiness disappeared the moment I walked in his office six months back. The problem was – his definition of a Director's Assistant was poles apart from mine. A DA to him was simply a glorified servant, who could speak English to attend his calls (mostly from his angry ex-wife), make perfect cappuccinos, time his medicines, order his food, remind him to eat, then get it heated when it went cold, at times serve him, hold his luggage, buy him gutka, clip his write-ups, clean his desk, stack his scripts, make playlists for his iPod, nodding a yes to whatever was asked and be a punching bag and get ranted upon by him whenever he wished to vent out his negative energy. But I had no complaints because one film with Rizwan Qureshi on your resume could make your career go ballistic. It had been three months now that we were shooting his war biopic in the remote forests of Himachal Pradesh and more than a week since I had spoken to Hrida.

"Lemme know if you've found someone new because I am about to" and a teasing tongue, the message from her beeped in. I smiled as I read it.

"Arjun! Where the fuck is my cappuccino?" I heard Rizwan scream on the PA system. I ran with the latte.

"Rizwan coff..." I swallowed rest of my words, looking at his furious eyes.

"What? Do I look funny to you?"

"No..."

"Then why the fuck are you smiling?" Shit! I had forgotten to wipe the smile of my face.

The worst part of the location was the place where our residential tents were built. It had no cellphone reception, so for anyone to make a call, they had to walk a kilometre uphill through a dark rainy forest. It was a night shoot, so after dinner, Rizwan went for his power nap, I made a wild run for the hill for the network. I just had a twenty minute window but I had to take the risk as it was her birthday *and* my only chance to call her. I dialled her number covering the phone from the rain.

"Pick up, pick up, pick up..." I muttered as the ring went through.

"Are you calling to break up?" she said goofily.

"Happy birthday, Sona..."

"So you remembered!"

"Please lose the sarcasm, I don't have much time." I checked my watch. I just had three more minutes to talk after the run uphill had already burnt my eight minutes.

"Okay, sorry sorry," she said. "How you been, kiddo?"

"I'm good... specially... now after listening to your..."

"Yuck, cheesy bitch!" she giggled. I smiled.

"I love you..." she said. I felt my heart skip a beat. The intensity of the wanting to be with her right at that moment was unexplainable.

"I love you too..." I said exhaling heavily. My tone gave away the sadness.

"What's wrong, Arjun?"

"Nothing, I'm just missing you too bad..."

"And?"

"And the mosquitoes, and rains, mucky location, bad food, back pain... that's it!"

"And?"

I paused.

"And, I have no idea what I'm doing with my life. I don't know how running behind him with his coffee and holding his snot-dipped tissues will help me. I feel like his servant. As for the money, the roadside labourers earn more money than me. I sometimes feel I made a mistake quitting engineering."

"Shut up... I know how you feel but you knew this would happen. No one jumps to the director's chair that easily. Your father is neither a Kapoor nor a Khan so chill, things will take their own course. For now you are doing great, trust me, not many people have the guts to break free and chase their dreams. I'm proud of you. Just switch off the brain and slog, bitch!" I smiled at the love and assurance in her voice.

"I'm sorry I didn't mean to botch your birthday with my ranting."

"You are more important to me than the birthday. Just don't lose your shit."

"I love you..."

"Ya thanks... Don't you have a shoot to go to?"

"Shit! I am screwed, bye bye bye... I'll try to call you soon..." I said beginning my run back to the tents.

Splashing and stumbling through the dark mucky woods I reached Rizwan's tent. I ran so fast that I could barely breathe, but thankfully I was in time. In fact, I was thirty seconds early. I waited for the alarm on my wrist watch to go so that I could go and wake my lord up. Waking him a second before he wanted me to could mean abuses for dinner, or maybe a few slaps too. The alarm beeped and I entered his tent. My heart stopped beating and dropped in my stomach when I saw the empty bed.

"Holy fuck! He woke up before time!" I felt a lump in my throat. I ran hysterically towards the set.

"Rizwan sir?" I asked a spot boy on my way.

"Set pe gaya hai, dhoond raha tha tereko!" he slurred with gutka stuffed in his mouth.

They had already begun shooting when I reached the set. How long had he been up or didn't he sleep at all? I waited silently behind him thinking of believable excuses to make to him once he was done. But what good are reasons if he doesn't even listen to them.

"Cut, OK, moving on," he yelled on the PA system.

"Where is my phone?" he asked me coldly. I handed it over to him. He glared at me before staring into it. My eyes were glued on him studying his mood.

He said without looking at me. "Give my stuff to production, and leave," and got back to explaining the shot to the actor. I rushed to his tent and gathered all his things and put them in a bag. I handed it to the production manager. I had no idea what leave meant so I went and took my place behind him again. It felt incredibly light after my body was relieved of all the slinging bags.

"Why are you still here?" Rizwan asked after ignoring me for a while. "Didn't I ask you to leave?"

"I-I don't understand."

"Allah! Leave means leave. Go, go home. You are fired," he said raising his voice."

I was dumbstruck, and perhaps my expression said the same. He asked again, "Do you understand now?"

"Rizwan, please listen to me at least..." I managed a whole sentence without him cutting me short. Unfortunately, for me that lit a cannon aimed straight at me.

"Listen to you? Listen to you?" He mock laughed. "No my friend, I don't listen to anyone. I paid *you* to listen to me which you didn't and that's what's gotten you fired. His rising volume got more and more attention from the busy crew. When I asked you to wait outside, you were supposed to fucking wait outside and not wander off."

"Rizwan but I..."

"When I say leave, *you leave, just fuck, the bloody off...*" he ragingly turned to me and pushed me to the ground screaming hysterically at me in front of four hundred people.

"You..." He caught hold of a spot boy.

"If I see him on my set ever again, you will be fired. Drag him out of here right now," he said and stormed off. All the eyes stared at me with sympathy. The guy assigned with the job of kicking me actually walked to me to carry his orders out. Rizwan had left no *kasar* to strip me of my dignity, so

I hurriedly got up before I was actually dragged out of the location.

After five long hours of an agonising drive in the clattering old jeep from the location in Himachal, I was dumped at the Chandigarh airport and left to fend for myself. I sat there with my soiled clothes and broken dignity, wondering if my mistake deserved such a brutal affront. Three more hours at the airport, two hours in the flight and one hour in cab from the airport to my house later, I still couldn't understand whats and whys of what had happened to me.

Cut to 2004:

I ignored the whirring of the phone as I stared at my marksheet. I was still a subject short to make it into the third year. I had again flunked five of the ten subjects I had appeared for. But somehow, I felt relieved about losing another year for I had no intention of going back to the hellhole. The phone started whirring again and I finally picked it up.

"Where the fuck were you all day?" Raghu screamed. "Are you alright?"

"Ya I am."

"Don't worry... we'll work something out next time."

"There is no next time."

"What do you mean?"

"I'm quitting."

"Tell me you are kidding."

"I am not."

"Chal theek hain..." he said.

"Poncho! Dinner!" my mom yelled.

"I got to go, man," I said.

"Ya okay."

"Bye."

"Listen..."

"Bol..."

"I broke up with her finally!"

"Kanya??"

"Ya, bloody mind molester," he said, and I laughed.

"See you at James' after dinner?"

"Yep, bye."

"I'm telling them tonight..." My message to Hrida read. I hit send as I pulled the chair at dinner table.

"Luck with it..." came an instant reply.

The dinner was served and according to Mom's new rule book, no one was allowed to talk at the dinner table. Apparently some health guru had advised against it in an article that she read in a magazine. So from that day on, I was yelled at and Dad was cold stared at if we tried to talk. Hence it was a silent table. It took me three miserable years in engineering to muster the courage to tell my parents that I wanted to quit. And now when I had decided, I just wanted to get done and over with it as soon as possible. I stared at both of them earnestly gobbling food. Dad caught my eye and bounced his eyebrows at me to ask what happened.

"I dropped another year." I heard Mom's spoon crash on her plate as I said that.

"And I am quitting the course."

A full minute of silence later Mom spoke. "Have you lost your mind? Did you even think before you opened your mouth?" Mom said, clearly demeaning what I said.

"I know what I'm saying. I have wanted to say this for three years now," I semi stammered.

"Who puts these ideas in your mind?" Mom said,

"I am not a child." I paused looking at her blazing eyes, "I don't need people to give me ideas to live my life."

"We are not having this conversation with you."

She looked at Dad for help but he didn't respond.

"I can't allow you to throw your life away."

"I am not asking you allow me, Aai. I have decided."

"Arvind you put some sense in this boy before I thrash him," Mom said.

"I'm sorry to let you down Dad but I can't bear it anymore. I don't want to do it. I never wanted to do it."

"This is the girl speaking, isn't it? She tells you to do all this, doesn't she?

"Damn it, Aai..." I pushed the chair back and stood up. "Why can't you for once keep your conspiracy theories aside and listen to me? I said I cannot bear it anymore. Every passing day in the course makes me feel worthless. Why can't you simply understand?"

"And what about what I want? What about my plans for you?"

The conversation suddenly transformed into a melodramatic screaming sequence.

"I don't care what you want!" I screamed back. "I *will* do what I want!"

"Not under my roof Arjun!"

"Fine! I'll leave then!" I said and stormed out of the house.

The sound of the door echoed in my ear, even as I pulled my bags out of the cab after Rizwan's thrashing. I was feeling so dirty both physically and mentally that all I could think of was crashing in a hot water tub. I startled my mother as I entered opening the door with my key.

"God! Poncho!" She freaked out seeing me.

"What are you doing here? You were not supposed to return for another fifteen days?"

"Ya, Rizwan fell ill, he is in a hospital." I wondered if Mom would be happy or sad knowing that I had been fired. Either ways I didn't want her to experience any one of those emotions, so I lied.

"Where is Baba?"

"Work, where else?"

"Okay," I began to walk to my room.

"I'm fasting so I didn't make lunch. Tell me what you'll have."

"No, don't bother. I'll eat out with Raghu."

"You sure?"

"Ya, ya." I disappeared in my room and locked myself.

I watched the ceiling fan go round and round with droopy eyes. I was tired and drained but my brain refused to let my eyes sleep. Every time they dozed, the subconscience mind woke me. The problem was, after getting a job with Rizwan, I was so cautious of not making any mistakes to lose it that in past six months of working for him, I had trained myself to be awake at all hours in case he wanted me. But now the job was gone, leaving me behind with an over chary mind. Since all my attempts to sleep failed, I dragged my feet to the balcony and lit a cigarette to divert my mind. I had a terrible itch to call Hrida but it was her birthday and I had no intention of ruining it. Instead, I called Raghu.

"And the big guy calls after three months!" he said audibly pissed.

"Hey man, sorry I didn't..."

"Oh don't bother, I'm not your boyfriend anymore..."

"Yes, and yet you sound irritated." I said goofily, " Sorry baby!"

"Bitch..."

"Really sorry man, got buried in work."

"I understand, how you been?"

"Good."

"Wait a minute," he paused, "Why are you calling from your landline?"

"Because my phone conked out."

"Fucker, you are back!"

"Ya."

"So why are you at home? Come here and help me plan the party for your girlfriend."

"Where?"

"My house, man. Raunak is on tour with his wife so it's a lodge!"

"Why do you call him by name, man?"

"Shit this surprise just couldn't get any better. Hrida's going to lose it." I could almost see the glint in Raghu's eyes. Organising hit parties gave him kicks.

"She's been missing you like hell lately. I just can't wait to see the look on her face." I smiled, imagining her smiling. "Just come fast, bitch!"

The party rocked as expected. Raghu's living room was cleared of all the furniture to make way for the dance floor. Since it was Hrida's birthday, everything from the cake to the menu was vegetarian. There were two separate bars. One served alcohol and fillers while the other provided milkshakes and cold coffees for Hrida and her teetotaler friends. The ambiance created by the rented party lights gave the house the correct look of a club. Raghu had over zealously invited everyone Hrida knew – her friends at school, college, office. The bastard made sure only her girlfriends came and the guys who were present were only there because their girlfriends were invited. The thing was that Raghu was on a dry spell ever since he had dumped Kanya.

Shashank and Neha were supposed pick Hrida up from work and bring her to the party. I, in the meanwhile was gift wrapped with ribbon, and was hiden in a closet in Raghu's room. I found it amazingly retarded but if all that meant making Hrida smile, then what the hell. I only hoped she wouldn't freak out. I heard muffled screams and voices wishing her as I stood between the stinking clothes of my beloved friend. It had been more than three months that I had seen her so the excitement of meeting her shot my pulse. Hrida's giggling got clearer as Raghu brought her in the room.

"What? You arranged a party but didn't get a cake for me?" She said giggling.

"Ya, I was kinda short on money so got you a gift instead." Raghu said.

"Raghu, what are you do...?"

"Shut up... Just close your eyes." Raghu scolded. "No peeking, *comprende*?"

"*Si, Si,*" she goofed.

"Now slowly, walk, one, two, three, enough." Their voices were very close now "This is the handle, now open the door."

She opened it and a smile propped my face as I saw her.

"Now your eyes!"

She did and the crowd screamed. Her eyes widened as she saw me. She covered her face with her hands and looked at Raghu, then at me again.

"Happy Birthday..." I said walking out of the closet.

As a response, she threw her arms around and hugged me tightly. I hugged her back. The intensity of the hug said how much she'd missed me. Not that I hadn't missed her but I had never seen this vulnerable side of hers before. With her breathing going haywire, I could tell she was crying. The best part about best friends is that they understand even slightest of change in your expressions so when I looked at Raghu for help, he shooed everyone away from the room, leaving us alone. A few more minutes later when she released me, there was a huge grin on her face.

"Shit you really *are* here!" She slapped my arm as she wiped her eyes.

"You might need an expert hand at doing that," I said pulling the handkerchief to straighten her ruined *kajal*.

"Raghu did this to you?" She peeled the bow pasted on my head as I bent down to wipe her eyes.

I looked into her eyes, and that very moment everything else went for a toss. God, she was beautiful. I exhaled heavily as I ran my thumb through her lower lip. She held me by the neck and kissed me. The intensity of it no lesser than the hug, but why would I complain.

For some reason that night I couldn't take my eyes off her the whole time. Hrida indeed possessed the power to instantly flush all my pains away. I felt like stabbing her hyper enthused friends after the cake cutting when they pulled her away from me to dance. I picked my glass and took the corner of the room to get a better view of her. To me, everybody else in the party was invisible. She caught me looking at her and ordered me to the dance floor. I laughed it off, it wasn't my day. The party took its patented course of people getting wasted and exhausted from dancing and continued for another three hours after which Raghu, Shashank and I had to parcel the girls to their homes.

"At times like these, I so badly wish I was single," Shashank said.

"Dude! Be careful what you wish for," Raghu said opening the door with his key.

"Hey baby, you still awake? I thought you'd be half dead by now," Shashank said to Neha as we entered.

"You think I'd miss *the night* with you for sleep?" She instantly got off the couch and hopped towards the bedroom. Shashank followed her nodding his head in fake embarrassment.

"Behave yourself guys, its my parents' roo..." The door banged before he completed his sentence.

"Fuck..." Raghu paused dramatically, "Twenty-nine girls I invited... and not one of them looked at me."

Hrida and I laughed.

"No Hrida, seriously, look at me!" He stood up and turned round and round in front of her. "Do you think there is anything wrong with me?"

"There is nothing wrong with you baby. I told you it's Kanya. She's cast a spell on you. Go beg her for her forgiveness and everything will be alright," Hrida said. I laughed.

"Don't you guys have some making out to do? Get off my couch. I really need to sleep." He snapped pulling us from the couch. We hugged and kissed him.

"Thank you, baby," I said to him before entering his room.

"Have fun kids!" he yelled.

I slid my hand through her waist and hugged her from behind as soon as we entered Raghu's room. I closed my eyes, rested the lips on the back of her shoulder after nuzzling on it for a while. Her body smelled so soothingly intoxicating that she could have pacified a raging bison if she willed. Ever since I met Hrida, I'd always looked to her for emotional restitution whenever anything went wrong. She had taken care of all my paranoia and ever hurtful life and stood by me. I just wanted to stand there holding her like that forever.

"Thank you, baby," she ruffled my hair stretching her hand behind.

"Mmm…" I said loosening the grip on her waist for her to turn.

"I never thought I'd be so cheesy but the past three months felt empty without you," she said impishly and hugged me. "I love you."

"Thank you," I replied.

"Thank you?" She raised an eyebrow. I nodded yes and stiffed my lips to control the smile. I felt an excruciating pain as she stamped on my feet, then placing her other foot on me, she ordered, "Walk me around."

"I hope you understand I'm not Stallone and you are not feather light?"

"I know, it's a punishment."

She giggled as I oscillated sideways to rotate around myself. Then three extremely heavy steps later, I crashed on the bed with her in my arms. Even though my feet hurt like hell it was totally worth it.

"I love you…" I said planting a kiss on her cheek.

"And I am sorry."

"For?"

"For saying thank you which is Hrida's patented reply."

"And?"

"And I love you," I stared at her with love-struck eyes. "A lot."

"Cheesy sala, come here..." she pulled me close and bit my cheek. I held her close.

"How's office?" I asked.

"Oh that reminds me, where is my phone?" She hopped off the bed.

"It's fun as usual," she said as she rummaged through her purse to find the phone. "Ah, finally!"

"What are you doing?" I sat up folding my legs.

"Putting up a mail for tomorrow's leave. I wanna spend as much time with you till you are free."

"Hrida, wait."

"What?"

"I have to tell you something." The bitter reality came back.

"What's wrong?" After a brief pause, she asked again, "Hello? What?"

"Rizwan fired me last night."

"Shit! But why?" She sat on the bed.

"I kinda screwed up." The rancidness of humiliation resurfaced as I told her what happened.

"What an asshole! I can't believe he pushed you."

"Tell me about it."

"How can someone be such a dick?

She climbed up and sat facing me folding her legs.

"I think it's something to do with me, people just hate me." I stared at her cuspated fingernails as I pressed my thumbs against them to inflict pain.

"I know how you feel right now. Had I been you, I might have killed myself. You are still doing good, I'm proud of you."

"I thought I'd learn something and find some footing after this job, but all I did was clear dirty plates and get nowhere.

What's worse is that he fucked me in front of all the contacts I made, so even if they give me a job, I'll always be the guy who got publicly screwed by Rizwan Qureshi."

"Oh come on, lose the crap. No one remembers. Big deal man, you lost one you'll find another one."

"You know I thought I'll never have to lie to Mom and Dad about anything again, but now I have to."

"So don't lie, tell them what happened."

"What do you think will happen then?" She looked at me blankly.

"Last thing I need right now is a I-told-you-so lecture from Mom." I was so frustrated that tears poured out of my eyes without permission.

"Arjun, listen to me." She pulled my head up to level with hers, "What happened has happened, you cannot undo it, it was your fault but you didn't deserve what happened, and this possibly is not the last time something like that will happen. I mean come on, it's the industry, it is known to do cruel things to people."

"I bloody burnt myself for two years to get it." My tears continued rolling out.

"I know that job meant a lot, but that's not what you want to become in life. You'll find another that will inch you forward."

I nodded yes wiping my tears. "Come here!" She pulled me to hug. I dabbed my nose with my sleeve to wipe the snot away.

"I love you," I said.

"This is gonna cost you much more that a plain love you," she said planting a kiss on my cheek. "Yum, *thoda namak zyada hai* but I'll make do with it!!" She goofed.

I held her face with my shivering fingers and rested my nose on hers. The dumb heart of mine as usual began its somersaults as my lips brushed hers. It had been four years with her but I could never figure what about her turned my life upside down. The effect that she had on me was inexplicable: one look, one smile, one kiss from her is all it took for the internal architecture of my body to crumble. I shifted my hand from her face to her hair for the grip and kissed her upper lip. Shivers ran down me as she reciprocated by nibbling my lower lip. I slumped on the bed and she slid herself on top of me. She pinned my hands and tussled with my t-shirt to kiss my collar bone; a while later, in a fit of excitement, she pulled it off me and threw it on the floor. My eyes squinted as she came closer to kiss me. I unzipped her dress, unhooked her bra, and held her down by her bare back. The smell and feel of her body rubbing against mine created an everlasting trance.

"Please stop..." Hrida whispered to me as I began to undo the rest of her clothes. I was so god damned zonked out of my mind that I didn't pay heed to her request, though now I wished I had stopped. What started as gentle snugly comforting intimacy turned into wild primal wanting. My eyes stared at hers while our bodies moved in sync. Finally the thing I had saved myself for from all the girls in my past happened. I lost my virginity, but somehow it wasn't the way I imagined it to be. It was far from a good feeling. Knowing that Hrida didn't want it, filled me with guilt more than any kind of pleasure. A part of me broke as I saw tears seep away from her eyes after we were done. I had asked her to trust me blindly which she did, and I blew it up. She awkwardly responded as I stretched my arm to hug. I prayed that Hrida was ready for whatever happened and I had not hurt her, but prayers are not always heard.

Next morning, I woke up to an empty bed. No message, no note from her.

She was gone.

Shit.

2012

7:30. I checked the clock when the blaring sound of the alarm woke me. I snoozed it and went back to sleep. It had been three months now that I moved in with Gayatri, and that meant I could afford sleeping an extra hour every day. Traffic in LA no more bothered me since I could walk to college and could party as long as I wanted, without the sword of commuting back home to Artesia hanging over my head. After Radhika's baby had come, her place was always buzzing with her in-laws and guests, making it highly tiring to live there. So when Gayatri suggested that I share the apartment with her, I readily agreed.

The alarm went off again, finally forcing me to pull myself out of bed, but sleep refused to leave my eyes. Only coffee can help now, I told myself and sauntered to the kitchen. I was so sleepy that I wished I could walk with my eyes closed.

"If it's coffee you are making, then I'll love to have some too." A heavily British accented male voice said startling me so much that it threw me off balance, leaving me grappling for grip on kitchen platform.

"Who are you?" I asked irritated.

"Eric, I...I was with your roomie last night," he said.

"H-hi..." I said and half smiled.

Going by his partial nudity and freshly minted hickeys on his body, he was definitely not just a friend of Gay.

Shit! she was cheating on Aneesh with this gora. Maybe not. Gay wasn't one of the girls who'd stray. He could just be her friend, or... Shit!

With all the random thoughts whirling in my morning mind, I handed Eric a mug of coffee.

"Why are you still here?" Gay asked as she walked out of her room.

"I have to have a coffee in the morning to help my bowels," Eric said animatedly.

"OK, whatever, just make it fast. I have to go to work."

The guy took his time to leave. Gay meanwhile ran on the treadmill, behaving as if he was invisible.

"I thought you were working today?" I asked, realising her treadmill run went beyond her usual schedule.

"It's Saturday na today, beta."

"Ya but you told Eric you had to, so I thought..."

"Oh yes his name was Eric, I was trying to remember."

She said panting "I lied..."

"OK." I had an intense urge to ask her about what she was up to with the gora, but it was none of my business. I got back to my workout. Yes workout. Another good thing that happened after moving in with her. I had initially evaded it, but Gayatri's persistent nagging forced me to give up. So much was the persuasive power of her nagging that she harrowed me into quitting smoking as well. But I had no qualms about it. I never felt better.

"You suck at telepathy..." she said.

"Huh?" I said pausing the push-ups, sweat dripping off my nose.

"I had to read your face to know..."

"Know what?"

"That you are itching to shoot me down with your questions," she said as she jumped off the treadmill and caved in on the couch wiping her sweat. I sat on the floor folding my legs. "So?" She asked.

"So... Umm... I don't mean to intrude."

"Skip the preface please."

"Who was the guy?"

"He was my attempt to give my body the physical attention it needs."

"You mean you slept with him behind your boyfriend's back."

"Wow, when you put it like that, it feels like I'm a premium quality slut."

"I'm sorry I..."

She began to giggle.

"It's alright, but yeah, it's pretty much what you said. Just that Aneesh knows about him and others if I do that."

"But I thought you guys loved each other."

"So?"

"So ideally are you not supposed be loyal to the person you love?"

"Ideally. Not when you stay five thousand kilometres away and meet only twice a year. Video chats don't satisfy you sexually, you know. Sex and feelings are mutually exclusive."

"Then why be in a relationship? Stay single till you find someone who lives closer."

"Love?"

"Your concepts are a bit ridiculous..."

"No."

"Why not?"

"Look, all my life the society preached me to save myself for the one true love, and when I found him, I have to stay away from him. It's been five years that we've been living away from each other. I am thirty-two and he is thirty-five and by the time life is gracious enough to bring us together, our bodies will be menopausal.

"So quit your job and go stay with him."

"Both of us have slogged our asses off to get where we are today, so giving up on either one of our careers is seriously stupid. We tried breaking up, but that didn't work. We kept getting back to each other every time we tried, but this open relationship thing worked for us."

"Ya, but doesn't it bother you?"

"At first it did bother us both, but now we've gotten used to it. If we had an option, we would have taken it but there isn't any, and sex with different people doesn't lessen our affection for each other. We are as much in love as any other couple. It's just sex that we outsource." She shrugged.

"Plus, it's not as if we'll be like this forever. For now, we are happy with this. We'll cross the bridge when we come to it.

"Honestly, it's too much to process."

"There is nothing to process... it's just sex."

"Hmmm... Who was the guy anyway?"

"Management trainee."

"Looked pretty gay."

"I know. Aneesh said the same thing."

"When did Aneesh meet him?"

"Ahh..."

She blew out air and took a dramatic pause. "Well, we have a ritual. Before and when we do it, we send each other snaps of the person..."

"Are you guys for real?" She took a bow. I laughed.

"Family is supposed to welcome the guests and not otherwise." Radhika said standing in my way placing her right hand on the door. The baby in her left arm blocked the other side.

"Sorry, I got traffucked," I smiled.

"Language... please... around the kid at least?" she said and handed me 'The Niece' and dragged me deeper into the dense forest of the guests.

Good food was one of the many perks of coming back to Radhika's house. Not that I couldn't take care of my sinner stomach but years of diligently standing besides 'The Mother' while she cooked brushed off some serious culinary skills on "The Sister". So the buffet that was laid graced such a variety of dishes that the watering mouths could fill enough buckets to bathe the whole of Los Angeles. The occasion was the sixth month birthday of the eight pound piece of flesh – my niece Kiara. The name was a bit wannabe for me, plus naming your kid after a cartoon character was supremely lame, but Radhika had fought off my disapproval and went ahead with the name.

As I roved my eyes around the party, I found nothing interesting. I looked at the decorated house, bunny shaped cake, delicious smelling buffet, enthusiastic neighbours, their riotous kids, desi relatives of Viren attempting an accent, lame birthday party games. Everything but what I was looking for – alcohol. Food, soft drinks and confectioneries weren't exactly my definition of a party. If it wasn't for the tutu-wearing baby Kiara, I would have made a run for it.

"What beta, you are not taking anything only? Your mother will think we *derived* you of food here?" Deprived, Kamal Aunty, Radhika's mother-in-law meant, "Take, take, how will you get *allergy* (energy)?"

"Yes I am. I am, wait I'll help you with the gravy," I smilingly said.

"Oh, no no beta, I am a *vegetable* (vegetarian)."

"I'm sorry I didn't know." I can speak Marathi too, Kamal Aunty, I thought of adding.

"By the way, beta I'm sorry the girl break your hard (heart)." What!! My sister's mother-in-law also knew about my devastation over a three-year-old break-up!

"But you don't worry, you are so young, I will find you a suitable groom (bride) here in Amreeka. And that too with a green card." She winked at me as she left.

I suddenly felt like all the eyes in the room shifted their focus on me, staring at me sympathetically. Had I become that guy who needs help to lead a normal life? I thought I was doing good with the moving on in life. I probably needed to exhibit my happy emotions a bit more openly.

Smile fool, smile. I told myself.

"What's wrong with you?" Radhika asked.

"What do you mean?"

"You are smiling."

"So, is that a problem?"

"No. Looks like you are faking it."

"Oh god! You need to stop dissecting every little thing..."

"Tell me when you are done pretending everything is alright."

"Everything is fine!"

"You probably think no one notices, but you've changed, Poncho..."

"Ya, because you can't be the same person all your life."

"I didn't mean it in a good way."

"What is wrong with you all of a sudden?"

"Because the person that I've been with in past one year is not the brother I grew up with. It's fine if you don't want to talk to me about what happened with Hrida, but you need to talk to her and get a closure. You think I don't know why you came here? Running away from Mom, Dad and everyone who loves you is not going to bring you peace. Arjun, throwing tantrums is not going to bring her back."

"Tantrums? Are you seriously kidding me?"

"Speak to her and sort your life when you go back, Arjun. That's all I'm saying."

"Speak about what, Didi? *I* broke up with her. I am not going back to her. It's the one thing I've promised her and I'm keeping my promise. Mom was right. I had to accept we were not meant to be together and I finally have. Don't worry, I'm fine..." I lied, but the last part of my argument finally scored Radhika's silence. When in an argument, quotes of people your opponent worships always help you win.

Later that night after hers truly, whiskey, failed to create the magic, I went back to my old friend in need, weed. It was a year since I had gotten baked so the first hit felt like I was shot by a shot gun. I had almost forgotten how it felt. I stood there with my back pinned to the wall, listening to my own heartbeat.

Radhika was right, I was pretending, but I knew no other way to move on. I thought plugging the memories and lying to myself would eventually ease things. In the past one year, film school had kept me so busy that I had no time to even feel the pain of my bursting bladder, let alone the pain of her not being around. But now with the course in its final phase, time had made itself available for me. And with time came the plans for the future, and her absence in the future took me back to the past. Right from the moment that she had walked out of the cafe that night, I had an intuition that she'd come back after her anger subsided. The counting of time changed from hours to days to months to years now, she never came back. I never made peace with the fact that she was actually gone. I couldn't digest the fact that she didn't want to be with me. As time passed, the bitterness inside me grew. My immature pretentious pursuit of Devdaas-like self destruction only led me to an empty life.

"*Chutiya banaya khud ko...*" I grunted and pulled my hair. Then, as if to steal the thunder of my grunting, the sliding door of the balcony opened with a thundering noise and spooked me. I dropped the joint in fright as she stared at me.

"Bloody criminal!" Gay yelled.

"Gay... I was just... I'm sorry..." I said flustered. The lit joint lying on the floor was still breathing smoke into the air. I lifted my feet to stamp it to death.

"What the fuck are you doing?" Gay screamed again.

"I-I..." It was so fucking tough to respond to her that words barely made it out of my mouth.

"It's a crime to waste a joint..." she pushed me aside and leaned to rescue it, "Do you know how hard it is to get weed these days?" she said and coughed her lungs out as soon as she took a drag.

"Where did you get it? This stuff is good..."

She coughed again, "Really good..."

"Leo got it for me..." I said.

Gay looked at me with a disheartened face as I flicked the joint out of the balcony.

"I have more."

"My herooooo..." she fluttered her eyelashes.

"That goes in there... and... umm... then a fold... and ca..re.. fu..lly... roll... and..." I jutted my tongue out to tape the joint. "Yum... here you go, milady. Your joint, lean and mean..." I said while Bob Marley sang Ganja Gun in the background.

Silence swept the living room as she sparked the spliff and took consecutive drags while I preyed on passive buzz.

"What... brought... the need... of weed on... you?" she said pausing abruptly, "Is she back... in here." She knocked her index finger on my forehead.

"Ahh! The famous 'she' of my life, yes she is back." I rested my head on the couch and tapped on her hand for a drag.

"No!" she snapped, "I'm not sharing."

"Cruel bitch!"

"What do I say, the praises don't stop."

"I give up," I said and got up to roll again.

"I need something sweet, can you fetch me the gummy bears? Please?" I fetched her the box and sat back on the couch.

"Ganja ganja..." she sang along with Marley.

"Three years four months and nineteen days..." I said interrupting her. "That's how long it has been since I broke up with her..."

"I sense an 'and' coming."

"And I have been waiting for her to come back all that while..."

"Why?"

"Because I am a *chut*..."

"Really?"

"Yes."

"Okay!"

"I wasted eleven years behind a girl for this shitty loneliness."

"No one forced you, right?"

"That's what makes me the fool that I am."

"Okay."

"You know, I can count at least seven girls who I could have been happily with had I not been hung up on her."

"Did you count me? Because that would make it eight."

"No, I didn't. Wait a minute, are you saying..."

"Eww no... it was in the past that I waited for you."

"You did? How long?"

"Five years."

"What the fuck?"

"Yes, what the fuck..." she said and took a drag.

"So... I kinda know how you feel..." she continued.

"Shit Gay, I... I had no idea..."

"Hmm... Gummy bears?" I grabbed a handful from the box. 'Leave the purple ones, they are mine."

"I'm really sorry Gay," I said and hugged her.

"It's okay," she said patting my back, "Let me go to sleep now." She got off the couch and walked to her room.

"I seriously wish I knew. I would have done something."

"Well you could now..." she said stopping at the door of her bedroom.

"As in?"

"As in if you want we can... you know..."

"You mean...?" I said widening my eyes.

"Ya I mean." She shrugged. "Unless you are still saving yourself for some princess charming."

"No..."

"No?"

"I mean no, I am not saving myself for anyone but... no..."

"Okay, no problem. Good night." She disappeared behind the door.

I went to my room and crashed on the bed. I tossed and turned under the quilt, but the mind refused to shut down. I got out of the bed and went to Gayatri's room.

Your days of being a chut are over, I told myself before I knocked on her door.

"Gay?" I knocked again.

"The door's open," she said.

"How do I have to pose for the photograph for Aneesh?" I asked impishly. She smiled.

"That we'll think of in the morning. Now come to bed," she ordered.

I closed the door and followed the order.

I was seven years late but I was happy that I was finally graduating. The convocation ceremony at Los Angeles Film Academy was a rather unconventional one. Ten films cumulatively made by ninety students from acting, directing, producing, editing and other faculties were screened to a packed auditorium. Then based on the average of their popular votes, the films were rated on ten. The highest scoring film would be sent to the festivals at the school's expense. Though my film wasn't going to any festival, it ranked number three. It had been long since I had done anything to make myself proud. I wished Mom and Dad were there. I wished she was there. Ever since I dropped out of engineering, these three people desperately wanted to see me graduate, and now when I finally did, they weren't around. But Radhika made up for their absence. She along with her whole family applauded as I walked up the stage to collect my degree.

"Mom would have been so happy..." Radhika whispered into my ears as she hugged me.

"I know." I said as she kissed me.

"I saw your name in the picture, beta, what proud I felt I tell you." Kamal Aunty said and kissed my forehead. I touched her feet.

"Sir, can I please get an autograph?" Viren said holding a paper and a pen. I grinned and signed. "You know years from now this will sell for a million dollars," he said to Radhika holding the paper. I hugged him.

"Beta, this is Bhoomi. You remember our neighbour Mrs Gandhi. She is her daughter," Kamal Aunty said.

"Hi..." Bhoomi said extending her hand.

"Hi..." I shook her hand with a confused look.

"When I told her mother about you, she *invested* (insisted) to take Bhoomi to meet you. She is big fan of films."

I smiled.

"I told you I'll find you a beautiful groom (bride)," she said rather non-discreetly, pushing both of us in a conscious silence.

"I loved your film," Bhoomi said after musing for a while.

"I'm glad you did."

A message from Gayatri tinged on my phone.

"Sorry kid, running late, got stuck at work... see you in six minutes." and one sad, one happy smiley, her message read.

"It's okay, just make sure you kiss me when you meet." and a straight face, I replied.

"I'm sorry..." I said to Bhoomi.

"Oh no it's alright..."

"So what do you do?"

"I help my father with his grocery store. We are the biggest Indian place in Artesia."

"That's great..." It was extremely important that I went through this matchmaking meeting flawlessly, because I knew everyone from Radhika to Viren to his mother, even the baby, were closely observing me from a distance. Even though it was Radhika's mother-in-law who had introduced me to the girl, Radhika was the real mastermind behind the meeting. I, however, had my own agenda of proving to Radhika that I was normal and the after-effects of the break-up on me had worn off.

"Hi baby, I'm so sorry I missed it," Gayatri said and pecked me on my lips. "I'm sorry, sorry, sorry," she said kissing after ever sorry.

"I wish you were there, honey," I kissed her back, in full public view.

"*Sheee*...Honey?"

"Just play along," I whispered.

"Bhoomi, this my girlfriend, Gayatri." Her face flushed.

"Hi..." she said.

"Poncho?" Radhika entered the scene. I *knew* she had been watching me, I mentally fist-pumped.

"Didi... meet Gayatri. She and I are..."

"Radhikaaaaa... I finally get to meet you," Gay jumped on Radhika and hugged her before I could complete my sentence.

Poor Bhoomi. She stood there dumbfounded.

"Gay, this is Viren bhai, my brother-in-law," I said.

"I've heard so much about you guys, Poncho keeps talking about you guys all the time. Where is Kiara?"

"He never told us about you?" Radhika said, "Wonder why that is?" She turned to me; I smiled sheepishly. Even though Gay was doing a great job, it was Radhika we were pitted against, so it wasn't going to be easy.

"Really?" Gay said, "You and me will have to talk later at home, understand?"

"Yes." I pretended to be scared, "And here comes the baby."

"Aww she is so cute, can I please kiss her?" Gay asked Radhika.

Kamal Aunty looked on a bit disappointed.

"Sorry, Aunty, I should have told you about Gayatri."

"Oh come on, beta if you are happy it doesn't mind (matter)," Kamal Aunty said.

"Gayatri, she is Kamal Aunty, Radhika's mother-in-law." Gay promptly touched her feet.

"Oh no need, beta." Gay smiled. "What do you do, beta?"

"I work for Technocom. They provide cellular service."

"Oh nice... and where are your parents from?"

"Mumbai..."

"Poncho, what time is your flight tomorrow?" Radhika asked.

"Two o'clock I guess, not sure I'll have to check," I said.

"Let me know, is your packing done? else I'll come to help in the morning."

"It's done. Gayatri took care of it, I'll see you at the airport directly."

"Cool. Let's leave," she told Viren.

"Why aren't you guys waiting for the party?" I asked.

"It's late. I better rush back home before the baby gets cranky," Radhika said, "It was nice meeting you, Gayatri. Come home sometime. Even if Poncho is gone, we are here."

"Oh sure, I'll come," Gay said.

"Take care baby, I'm proud of you." Radhika hugged me.

"I love you," I said.

After all of them left, I exhaled in relief.

"What did you just make me do back there?" Gayatri asked.

"Save my ass from getting married to a grocery store owner's daughter."

"Whatt?"

"Run run run, we'll be late for the party," I said and pulled her with me.

"Get a room, you guys!" Leo's drunken voice yelled in my ears from three inches away, while drunk me and drunk Gayatri chomped on each other's lips on the dance floor. I pushed him away as soon as he handed me my drink.

"I've never done this before, you know," I said taking a break from kissing her.

"What?" Gayatri said breathing heavily.

"Making out in full public view..." I said as she circled her tongue on my neck, her fingers griping me by my hair.

"Okay..." Gay said. Her antics were blowing my mind beyond explanation, I gulped the drink in one go and chucked the glass to lift her by her butt.

"I haven't done it in a loo after we did it in college. Come on, let's go..." she said and dragged me with her.

"Where?" I slurred.

The ladies room was buzzing with girls. All eyes stared at me as Gay pulled me by my arm into one of the cubicles.

"Shit! That bloody hurt, you vampire!" I wailed in pain as she bit my neck not so gently.

"You've been a bad bad boy," she said in a Russian accent.

"Ooooooo... what are you going to do to me masterrr?" I replied as she pushed me on the toilet seat. Even inside the loo the music from the dance floor could be heard clearly, Gayatri began her pelvic thrusts to the beats, occasionally running the nail of her index finger on my face. She looked so godfasakenly hot that I slid my hands across her waist and pulled her towards me. She pushed me back.

"No touching... okay?" Gayatri ordered her voice full of lust.

"Why?" I whined.

"Because the master says so." I inhaled heavily and blew the air out.

The cubicle of the loo had officially transformed into a private room of a strip club as she began her lap dance on me. With her body thrusting against mine and her hands running all over me, it was getting horribly hard to control myself from keeping my hands off her. I gave up my resistance and fiercely turned her around holding her by her hair and began to kiss her violently. Though the pheromones from our bodies did an amazing job of trancing us, the stench and the congested area of the cubicle was killing the buzz.

"I don't think this is good idea..." I whispered in her ear.

"Ya, my butt's cramping too... Let's fuck off from here."

Both of us ran out of the club.

Mumbai or LA, cabbies everywhere play a hard to get hot lass. It was past midnight, so hoping to get a cab was like asking to legalize marijuana. She removed her heels and prepared to walk, for next twenty-three odd minutes, Gayatri and I brisk walked holding each other's hand. As we neared the building of our apartment, I let go of her hand and began to run and she followed me. Rushing through the pavements and stomping heavily on the stairs to climb up, huffing and puffing I struggled with the keys to open the door.

"Fuckkkkkk." I grunted in frustration as I dropped them a couple of times before I finally unlocked it. The door banged open as Gayatri pounced on me and pinned me to the wall resuming the wild kissing. I clamped my hands to her butt and carried her to the living room. Her body smelled so heavenly that I felt like kissing every square millimeter of it. She, in the meanwhile, ripped the buttons of my seventy-three dollar shirt. In normal circumstances, I would have battered her to death for it but at that point of time, her furious passion had zonked me out of my mind. I unzipped her dress carefully and crashed on the fluffy rug on the floor with her in my arms. The clothes left on our bodies perished subsequently as the romping progressed. Nothing about Gayatri had changed in all these years, except for a few tattoos in explicit places. They might have existed even when I was with her. I wouldn't know since I had never gone beyond second base with her then. Since it was my last day in LA, we spent the rest of the night pleasuring each other in every possible corner of the house – living room floor, kitchen platform, bathtub in my room, and finally concluding on the bed in Gayatri's room.

A huge thud woke me up the next morning. I saw a guy pulling a suitcase out of Gayatri's wardrobe. I knew I had to shout for help, but I was so tazzed by sleep that by the time my brain registered anything and opened the mouth, the suitcase was out of the bedroom. I helplessly looked around for Gayatri since she wasn't in bed.

"I'm so sorry, dude. I was just taking some of my stuff out," he said as I continued staring at him with sleep-glutted eyes.

"Arjun right? I'm Aneesh, please sleep. We'll catch up later." I hardly managed a smile before he left the room. Thank god for the quilt for I was practically naked under it. I caved my head back into the pillow and went back to sleep. A few minutes later, a voice yelled in my head "Aneesh! Gayatri's boyfriend is here! Wake up, wake up wake up!"

I woke up, hurriedly got dressed, and walked out of the room.

"You are up extraordinarily early today..." Gay said.

"Shit... I'm so sorry I woke you up!" Aneesh said.

"It's fine." I croaked, "Hi again, we finally meet." I extended my hand to him.

"Ya man, finally."

"I'll just freshen up and be back..."

"Sure sure," he said.

"Coffee?" Gay asked.

"Will love some..." I said and smiled at her before entering my room.

I locked myself in the bath, sat myself down on a bathtub wall and began staring at things. It took a while for what just happened to sink in. I mean Aneesh actually found me naked in his girlfriend's bed, but he didn't have a single frown on his face. In fact, the guy was more concerned about disturbing my sleep. Hearing about the concept of an open relationship was weird, but witnessing one so closely was altogether a different level of weird. *I* felt guilty about the whole set-up when I walked into the living room, but both of them were at such ease with it that they behaved as if nothing had happened. It was indeed love that had kept both of them together for so long, otherwise their arrangement was a perfect recipe for a classic disaster. The price you pay for love, I thought. Wow!

"Hey..." I said, interrupting an after joke laughter between both of them.

"Hey buddy, come sit," Aneesh said.

"I'm so glad I got to meet you before I left," I said.

"Me too man, ever since I started dating her, I've heard about Arjun and Arjun only."

"You're bluffing."

"No, I am serious. You are the case of one that got away for this one here."

"You were the reason for our first break-up," Gay said, as she handed me the coffee mug and the breakfast plate to Aneesh.

"God!!! This is so embarrassing." I said and buried my face in my palms. Both of them laughed at me.

"You know, we were actually each other's rebounds." Aneesh said. "I was tending to wounds of my break-up when we first hooked up." He said, while chomping on to the piece of bacon.

"Ya we'd drink and cry to each other for hours and then fuck," Gay said.

"Language lady!" Aneesh hush snapped.

"What? This bitch doesn't mind. Do *you* bitch?" I smiled and shook my head in a no.

"I was so jealous of you that the jealousy doused the grief of my break-up." Aneesh laughed. I laughed. Then they kissed.

"But it's good to see you guys together like this," I said.

"It's crazy, I tell you, sometimes I wonder what's kept us together for so long." He burped indiscreetly as he finished his breakfast.

"Well, what's important is there *is* something that's keeping you together."

"True that bro," he said as he took his plate to the kitchen.

"Here, spray some." Gay said handing me an antiseptic spray.

"Where?" She touched my neck, and I asked "Why?"

"Because you look like a victim of domestic sex abuse," She whispered.

"Guys you know what, we should go out partying tonight. What time is you flight, Arjun?" Aneesh said.

"I don't know. Two o'clock I guess," I got up to go to my room.

"Why haven't you still checked the ticket?" Gay yelled. "Where is it?"

"What?" I yelled back from the bathroom as I sprayed the antiseptic.

"Your ticket, you dumbass."

"In my sack somewhere." Gayatri had indeed left me looking like a raped wife.

"What the hell!" She screamed at the top of her voice, I ran out of the bath. "Arjun????"

"What?"

"It's a two PM flight!"

"Ya so... Why are you... oh bloody shit..." The wind knocked out of me as I realised my blunder. I had made a common hareheaded mistake of assuming *PM* as night.

"Shit..." Aneesh said.

All of us paused and stared at each other in horror.

"It's ten we can still make it," Gay broke the silence.

"I'll go get a cab," Aneesh said.

"How can you be so fucking dumb, Arjun?" Gay scolded me, "Seriously."

"Its no big deal, Gay, I'll postpone it, chill."

"Are you mad? Why do you want to waste money for just twelve hours? You are anyway packed."

I was so stunned by the fall of events that I stood there unable to move.

"Run, get ready fast. I'll call Radhika." She pushed me into my room.

One hour fifteen minutes after realising my blunder and hurriedly stuffing my bags, I reached LAX. Even though I was slated to leave LA that day, I wasn't prepared for the abrupt exit I was about to make.

"You are the limit, Poncho. How dumb can you get?" Radhika said as I pulled the bags out of the cab.

"Please don't lecture me anymore. Gay has chewed enough of my ears already."

"Okay fine. Here, put this in your bag."

"What is it?"

"Some stuff Mom asked me to send."

"I am not going home if that's what you are suggesting."

"Ahh whatever, just courier it home," she gritted her teeth.

"Bye bye, Baby Ki," I said to the baby kissing her. "Come soon to Mamu, okay?"

"Bye, Viren Bhai. Thank you for everything. Say sorry to Kamal Aunty, I was going to come home but..."

"It's fine kiddo, you be good," he hugged me.

"Don't go Poncho baby," Radhika jutted her lower lip and the tears appeared. I hugged her.

"You should go Poncho, you are late already," Viren said.

"Yep. Bye, Didi and see you soon," I said.

"Speak to Hrida when you go back," Radhika said as she let me go. I nodded.

"Hey man, have a safe flight," Aneesh said.

"Sorry for all the hassle I caused you."

"All good bro, you take care," he said.

"Bye." I smiled and wheeled the trolley.

"I still think I should postpone..." I said to Gayatri.

"Shut up and get lost. I'm done with you," she said and kissed me in front of Aneesh, for a nice ten seconds. "Shit... I'm going to miss you so much."

"Me too baby, but I'll come back soon," I said looking at her moist eyes.

"No, don't."

"Why?"

"Because, I still love you."

2009

Raghu and I stared at his smiling face as he hurriedly walked out of the arrivals at the Chhatrapati Shivaji International Airport. Usually receiving someone at arrivals in Mumbai is a supreme pain in the ass, considering all the front rows of the eternally makeshift steel railings are occupied by placard holding, sleep-deprived oversmart pick-up drivers, making it impossible for your arriving passenger to spot you. That day, however, it was least of our concerns. Shashank had spotted us the moment he stepped out. What both of us were spooked about was the news we were about to give him, rather the news that Raghu was about to give him. I had made it clear to Raghu on my way to the airport that I wasn't going to be the one to do it. I looked at his smiling face for the one last time as he walked to us in his casual grey T-shirt, black track pants, Superman flip-flops and a gym bag slinging from his shoulder.

"How have my bitches been?" he said and hugged us both.

"Missed you slutty," I said as he released me from the hug.

"Me too. Wassup Randy?" he said to Raghu, strangulating him between his biceps and forearms. "What's wrong with him?" I shrugged with an awkward smile.

"He has that constipated 'my-girlfriend-dumped-me' look on his face. Someone dumped you again Randy, haan?" He said kissing Raghu.

"No, Arrgghh... Leave me..." Raghu said trying to free himself from Shashank's grip. "What fucking took you so long? And what happened to your luggage, did the airline rob you of it?"

"Ya something like it. Asses left it in Frankfurt," Shashank giggled.

"What the fuck?" I said.

"It'll be here day after tomorow." He smacked his palm on his forehead, "I'm sorry I totally forgot..." He turned to a girl standing behind him,

"Guys, this is Natasha, and Natasha this is Raghu and that's Poncho."

"Hi, Arjun." I said waving at her. I was so preoccupied with the noxiousness of the news that I didn't notice the orange skinned Spanish hottie standing right next to Sachdev.

"RA-goo and R-jun... nice names," she grinned.

"Guys, come let's get her a cab," Shashank said as he led her to the taxi stand. RA-goo and I followed them.

"How much should I pay him?" she asked Shashank

"Don't worry, I'll fix it for you," he replied.

"You are such a sweetheart," she said and stroked his cheek. Shashank grinned.

"I know that fucking grin, I bet he has a boner in those tracks right now," Raghu said to me semi-irritated.

"I guess it's fair, he is not gonna smile for a long time after you tell him," I said.

"I know I have to tell him so don't bug me," Raghu snapped.

"Boss? JW?" Shashank asked the cab driver."

"Yes," he replied.

"How much?"

"By the meter," the cabbie said.

"Okay," he said and turned to Natasha, "It shouldn't be more than three hundred rupees."

"Thank you so much!" she said and hugged Shashank before sitting in the cab.

"I'll see you day after," he said and the cab zoomed off.

Raghu stared at him as we walked towards the parking.

"What? I was just trying to help," Shashank said and grinned ear to ear.

"Who was she?" I asked.

"I met her in the flight and her baggage got misplaced like mine so..."

"So you just clung to her," Raghu muttered.

"It's the other way around actually." Shashank winked.

"Lucky bastard." Raghu said shaking his head in disbelief.

"Where to?" I asked starting the car.

"Pyaasa..." Came from Shashank

Throughout the drive from the airport to Pyaasa, Shashank blabbed about New York, his college, food, cars, girls, parties, systems in the US, leaving little room for Raghu to open his mouth. The only time he paused was to light a cigarette. The excitement with which he spoke of his time spent in New York was probably what demotivated Raghu to open his mouth. Finally, twenty kilometres, two hours, and seven large pegs of Jack Daniels later, Raghu managed to open his mouth.

"I, I, I have to tell you something..." Raghu said slurring heavily, "You are my brrrotherrr, Slutty," he said and hugged Shashank stretching across the table, knocking his glass down. "I love you..."

"I love you too, Randy." Shashank said taking a sip. "I wish you guys were there with me in NY... It was just..."

"I have to tell you somethinggggg..." Raghu broke down while he still hugged Shashank across the table.

"I have to tell you somethinggggg..." Raghu's whining continued.

"What is it man, what's wrong?" Shashank said ruffling Raghu's hair. His expression changed realising something serious was up.

"Fuck *Bhenchod*, this is not fair." Raghu returned to his seat. "You are an unfair man. I hate you, you hear me, I hate you." He said looking up at god. Then crying dramatically, he threw an ice cube at his imaginary god in the celing, the ice cube landed back on his head.

"Dude what the fuck is up?" Shashank asked me as Raghu rested his folded arms on the table and dunked his head in them. As always, the bad karma of breaking bad news to someone came to me.

"You remember Pandit?" I said trying to put it as lightly as I could.

"Who?"

"RD 350, chopper goggles, remember?"

"That racer Pundit?

"Yep, the guy you thunder bashed at Danny's party," I said.

"I'm going to kill that fucking bastard, I swear on you my brotherrrr," Raghu sprung up and turned to leave.

"Shut up and sit down." I said pinning him back on his seat.

"Okay, I'll order a hit on him," or something like that Raghu muttered and began to dial a number on his phone.

"What about him?" Shashank asked.

"He saw him with Neha at Red Oaks three days back," I said pointing at Raghu with my nose.

"They were dancing thisssss closely." Raghu brought his palms close to each other to show the proximity. "Bastard's hands were all over her." I saw Shashank's face go pale.

Shit, I hated such situations.

"I'm sorry man Shashank, but we had to tell you," I said.

"You just say the word and I'll take care of him." Raghu stood up oscillating side to side.

"Wow!" Shashank said and emptied his glass. "She moved on quite quickly."

"Moved on? What do you mean?" I asked. Raghu paused swinging.

"Hello boss??" Raghu said knocking his knuckles on the table in front of Shashank.

"We are not together anymore." Raghu and I stared at each other. "We broke up six months back."

"Why?" I asked.

He shrugged coyly.

"Abey why? what happened?" Raghu asked impatiently.

"Look, I don't want to explain the whole thing. We had issues and our wants couldn't mutually coexist," Shashank said.

The waiter returned with the second round of our drinks.

"Abey yaar slutty, not again!" Raghu whined.

"Yeah, I mean you guys were together for more than six years. I thought you loved her."

"There is nothing such as love, Poncho. It's about compatibility. As long as you get what you want, everything is rosy. Once your interests conflict, all of it disappears," Shashank said.

"And it took you six years to realise that?" I slurred.

"Yes..." he said sipping his drink.

"I bet there is a third angle to this story," Raghu said to me.

"I know you guys think I'm a slut, but no, I didn't cheat on her."

"But seriously man, didn't you feel any guilt leaving someone so close? How can you be so unfazed?" I asked.

"I don't understand why you guys are grilling me over this; it was her decision too."

Finally Shashank slurred. "If she can move on so quickly and start seeing someone, why can't I?"

"I'm telling you Poncho, this guy is the culprit," Raghu said droopily. "I don't trust him a grain bit."

"Fuck you!" Shashank yelled at Raghu. He was already asleep.

I whistled to the waiter

"Repeat one large and get the bill," I said.

"Make it two," Shashank said. I looked at him.

"Don't look at me like that."

"Like what?" I asked.

"Like you are accusing me of all this."

"Then convince me otherwise."

"I don't need to convince anyone. Whatever happens, I'm not going to publicly discuss my personal life. Go ask her if you want. She is free to yell about it from a mountain top. All I'll say is that we had issues," Shashank said and pounced on his drink as soon as the waiter brought our order.

"And issues can't be solved? You were together for *six* years, Shashank?

"The amount of time spent together has nothing to do with this. You can never change the way a person thinks. He is what he is."

"I really thought you guys loved each other."

"For the Nth time Arjun, *there is nothing such as love!*" he yelled. "It is just an overrated concept blown out of proportion by romantic movies. It's all about convenience. The moment problems creep in, everything changes."

"Whatever! I hope you don't regret it," I said tilting sideways to remove my wallet to pay the the bill.

"I thought at least you'd understand me. Anyway, it's over and I don't wanna talk about it anymore." He got up to lift Raghu. "I hope that you'll respect it at least."

I didn't respond, but I never spoke of it again to him.

"Hi..." I said as Hrida entered the cafe.

"Hi..." she said pulling the chair, her tone bland.

"How was your day?"

"Good. How was your shoot?"

"Fun as usual," I said.

"Okay," she said and dived into the newspaper lying on the table.

Ever since my blunder on her birthday a year-and-a-half back, Hrida's side of the conversations were smileless and limited to monosyllables and sentences framed with minimum words. Silence had become a substantial part of our relationship. If at all there was any talk, my day at work would mostly be the topic of the conversation. Hrida's smile which was the highlight of my life, was replaced by an occasional awkward half-hearted smile. Holding hands and hugs, kisses had disappeared, giving way to distant behaviour. All my love yous were replied with thank yous. Frequent snapping at me for miniscule reasons and random fights were the new in-thing. Meetings were diminished to twice, max thrice a week. Make-out sessions, which happened only twice in that period, felt like I was kissing stiff responseless lips of a motionless corpse. In the initial days when Hrida began staying aloof from me, I thought things would return to normal once the phase passed. With each passing day however, things deteriorated to the core. Most of the girl population in my generation had no qualms about losing their virginity, but I found that one girl for whom it was important, and screwed things for her. I horribly wished I could do something to bring her smile back on her face.

"Arjun? Hello?" I saw Hrida waving the menu in front of my eyes.

"Huh, ya, sorry," I said returning back from my guilt trip.

"What is wrong with you?" she asked irritated.

"Nothing, some work stuff."

"What are you gonna have?"

"The usual."

"Then order, I'm not having anything," she said and went back into the newspaper

"Why?"

"I don't feel like it," she said without looking at me.

I waved at the waiter and mimed my order to her. She smiled back.

"At least talk?"

"You talk, I'm listening," she said, her gaze still in the newspaper. "I don't have anything to talk about."

"We are practically meeting after a week now, yet you have nothing to say," I said.

"Now is it my fault if I can't think of anything to talk about?" she snapped and glared at me.

Hrida's indifference was extremely annoying, but there was no way I could make it go away. Thirty minutes of silence later, I swallowed the latte and my pride and made yet another attempt to revive the conversation.

"I met Shashank yesterday."

"Oh wow, nice. How's he doing?"

"He's good, seems totally smitten by New York."

"Nice." And came a smile, it wasn't for me. It was for New York, yet my stupid heart somersaulted looking at it. "I'll meet him soon," she said and waved at the waiter to ask for water.

"What happened?" she asked gazing at me.

"Nothing, why?"

"You've got that I-have-to-tell-you-something look on your face."

"What is it?" she coaxed after moments of silence.

"Shashank and Neha broke up."

"Okay," she said.

"You knew about it," I said studying her reaction. "And you didn't feel the need to tell me?"

"Neha told me because I'm her friend, not your girlfriend. If she tells me something in confidence, I *won't* tell anyone."

"I'm not just anyone."

"This is not about you, Arjun. How does it matter if I told you or not."

"How it matters is if I knew about it, I could have done something about it."

"Then do it now," she snapped.

"It's too late, your friend is already seeing someone else." Hrida's face flushed, suggesting she obviously didn't know about Neha and Pandit.

"Well it seems your 'friend' doesn't tell you everything after all."

Long silence followed.

The waitress got the water.

"Okay, maybe I should have told you," she said taking a deep breath, "Sorry."

A sorry from Hrida after dunno how long! I responded by nodding my head.

"What does Shashank have to say about the break-up?" she asked.

"The same old bullcrap of how their wants couldn't mutually co-exist. Every time he breaks up with someone, he has had this patented line in his pocket. On top of it, he expects me to understand."

"Maybe there is a reason for him to say that."

"What's there to understand? You can try to understand if there is a concrete reason." I said, "I can't blindly trust him just because he says they had issues."

"I sort of agree with Shashank, but if you love someone, you should be prepared for the person in totality."

"What love? All of a sudden, he doesn't believe in love. It's all about compatibility, he says. Okay, agreed, but does it take six years to realise that you aren't compatible?"

"Oh come on," Hrida said.

"That's what. It took me six months to figure that our relationship isn't working, so I know how it works."

A sonic wave of silence swept our table as soon as I said it. I had to say something to resuscitate the situation. "I mean, you can tell if a person loves you or not."

Dead silence.

"Hrida," I said and stared at her, waiting for her to level her line of sight with mine. "Do you love me?" I asked after she looked at me, and a second later regretted asking it. She dunked her head back in the newspaper.

"Can I not even get a reply?"

"Don't go there, Arjun, it's not worth it," she said glancing at me for a fraction of a second.

"Why?"

"Because I don't want to lie."

"Then don't, why would you need to lie anyway?"

"Because you won't like the truth."

"Just give me an answer."

"I don't remember what you asked."

"Don't bullshit me, Hrida."

"I'm serious, I don't remember."

"OK, fine, I'll ask again." I said breathing heavily to calm my rising temper.

"Do you love me?" I asked swallowing my pride yet again. "Do you want me to repeat it, or once is enough?"

"No."

"Then can you *please* answer me?"

"I don't know."

"What the fuck do you mean you don't know?" I finally lost the grip on my anger. "It's either a yes or a no, why are you being such a prick about it?"

"Because you are a bloody moron and you don't understand that I don't want to hurt you," she yelled back. "The answer you want is *no, I don't love you.*"

I knew the answer the moment I had asked the question, maybe even long before I asked it. Every time I had this conversation with her in my head, I had wished the answer was yes. In spite of knowing it in the back of my mind, the confirmation from her left my innards in total chaos. I knew I was the reason behind it, yet looking at her calm and unperturbed face I felt a feeling of intense hatred and anger. It was like she felt no pain or hurt over it.

"How could you do it to me?" I asked in the utmost accusatory tone.

"How could I do what?" she asked tone of her voice in sync with her unfazed reaction.

"Not love me? Lose all those feelings for me? Fall out of love? How could you let it happen?" I had no idea what I was saying as my mind played the visuals of life without her on loop.

"This is not fair, you cannot do this to me," I murmured, not sure if I addressed it to god or to Hrida.

"How could I do it? How could *I* do it?" Hrida almost screamed. "You should have thought about it before raping me, you fucking bastard," Hrida said as her eyes blazed hatred for me.

Silence.

"*You* asked me to trust you blindly; was it my fault I did? In spite of asking you to stop, you did what you wanted to, wasn't that unfair???" Tears appeared in her eyes. Hrida's words had stunned me.

"So whatever happens to you from now on, you don't get to call it unfair because you deserve what you get."

She pressed her palms against her eyes to stop the tears and began to breathe heavily.

Hrida was clearly disgusted by my existence in her life. It felt like someone had stabbed a pair of pliers into my chest and pulled my heart out. She not loving me meant only one thing – everything we had was over. The relationship was the only plausible thing left in my life, and with it gone, I would be left with all the half-baked dreams. The way the relationship had changed was so unreal that it felt like a bad dream.

"*You raped her!*" Voice Two screamed.

"No, I love her. I have never done anything to hurt her," Voice One said.

"Keep telling that to yourself, she clearly thinks otherwise. Her love for you is gone." Voice Three scorned.

"And because you love her, you are allowed to rape her?" Voice Two said offensively.

"It's a shame that a girl loved and trusted you with all her heart and you raped her," Voice Four said.

"*I didn't rape her*!!!!" Voice One wailed.

"Didn't she ask you to stop?" Voice Two screamed again.

"Didn't you see her tears?" Voice Four said.

"I didn't mean to... I was just distraught because of Rizwan... all of this is not true... I was happy to see her, I got carried away. But I love her. It was not rape." Voice One tried everything it could to convince the others.

"Did she ask you to stop or not?" Voice Two asked.

"Yes." Voice One surrendered.

"Then it is a rape!" Voice Two declared.

"You raped her!" Voice Three and Four declared in unison.

"Shit! I raped her." Voice One finally gave up after its every possible explanation led to one word. Rape!

Tears started rolling down my cheeks as I knew I had screwed up, but rape is not how I ever looked at it. But what I thought was not of any importance.

"Why didn't you tell me about it earlier."

"What difference would it have made," her eyes welled up again. "What I have lost is lost forever."

"I'm truly sorry for what I have done." I said putting my hand over hers. She cringed at my touch. It felt like a part of me broke. I would never forget the look on her face when she cringed.

"I love you more than my life," I said.

"Why don't you just spit on my face than say you love me. It is all the same." She said, "Your sorrys, or love yous mean nothing to me. You are just somebody that I'm ashamed to say I once loved."

The disgust for me was so apparent from the way she was speaking, I realised there was no way to get her back.

"Ever since I've met you, I have loved you more than anything in my life. I could never imagine hurting you but no matter how many justifications I give, what I've done is irreparable. I guess I've ruined the beautiful thing we had all these years. But Shashank was probably right; you cannot ruin your life because you are with someone for a few years. I don't want to screw the rest of your life," I said fighting the tears.

"I can fight the world but not you for your love. So I guess it's time I let you go your way." I looked at her knowing I was not going see her ever again. "I'm sorry I broke my promise once, but I promise you, you won't have to see my sorry face ever again..."

"Have a good life..." Tears poured out of my eyes as she blankly got up and left without saying a word. I sat there as Hrida walked out of the cafe. I watched her go till she finally disappeared out of my sight, her last words ricocheting in my ears.

"You are just somebody that I'm ashamed to say I once loved."

She left me with the same numbness I felt when I saw her seven years back. Only this time, I felt bitter emptiness inside me. I left my bike at the cafe and began walking; barbaric riots had broken out inside my head.

It had been more than an hour that I had been walking. My legs had began to hurt, but it was nothing compared to the pain my heart felt. The look on Hrida's face as she left kept flashing in front of my eyes. "She felt nothing, she didn't love me, she will come back..." the endless conversations continued in my mind.

I rang the doorbell and stared at the door till she opened it.

"Arjun ya, it's 1.00 a.m.!" Devika whined, I stared back with tears in my eyes. "Hey what's wrong?" she said.

"I broke up with Hrida." I said and hugged her.

She hugged me back.

74 *Ext. Kala Ghoda, Mumbai-Evening* 74

The atmosphere is a festive one, people crowding for the live concert, vibrant street festivals are in progress, food stalls, art fair, huge colourful set-ups of artifacts are displayed. We see Siddhartha giving final touches to his installation. It's a huge fifteen-feet bleeding heart. He suddenly realises Ananya is watching him from a distance. He angrily stares at her and turns to leave.

> Ananya
> Please don't make me follow you
> ya, the leg is as it is killing me.
> (She limps a few steps to follow him)

> Siddhartha
> I'm just doing my job, don't follow if
> it's hurting.
> (He continues to move around)

> Ananya
> But I'm here to talk to you.
> (She continues limping behind him)

> Siddhartha
> Just stop please! I can't see you
> limping like that.

                    Ananya
        Then you stop skittering around.
            (Siddhartha stares at her)
        Please?? I want to apologise for what
        I did to you, I feel really bad.

                  Siddhartha
                Ok! Apologise!
              (He says blandly)

                    Ananya
        Do I have to do it here? I mean if
        you don't mind, we can go somewhere.
        (She smiles impishly, He nods his
            head in disbelief and smiles)

74A EXT. Kala Ghoda, Parking Area,
Mumbai-Evening 74A

We see both of them walking towards a car. Ananya is
limping with a plaster around her right leg. Siddhartha
presses the autocop, the car beeps to unlock. It is
a two-seater, yellow electric car. Ananya stiffs her
lips to suppress laughter.

                    Ananya
                That's your car??

                  Siddhartha
            Yeah, why what happened?
        (She covers her mouth with her hand
                to control herself)
                    What?

```
                    Ananya
        Nothing, it's just that my bike
             is bigger than your car.
      (She bursts out looking at flushed
                  Siddhartha)

                  Siddhartha
    Hey! You want to say your sorry or not?
                (Mocks anger)

                    Ananya
                   Yes yes!
```

The doorbell rang as I typed in the last words in the laptop. Thanks to the lack of job offers, I had been busy completing my film script for more than three months now. I hadn't exactly envisioned a red carpet welcome for myself, but after film school, I thought finding a producer would be much easier. The reality was contrary to that. Three producers I met loved my script but rejected me since I had no star to back it. I wondered how I was ever going to make it to the director's chair. To make things worse, I was jobless and broke since I had blown all my saved up money up on the film course. It was getting tougher by the day to survive in the city. If it wasn't for Ashwin, I would in all possibility be sleeping on the pavements of the city. He on the other hand, was more than happy to keep me. After I left for LA, Tamsin had gotten pregnant again, not because Humpy forgot to wear protection, but because both of them wanted it. They got married and moved out, leaving Ashwin alone in his huge house.

"Wassup man?" Ashwin said as I opened the door.

"Typing, what else?"

"How much did you write?"

"Not much, three sequences..." I walked back to the writing table to switch off the laptop.

"Not bad..." he said spreading the take-out boxes on the dinner table.

"You wanna read?"

"Yeah... after dinner, come let's eat."

"I need a field job, man. Sitting at home is frying me crisp."

"Hmm... How long do you think you'll take to complete it?" He said and gobbled a spoonful of rice.

"Dunno, a week may be, max two, why?"

"There is this film happening in BFE and the 1st AD has bolted." He paused to swallow, "I can put a word for you if you want."

"Your company? But I thought you said they are not doing anything else... oh fuck... are you quitting?" I looked at him spooked.

"Yep!"

"But why??"

"I told you about the meeting with Rohan Rastogi right?"

"Yeah?"

"His manager called today. Dude's given me bulk dates for next month."

"That's awesome news."

"I know."

"But isn't it a bit unprofessional to dump Divya like that?"

"Dude, I've slogged for eleven years." He paused to drink some water. "Balls I care, it was a choice between my career and their films."

"Abey, but won't your producer uncle get a stroke?"

"That is why I'm giving *you* to him," he said cheekily.

"What will you tell him?"

"Anything man. I'm getting operated upon, mother's ill, grandfather died. I'll think of some believable reason."

"Are you sure this is a good idea?"

"Come on, you'll love it there, it's a romcom and there's Neera Dutta." That last part fixed an ear to ear grin on my face.

"Yes, I'll love it," I said, more to myself.

"I think you should add extra two days to the schedule," Rakesh Kapoor said putting the schedule sheet on his desk.

"I have, in fact, going by the number of scenes left to shoot..." I abruptly stopped as Baby, Rocky's assistant, banged the door open.

"Boss!" She almost screamed.

"God baby, don't you knock?" he growled.

"E-News, now!" she panted.

"Shit, what happened?" he asked. She cringed in horror. Rocky punched the remote.

"This happened in broad daylight. When the famous film director Divya Rao was with her female friend at Cookies, a regular joint for Bollywood celebrities, superstar Neera Dutta stormed in and emptied a whole glass of milkshake on her head." A reporter of an entertainment channel was jumping with hysteric excitement as if Ranbir Kapoor had asked her to marry him.

"When was this?" Rocky asked Baby with equivalent horror in his voice.

"Today morning."

"Remember you are watching this exclusively on E-News," the reporter's corny bragging continued while the video of Neera emptying the glass on Divya played on loop.

"Call Shreya. Find out where Neera is right now."

"I did. She's shooting an ad in Mehboob."

"Get my car." He began to leave.

"I'll see you later," I said and began to gather my things.

"No, you come with me," he said dialling a number on his phone. "I need someone with me."

"OK," I said unsure of how I could help.

"Divya, what the fuck did you do?" Rocky screamed on the phone, as he called for a lift.

"Couldn't you fucking wait for another month?" I followed him into the lift quietly.

"I've got fifty crores running on this movie. I will mince you if anything goes wrong. Drive your sleazy ass to Mehboob right now." He hung up before any reply came from the other side.

What can you say about a twenty-six-year-old girl with a face of an angel, a deep dimpled smile that got both male and female population of the country weak between their knees, intense dark brown eyes that spoke more than her mouth itself, red luscious lips that could make your heart weep thinking how you'll never get them, a chiselled micro-maintained body that will make you gawk and drool? Well you don't say anything, you just shut up and watch. Neera Dutta, the only daughter of legendary filmmaker Ramesh Dutta, was adopted by the whole film fraternity as their own child after his early demise. Rakesh Kapoor was one of them. He launched her in one of his super budgeted films and made sure her debut sky-rocketed her career. It did. I, like the rest of the country, fell instantly in love with her. Her flawless acting had made sure people felt all the emotions she wanted them to feel. Ever since my first encounter with her in the theatre eight years back, I had longed to see her, and now all thanks to Ashwin, I was going to be around her for a whole twenty days. Even though the timing was horribly wrong, I was going to meet her for the first time. My heart skipped a beat as Rocky steered the car into the gates of the studio. Neera was known for being short-tempered, but what cost Divya the milkshake bath was not known. Whatever it was, Rocky prayed it hadn't cost him his film.

"Shreya baby, how have you been?" Rocky hugged Shreya, Neera's manager, as soon as he got out of the car.

"I'm good Rocky," the squeaky voiced Shreya said.

"Where is the kid?"

"She's inside, come." Shreya took Rocky's hand and pulled him inside, he signalled to me to follow.

Rocky's muscle in the industry was evident going by the silence that struck the shooting floor the moment he stepped in. All the heads turned and followed him as he walked straight up to where Neera was sitting. He patiently stood by her chair as she intently read something on her phone. It was dark and she was sitting with her back to me, so I could barely see her, yet the gravitational force stopped working on my body, making me virtually float in air with happiness. I was hardly a few feet away from the girl who could give half a country a stroke with just her smile.

"Neera?" Shreya said meekly.

"Hmm?" Neera responded

"Rocky..."

"You got a minute for me, kiddo?" Rocky said warmly.

"Shit! How long have you been standing here?" Neera sprung up seeing him.

And I finally got to see her. A single ray of light falling on her face, God. She was a goddess.

"Question is how long can I wait for you," he said as they hugged.

"Okay, how long can you wait for me?"

"Forever..." he said. She giggled.

"Come, let's go to my van."

"No, get done with your work, I'll wait here."

She stared at him. "I'm serious go!"

She smiled and left.

An hour later, when she wrapped her part of the shoot, she took Rocky to her van. A few minutes later, Divya arrived in her milkshake-stained shirt and walked straight in. In spite of the noise all around, Neera's muffled screams could be heard outside the van. I stupidly waited outside, awkwardly smiling at people who stared at me. Shreya saw the E-News reporter rightfully barging in and signalled the security guards to shoo her away. She had already created enough of ruckus.

My phone rang. Rocky.

"Come in." He said and hung up.

First thing I saw when I entered the van was a red-eyed swollen-faced tearful Neera. I felt like jutting my lower lip out and crying with her. What could have happened to cause her so much distress, I wondered.

"...ask her why she cheated on me with that tramp." Neera was saying sobbingly.

What the hell does that mean, I thought.

"Look, I know how you feel but..."

"No Rocky. Ask her, right now..." she sobbed.

"OK, Divya, why did you cheat on her?" Rocky asked diligently.

Silence.

"I'm sorry baby... you know we were drifting apart," Divya said.

"Shut up bitch... I never wanna see your face again," Neera screamed.

What the bloody fuck! Neera Dutta is a lesbian? No... no... no... can't be... she had that affair with that hero with what's-his-name...

My mind started consoling my heart which was crying hysterically. Neera was the superstar who every boy in the country wanted to be with. It was a given that she was unattainable, but even then, there was this juvenile hope in my mind that someday I might. But what I had just discovered shattered my heart into shards.

"I'm sorry it's gonna screw your film, Rocky, but I swear I'm never talking to her..." Neera was saying. "She broke my heart... I'm not coming back to shoot."

Rocky stared at me as if asking for help. I shrugged gingerly. Then suddenly his face lit up.

"Don't, if you don't want to kid. I have a solution for this," he took a pause and looked at both of them, "Him." He pointed at me.

Huh? What? Me? I almost blurted out.

"Arjun will be Divya's point man for you. Whatever she has to say to you will come to you via him and him only. I promise she'll never come to talk to you." I folded my hands and rested my chin on it to keep my jaw from dropping to the floor.

"Boss... but?" Divya muttered. Rocky glared at her in rage.

"He is good chap. He is a film school guy."

Neera for a fraction of a second looked at me from head to toe.

"Please do this for me, kid. It's just a matter of twenty days. Please please." Neera smiled at Rocky's almost begging tone.

"So it's a yes?" Rocky asked.

"Yes." Neera croaked.

"I love you, kid." He hugged her.

"You are on buddy! You better be good!" he whispered to me as we walked out of the van. "Cape Town, here... we... come..."

He heaved a sigh of relief.

42 EXT. Blackrock Castle, Cliff,
Cape Town-Evening 42

We see Heer and Abhay sitting on a wooden bench in the backdrop of the sun setting in the blue waters of the sea. Breeze from the sea is gently ruffling wisps of Heer's hair. She is distraught about something. Abhay calmly looks at the sunset while he drinks wine directly from the bottle. Both sit in silence.

Abhay

Hey?

(He turns to her)

He is going to be alright, OK?

(Heer's eyes well up)

You spoke to the doctor yourself,

he said the same thing, didn't he?

(Heer pulls her legs up and cradles

herself)

```
        There is nothing to worry about baby,
                      trust me.
        (She starts sobbing, Abhay put his arm
             around her and consoles her)

                        Heer
      I spent the last ten years hating him for
      leaving my mother for another woman, but
           I knew he was still there. I can't
         imagine life without him, I'll never
           forgive myself if anything happens
                       to him.
               (She bursts into tears)
```

"Cut!" Divya screamed to fight the wuthering air on the cliff. "Neera, baby, something is missing."

She began to walk towards the bench Neera and Kunal were sitting on. I followed her.

"What's wrong?" Kunal asked.

"I don't know. It's just not working, she..." Divya stopped midway seeing Neera walk away. "Oh come on!" she helplessly looked at me.

"Should I?" I asked.

"Please..." she said and walked back to the monitor.

Neera in all that while had walked quite far away from the shooting area. I darted behind her as the sun was setting and we were fast losing light. Fighting the wagging walky and controlling the script papers, I reached the spot where she was standing. The crying had splattered her eyeliner and screwed the makeup, but even then she looked breathtakingly gorgeous in the orange light of the setting sun. If it was up to me, I would have stood there looking at her forever. But as much as I hated to disturb her, I had to take her back.

"Umm... Neera..." I said meekly, She turned to me and before I could say anything else she started walking back to the bench.

"Walking Heer back to the set." I said in the walky as I walked her back.

The crew hushed to dead silence as she returned to her position next to Kunal.

"Dude, what's wrong?" Kunal asked me.

"The body language looks awkward, it's not in sync with the equation Abhay and Heer share." I said kneeling to level with line of their sight. "May be you can nuzzle on his chest after the lines." I said to Neera.

"Or you can kiss her hair?" I said authoritatively, both of them stared at me. I wondered if I had overstepped my limits, so I went silent.

"Cool," Kunal said and smiled. Neera nodded. I ran back to the monitor.

"Are we cool?" Divya asked.

"I hope so..." I replied.

When Neera said she will never talk to Divya again, she meant it quite literally. So after she snubbed Divya on first day of the shoot, Divya for next nineteen days stayed away from her, hence whenever Neera was shooting, I got to run the show. Whether it be rehearsing the lines or explaining the scene or giving her the cues, I got to do it all. Neera left no stone unturned to pick a bone with Divya. Apart from the snubbing while shooting or at dinner tables, Neera began flirting excessively with Kunal which completely fried Divya.

Cape Town on the other hand was treating me extraordinarily well. Warm weather, white sand beaches, unbelievably beautiful blue-watered coastline, traditional African street dancers, live music performing artists, delicious food – there was this permanent festive vibe in the atmosphere that made me smile. Neera's presence in all that made those twenty days the most memorable days of my life. It was funny how life had changed from minutely following the news reports on Neera's shooting schedule and then waiting outside studio gates to just get a glimpse of her which I never did, to sitting three feet away and rehearsing lines with her. Finally, the laws of attraction had gotten to work. All those years of slogging seemed to be finally worth it. Taking up this project from Ashwin had turned into the most fulfilling assignment I had ever taken up.

The atmosphere on the set on the last day of shoot reminded me of the final exam day in school, just before summer vacation started. Everyone in the crew was frolicking, anticipating their return to their beloveds. Work was almost over and it was time to return home, but a sudden sadness ran through me as Rocky announced wrap of Neera's part of the shoot. I knew the amazing time around her was going to end someday but I wished it never did. I stood there heartbroken while the crew clapped and cheered for her. She hugged Rocky and then Kunal. I saw Divya's face turn red as Kunal's hands slid down Neera's back to her butt when he hugged her. Even if you are the one to break-up, it always hurts to see your ex with someone else. In this case, Neera was deliberately screwing with Divya's mind. She was royally successful, but little did she know that poor Kunal would have to suffer for it.

"Is the horse I asked for here?" Divya asked me.

"Yes."

"Okay, get it ready, I'll go get Kunal," she said and left in a huff.

Rocky had approved of the horse, even though it was a last minute requirement. We had waited three hours for it, but if it was for the betterment of the film, Rocky would have provided her even with a dinosaur if she had asked for one. I knew Divya was up to something since the horse fitted nowhere in the script.

"Are you sure it'll look nice?" Kunal asked Divya as she walked him to the horse.

"You bet your ass it will," Divya said boastfully.

"No, I mean it shouldn't look corny."

"Dude! You are the newly crowned prince of the industry, just go topless and show them your washboard. The girls will go bonkers," Divya said.

Poor guy took the bait. He instantly dropped his shirt and jumped on the horse. For the next forty-five minutes, Divya made him ride the horse in every direction of the sandy beach. When all of the land was covered, she asked him to ride in the choppy waters. The initial smile on his face disappeared in the first fifteen minutes of the ride, leaving behind a pain-stricken face.

"What the hell are you doing Kunal?" Divya screamed on the mike.

"Haven't you gotten anything good yet?" Kunal said in a pitiable voice. "My balls have started hurting."

"Almost done... a few more rounds. just keep up the attitude," Divya said..

From Divya's face, I could tell she was deriving much pleasure out of his pain. More than half an hour later, when she finally let him get off the horse, he could barely walk.

"That's for touching her with those sleazy hands." Divya murmured and a smile appeared on her face.

"Okay people, thank you all for a wonderful shoot. *It's a wrap!*" she announced.

The clapping and cheering began.

The wrap party later that night was a glamorous affair. Rocky's team had booked a three-storeyed club exclusively for the crew. Alcohol, food, music – the basic party ingredients were of premium quality. Rocky had made sure every single member in crew was personally invited. It was his way of thanking the crew for their hard work they put in on the film. After, the initial formal drinks with the heads of departments, Rocky took a bottle of tequila from the bar and joined the technical crew on the dance floor. He had no reservations about their status or class. He danced with the technicians, spot boys, lightmen without being conscious. He hugged them, kissed them, pushed shots down their throats, clicked snaps. It was this grounded and humble attitude of his that people instantly fell in love with. I was glad I got to work with him. He caught my eye and camel-walked towards me.

"Thank you, buddy!" he slurred in his rugged voice as he fixed the bottle to my mouth. "I owe you one," he said and bear hugged me. He blew a kiss at me as someone from the dance floor held his hand and pulled him away.

I gazed around at the happy faces. It was a full house. Divya's new girlfriend had flown down from Mumbai. I recognised her from the milkshake bath video. Everyone was there at the party, except for the lead pair of the film. I could understand Kunal's absence considering what Divya did to his balls. But why was Neera missing, I wondered. At that very moment, all the heads on the dance floor turned to the club's entrance. She stood there looking as ravishing as ever in a silver backless dress and high heels. I grinned.

Rocky greeted her with a hug and pulled her to dance. Neera's face flushed seeing the girl Divya left her for. I don't claim to understand the dynamics of a lesbian relationship, but how could anyone dump someone like Neera who was the definition of Miss Perfect, and that too for a hideous Gothic chick.

A few glasses of vodka, loud music and accumulated pain of watching Divya dancing with the other girl later, Neera took to the floor. Since there was no Kunal to cling on to, she found a gora from the local crew to dirty dance with. This time, however, her genius plan to boil Divya's blood with jealousy failed. Divya left the moment Neera began her antics. Everyone around in the party was piss drunk to notice the tears seeping out of her eyes as she left the floor.

Although it was none of my business, I followed her to the roof. She sat on the wall crying. The view from the glass walled entrance to the roof was hallucinatory. Billions of tiny colourful lights twinkled at the foothill of the far away mountain at Camp's Bay, needless to mention Neera whose silver dress glittered in the red and blue dancing light of the club's huge hoarding. I waited for her to stop crying, but it continued till my drunk body could no longer stand, so I walked to the wall and sat beside her. She looked at me and bounced her eyebrows to say hey. Tears still passed out of those heart-stopping Bambi eyes. I smiled back and offered her the bottle of vodka I had flicked from the bar.

"Thanks," she said twitching her eyes as she gulped a mouthful of it.

"You are welcome," I said and gave stiff lipped smile.

Neera Dutta, India's superstar, was sitting three feet away from me, drinking vodka from my bottle and crying, for real. Stars are always expected to smile, be happy and look beautiful. The moment they lose their masks, it becomes news. What these news hungry bozos fail to understand is they are humans too and their pain is as real as anyone else's. It is nobody's business to know what they do in their personal life.

"I thought you'd cry differently in real life." I said looking at the twinkling lights, "But either way, you don't look good." I turned to look at her as she chuckled wiping her eyes.

A few minutes of silence passed and she broke down again. I know how it feels after a break-up, pain comes in waves when you keep realising that the person you wanted to be with is no longer with you.

"I'm pretty drunk, you know." I said and took a sip from the bottle, she looked at me with confused teary eyes, "So I can't think of many things to cheer you up."

She chuckled again. "You probably don't need me to..." I ate rest of my words as she began to nod excessively.

"Nothing like that," she croaked. "I'm glad you are here." The last part shot my pulse.

"Its just that it's... just... just..." she gritted her teeth.

"Painful... I know, break-ups suck," I said. She took a sip of vodka.

"Like contraceptive pills, they should make a pill to annihilate the *after break-up repercussions*. I'll promote it for free," she said.

"Yeah it'll be like the best break-up gift." I laughed.

"Seriously, it is so painful. I feel like killing myself."

"Ugh... tried that once... bad idea..."

"You did?"

"Yup!"

"Break-up?"

I nodded yes.

"How long were you dating?"

"Seven years."

"Yikes!" She swigged a few millilitres and passed the bottle to me. "What was her name?

I cringed.

"I'm sorry I shouldn't..."

"No, its fine. I just realized I haven't said her name out loud in a long time."

"You really loved her bad."

"Hrida, I still love her." I took a deep breath. "But it doesn't hurt that much anymore. More than my love for her, the pain was out of the fact that what I wanted didn't happen, so I just made peace with it."

"Wow." She said and smiled. "Do you always analyse everything so much?"

"Well not exactly, but when my *Devdaasgiri* cost me all the people important to me, I had to."

"Ahh... I feel so much better."

"Knowing I got dumped after seven years? You are cruel."

"No, no no... it just hit me that I was upset because she cheated on me. I'm not sure if I even loved her," she said, more like talking to herself.

"Poor Kunal!" I mumbled.

"Huh?"

"His balls got caught in a crossfire between you and Divya for no reason."

"As in?"

"Divya sort of took it out on him for flirting with you."

"So my plan worked... It did set her off..."

"Yes, but why should he suffer?

"Ahh... whatever, he's a sleaze ball anyway." Both of us laughed.

Silence swept the scene as the chilly breeze hit us.

"Thank you!" she said.

"For what?"

"For making me smile."

"Oh that, don't mention it. You've made me smile for so many years. I'm just returning the favour." She blushed.

"I like you..." she said and grinned.

"You are drunk. Here, take the last sip." I passed her the bottle.

"No I am not," she emptied the bottle and moved closer to me.

"Don't tell me you are gonna kiss me now."

"How you wish." She raised her eyebrow. "I came close to listen to your story."

"What story?"

"Your script, you wanna direct someday."

"What makes you think I have a script for you."

"I can tell from the way you look at me."

"You are drunk; you are not gonna remember any of this tomorrow. Why should I waste my energy?"

"Try me..."

"You better not be messing with me..." I muttered to god looking at the sky.

He wasn't. It was really happening. I took a deep breath and started.

"So there is this girl, Ananya..."

All I wanted to do after my return from Cape Town was crash on my bed and sleep for like a hundred years. Little did I know what was waiting for me at home. In the twenty days that I had been away, Ashwin had converted the house into his office. Practically every room in the house was occupied by Ashwin's staff. Schedule boards, laptops, desks, set models, costume stands had replaced all the furniture in house. My room was converted into an audition room. The bed that I was looking for had disappeared. After wandering around the house between strangers, I found all my stuff neatly stacked in the balcony beside the best friend of my back pain, the couch. That was to be my bed. I was so drained that in spite of the gaggle and the cramped couch, I instantly fell asleep.

Three hours later, the blaring of the ringing phone woke me up. It was Rocky.

"Hey boss!" I said with a choked voice.

"What did you do buddy?" his voice yelling adjacent.

"I don't understand...

"Neera called a minute back."

"Yeah so?"

"She said you narrated a script to her in Cape Town," he sounded annoyed.

"Yes I did."

"Why would you do that? Don't you like me?"

"I... I..."

"I was gonna go on a vacation after *Heer*, but you screwed it."

"I don't understand."

"She liked it, you duffer!" He began to giggle, "She wants to start it as early as possible."

I rubbed my eyes to confirm I was awake and not dreaming.

"Hello?"

"Yeah boss I'm listening..."

"So when can I read?"

"I'm kinda still writing it."

"Okay then, you give me the final draft. I sign you then. Deal?"

"Yeah."

"Say deal..."

"Deal." I smiled.

"Get to work now."

"Hey boss."

"Yes?"

"You remember you said you owe me one?"

"I do..."

"Can you get me a place to live?"

"Consider it done. Pack your things and get ready to move."

Five days after the call, I was staring at the key.

Godrej / 85163, a steel key.

I kept staring at it as I stood at the door. A big wooden double door with a grill. The door to my first apartment. Rented, yet mine.

2012

I have to confess I love sleeping more than anything else in this world. Especially when it is a cold December morning. Being sandwiched between the warmth of a thick furry quilt and the bouncy bed feels heavenly. I lay there on my stomach with my face caved in the softness of the pillow, drool flowing out of the mouth while my lips locked themselves with the pillow. My right hand and leg hung down from the bed, while my left hand was tucked under the body and left leg sliding slowly all over the bed feeling the satiny smoothness of the bedsheet. I had no intention of giving up the romping with my bed, but then I heard Radhika scream hysterically.

"Poncho!" With my barely open eyes I saw her charging at me, "What the hell is wrong with you???" She said shaking me vigorously.

"There are twelve hundred people waiting for you and you're still laying half-naked in your bed?" She semi-slapped my face multiple times to wake me.

"Waiting for what?" I groggily snapped.

"Your wedding!" She stared at me with the scary eyes.

"What?"

Flash!

I was standing topless on the stage in front of twelve hundred people, in my polka-dotted satin boxers.

"Dude what the fuck?" Raghu hushed looking spooked. "Why are you in your boxers for your wedding," he said to me.

"What wedding? I never agreed to marry anyone!"

"Shit! SHE's gonna kill you man." I looked at Shashank's panic-stricken face as he said it.

"Who the hell is SHE?" I jumped frantically to look at the face of the girl standing on the other side of the traditional cloth held between me and her. All I saw was a long ghoongat.

Flash!

"Dad!" I called out at the top of my voice as I ran towards him, "Dad, I'm not ready to get married."

"Clearly..." he snubbed looking at the half naked me from head to toe.

"Baba I beg you, please help me." I pleaded, "I don't want to get married."

"You know I can't help you." He said and disappeared.

Flash!

"Aai, what the hell is happening?" I said to my mother after I found her standing between the statued guests.

"Your wedding Arjun, remember you agreed to get married?" she said.

"Yes, but not blindly." I said freaking out.

"You said you'll marry whoever I choose for you."

"Aai, what is wrong with you? I haven't even seen the face of the girl you are forcing me to marry!"

"You have to get married, Arjun." Her voice suddenly turned rugged like a zombie.

I ran.

Flash!

I was crazily running from one door to another but every exit door of the banquet was locked. All the guests who were statued all this while transformed into zombies and began walking towards me with wedding garlands in their hands, mumbling *"Marry Arjun marry!"* Finally some of them caught me and dragged me to the stage where the faceless girl waited for me.

"No!" I wailed but it was useless. As the traditional wedding cloth came down, the girl in her long ghooghat zombie-walked towards me and tied garland around my neck like a noose. All the zombies began to clap.

"Aaaaaahhhhhhh!!! I screamed out loud as I woke up.

The rising sun, the mug full of coffee, the chilly December breeze and the extra spacious Italian window of my apartment helped the rotten aftertaste of the night's nightmare to subside. I sat there absorbing the view and the atmosphere as the elements worked their magic on me. No matter how horrendous the dreams, my subconscious mind showed me that the reality of my present day life was way more exciting. Pain and the imbecile pursuit of self-destruction had abandoned me and my career had rocketed after Neera signed my film. I had patched up with my Mom, Dad, and Raghu so my loneliness was executed. I had more things in life to look forward to than weep over the past. One of the immediate sources of excitement in the next two days was Raghu's wedding. I laughed at the visual of Raghu's bride whipping him to sit, stand, and roll like a circus lion. I wondered that if someone like Raghu could be ready for an arranged marriage, what was holding me back. Nothing was, so I probably did the right thing asking 'The Mother' to choose 'The Wife' for me. And the speed at which she was hunting for her daughter-in-law, I was sure I was not going to be single for long. I, however, had to find a date for Raghu's sangeet. I made another mug of coffee and knocked on her door after the doorbell refused to ring.

"It's almost been a month and your doorbell is yet to be fixed. Do you plan to get it fixed anytime soon??" I said and smiled at Aditi as she opened the door.

"Coffee??" I asked as she sleepily stared at me.

"What do you care...you anyway don't use it," she croaked.

"So I was right; you *are* pissed at me. I'm sorry I didn't reply to all those calls and messages." I handed over the coffee mug. "But really I want to make up for it."

"How? Dinner again?" she asked with glint in her eyes.

"Even better. Traditional clothes, dance, good music, good food, alcohol and of course, me..." I said the last part a little cheekily but it fixed an ear-to-ear grin on her face.

"Where are we going?"

"Raghu's sangeet..."

"And why the generosity of taking me along?"

"I told you I want to make up for disappearing on you..." she raised her eyebrow tuning the volume of rest of my sentence down, "...and the last I checked, it's a bad idea to pick up girls at family functions, so it's better to take your own date."

"Hawww! Dog!" She punched my arm.

"Be ready by seven, will you?" I said.

"I'll see what I can do!" she grinned.

"How do I look?" Aditi asked concluding, dabbing her under eyes.

"Would saying 'irresistible' suffice??" I said as I parked the car outside The Royal Lawns.

"So there is a good chance that I'll get to make out with you today, right?" She said gently clenching my collar. I felt a huge thud in my stomach as she came close. She probably meant every word out of her not-so-subtle flirting but no matter how godforsakenly hot her dusky body looked in that velvety deep blue cleavage and navel revealing sharara, I had no intention to eat the forbidden fruit.

"I... I..." I tried to fish words out of confusion ridden mind of mine.

"Shit... look at your face..." she began to laugh crazily. I was handsomely embarrassed realising she was joking.

"Ahh... you spooked me!" I said regaining my composure. "It's just that I've gotten a bit rusty with girls these days, so..."

"Yeah, that explains why you asked you mother to find you a girl." She said shooting a rotten face at me. "That's really lame, by the way..."

"Hmm... Let's go in..." I said to change the topic. I got out of the car.

"Seriously ya Arjun..." She ran behind me as I entered the venue. "I mean, look at you, you can totally score a blazing hot girl if you wish," she said stopping me in middle of the lawns. "Why marry someone you don't know or love??"

"Kid..." I said putting my arm on her shoulder, "Things like feelings of love, are too exhausting. It might be a heartbreaking news to you now, but when you get to my age, you'll understand."

"But Arjun..."

"Poncho?" Aditi swallowed rest of her words as my mother entered the scene, I swiftly removed my hand off Aditi's shoulder.

"Hi Aai..."

"When did you come?" she asked.

"Just now... Where's Baba?"

"He is with Raunak Uncle. Who's your friend here?" I could see intense suspicion in her eyes. "What's you name beta?"

"Aditi..." Aditi replied and touched her feet instantly. My mother gave a me a betrayed look assuming she was my girlfriend and I was on to depriving her of the bride hunting.

"She looks too young for you, Arjun..." her tone made her irritation rather conspicuous. "How old are you, beta?"

"She is sixteen, Aai..." I jumped in before she could make things any more awkward, "She is my neighbour..."

"Oh, I see..." A smile of relief propped her face.

"Yeah..." I gave her a sarcastic smile, "I'm gonna go find Raghu."

"Sure, it was nice meeting you, Aditi," she said turning to Aditi.

"Same here, Aunty." Aditi flashed her mindblowing smile before following me into the crowd of guests.

"So what do you suggest I do with her after I 'score' a blazing hot girl?"

"Oh come on! What era do you live in... you cannot really be serious about getting married to please your mom."

"No... but it's like a win-win for me. If I get to make her happy and find a good wife without making any effort, why not??"

"But why?" she semi-screamed with irritation.

"Because, my love, I've gotten rusty."

"I'll help you scrap the rust off you; just don't give up."

"Why is so important to you that I find love?"

"Because I want to believe that there are second chances for the people with broken hearts..."

I didn't say anything, so she continued.

"...And I owe you for saving me from Renzil."

"I give up." I said blowing air out, "So what now?"

She grinned.

"Let's find you a girl first..." She frantically looked around the venue for a couple of minutes, "There..." She said finally zeroing on a girl, "...the girl in the red saree at the bar counter."

"She looks old ya, Aditi."

"You aren't exactly a teenager either, so go, talk to her..."

"Promise me you'll stop irritating me if I speak to her?"

"I promise, now go score some booty..." she slapped my behind.

"I must be really out of my mind." I muttered as I began to walk to the bar counter.

"Hi, can I get a large of double black with ice and water?" I said to the bartender as I anchored my elbows on the counter. I checked her from the corner of my eye. The red low waist saree fit perfectly on a curvy, well-worked-out body. Golden brown hair tied in a bun, green eyes glinting warmth, diamond studded nosepin on a cute nose, blushing red dimpled cheeks, toothy heart-squeezing smile, pink perfectly carved tiny lips. I have to agree the girl was a total ten on ten. She smiled at me as she caught me looking at her.

"Hi..." I smiled back.

"Hi..." She said as her smile grew into a more complex one as if she knew me.

"You seem to love drinking," I said pointing at the two glasses she was holding.

"Something like it."

"Cheers!" I clinked my glass on hers.

"Cheers!"

"So are you related to Raghu?"

"I'm a friend." She said, "You?"

"Me too, his school friend actually."

"Really? I didn't see you at Shashank"s wedding."

"I… wasn't around then." I said taking a sip. "You know Shashank too?"

"Yeah a little bit." She smiled.

Not that I was trying to eyeball her cleavage or anything, but my eyes caught a glimpse of her *mangalsutra* that had been hiding behind her saree all this while. *She's married,* a voice yelled in me. Whoever she was married to was a lucky bastard. As for me, it was time to abort *'Project Finding Love',* for the moment at least.

"I'm sorry, it feels really stupid, my friend back there…" I said pointing at Aditi, who in the meanwhile was getting hit on by Raghu's cousin, "…pushed me to flirt with you. I didn't know you were married. I'm so sorry." Taking a sip from her glass she turned to look back at Aditi.

"Does it matter if I'm married?" She said huskily and moved a step closer to me.

"Yeah… *it bloody does…*" I stepped back.

"How Arjun? How does it matter?" She said and grinned, leaving me confused.

"First you bunk my wedding and then you have the balls to flirt with my wife?" I heard a familiar voice say before a mighty slap landed on my back.

"Yaarrr, Shashank!" I wailed in pain. "It hurt…" It was so painful that tears spurted out of my eyes.

"Does it, now? Bitch!" He said strangulating me with his long hand. "Haan? haan? haan?" Pressure of his hands around my neck increasing with every *haan*, "Do know how much it hurt me?"

"Arrrggghhh...I'm sorry I missed your wedding..." I managed to speak in a choked voice. "Please leave me..."

"Bloody bitch, at least tell me you seriously didn't think I'd let you go that easily." He was now punching me in my stomach.

"Fucker, let him go or he'll miss my wedding too and I won't even get a chance to hit him if he dies." I heard Raghu's voice saying. Shashank delivered yet another mighty slap on my back before pushing me away. I breathed in small bursts that was coupled with coughing. I bent down holding my knees. Shashank's outburst might have been a bit too nasty, but if it had been me in his place, I would have been only more brutal. It took a nice five minutes for the pain in the body to subside. I took a couple of deep breaths and stood upright. Meanwhile, everybody was staring at me.

"I'm really sorry..." I said smiling at Shashank.

"Come here, bitch!" he said and hugged me tightly. "Now we are even."

I had really missed him badly. Thank god everything was back to normal.

The sangeet after-party, needless to say, was an amazing affair. Considering the possibility that it was the last one Raghu would ever get to organise, he left no stone unturned to make it unforgettable. Huge draperied shamiyanas were erected over a ten acre lawn, the top DJ in town played mind blowing music, Mumbai's number one caterer served mouth-watering food and premium imported alcohol, and on call drivers waited to drop the drunken guests. The icing on the cake was, however, the personalised escorts he had hired to serve and refill drinks for the guests, and in some cases to give dateless guests company on the dance floor. It was by far the best Raghu-organized-party I had attended. It was its warm vibe that made it more special for me. I roved my eyes at all the happy faces around – Raghu, his to-be-wife Ruchika, Shashank, his wife Ragini, Mom, Dad, Raunak Uncle, Uma Aunty, and all our family members. Finally, I was around my people and there was no need to fake the smiles or hugs. The alcohol had done a magnificent job on me, so at the first opportunity, the bar girl in me erupted and took to the dance floor. The trademark down-market steps suppressed within me for all these years broke out making me the centre of attention. I had almost forgotten how it felt having fun with the people who you cherish the most. As the night progressed, the elders left, leaving us behind with never-ending alcohol and mind-trancing music. Raghu, Shashank and I were so busy bromancing with each other that we were totally oblivious of Ruchika, Raghini and Aditi dancing around us.

"Raghu!" Ruchika said interrupting his raunchy booty shake.

"Yes, yes, what happened?" Raghu said in a fright adjacent tone.

"Shall we go home?" she said stroking his back, "It's our wedding tomorrow, remember?"

"But I want to stay!" He looked at me and Shashank for help; Shashank nudged me with his elbow.

"I am not asking her. She scares me man, you ask." I slurred to Shashank.

"Pussy!" He said and macho-walked to her, "Can we please borrow our friend for just this one night. You can shred him from tomorrow on!"

"Please, please, please?" I jumped in to make my contribution.

"Baby, it's too late. Let him sleep he's got a long day tomorrow," Ragini said to Shashank.

"No, it is alright. He'll be fine." Ruchika smiled, as she shared a look with Raghu. "Have fun you guys."

"Hey Ruchika..." I said, "Can you please drop Aditi home?"

"Yeah sure... come Aditi," Aditi pecked me before leaving.

"Honey..." Raghu slurred to Ruchika as she walked away, "Can you please ask the DJ to fuck off?" She smiled and nodded yes.

"She's crazy for you Randy..." Shashank said making a drink. "...I can tell from the way she looks at you."

"I know, who could have thought I'd find love in arranged marriage." A smile propped on Raghu's face. "I sort of love her madly too..."

"Yes, that explains the 'Honey...' *Sheeeee* Raghu!" I said. "Cheap you have become."

"Aww honnneyyyy don't be jealous, come hearrr, come let me kiss you..." Raghu said as he pushed his weight on me.

"Oh yes honey, I'm coming, I'm comingggg too..." Shashank jumped on us as the laughing took over and choke-slammed us on the lawns.

"I missed you guys..." I said as the laughing died down, "...I was so lonely without Devika and you guys."

"Oh yes, where's Devika man, why didn't she come?" Shashank asked Raghu. I cringed.

"I had called her, she was being all weird, no idea why."

"What?" Shashank asked me sensing my discomfort.

"What?"

"Your face?"

"What about my face?"

"This bhenchod *pakka* did something!" Raghu jumped as the guilt took me over.

"What the fuck did you do Poncho?" I went silent.

"He fought with her too, confirmed." Raghu declared, "Chutiya Poncho she was the only one who stood by you, you kicked her too?"

Silence.

"What?" Shashank pushed.

"Even worse..." I mumbled, realising it was pointless to hide the reality. Besides, I had been carrying the weight of guilt on my chest for long. I had to share it with someone. "I got her pregnant..."

A minute of silence after I told them what happened with Devika, floodgates of abuses opened on me.

"Devika? Seriously?" Raghu was asking animatedly, "How could you?"

"What the fuck were you thinking, Arjun?" Shashank was relatively less agitated.

"I told you I wasn't thinking straight."

"Is that supposed to justify what you did?" Raghu said.

"How could you not even talk to her after it... she is 'Devika' man?" Shashank asked.

"I was so ashamed, I just couldn't face her. I screwed up big time, didn't I?"

"You literally screwed Devika!" Raghu chucked his glass and stood oscillating in front of me, "You listen to me Poncho, you are going to make this right, immediately, or the thrashing that Shashank gave you will be nothing as compared to what I'll do to you. You understand?" I nodded a yes.

A long period of silence later.

"Poncho..." Shashank said, "How was it?"

"You fucking bastard, she is like a sister to me..." Raghu threw a plate full of peanuts at Shashank.

The hangover in the morning after a drunken escapade is a royal punishment. What makes it worse is the lack of sleep. My head felt like a jamming ground for percussion artists. I stood on stage behind Raghu with a thumping head. God bless the man who invented glares, for it masked my red puffy eyes and saved me from public embarrassment. Surprisingly, there was no trace of distress or aftereffects of all the alcohol we drank on Raghu's face. In fact, he was glowing with happiness. I had never seen him having such clarity about anything in his life. I stared at Raghu in awe as he confidently clipped the mangalsutra around Ruchika's neck. I guess you don't need to prepare yourself for things like wedding. When the time is right, you just know it from inside. I looked at teary-eyed happy faces of Raghu's parents, contentment in the form of the tears trickling down their faces. Karan Johar was right, it's truly all about loving your parents. So now after Raghu, it was my turn to get my parents happy high on my wedding. I roved my eyes all over the venue, searching for prospective girls, who I assumed my overzealous mother would have already tapped for me. Yet again my glares provided me cover from being caught staring at girls standing between the sea of guests who were ready to pelt rice at Raghu and his almost wife on the mantra-ranting pundit's cue. My radar so far had picked no match when my eyes fixed themselves on the entrance as she entered, looking ravishing as always in the golden and red *anaarkali* suit. Without a single blink, my eyes followed the face I had known forever, till it made its way to stage through over-enthused guests.

"Sorry I'm late..." Devika whispered in Raghu's ears before she came and stood beside Shashank. "Hi guys... did I miss much?" She said looking at Shashank, my eyes still glued on her.

Finally the pundit was done reciting all the mantras needed to tie Raghu and Ruchika to each other for eternity. He took away the traditional cloth between the bride and the groom, and the barbarian pelting of rice at Raghu began. Our boy now was officially married.

It had been more than two hours that Devika was around but she hadn't spoken a single word to me. The reason, surely was my moronic response in the past, but I preferred to assume it was Advait, her fiancé who had accompanied her. Who Advait? Remember Mr Francisco? At last Devika's father had succeeded in convincing her into getting engaged to him. I waited for the rest of the seats at the lunch table to be occupied so that I would get a chance to sit beside her, but when the time came, 'The Mother' chose to put me on display to a bunch of kitty party type aunties. By the time I reached the table, the seat was occupied by Advait. Muttering abuses to my bad luck, I took a seat Ragini had saved for me.

"So Raghuvir?" Shashank said loudly enough to score the attention of all the ten people sitting at the round table. "What have you decided?"

"About what?" Raghu said meekly, fully knowing he was going to be ragged.

"About your name. I mean are you keeping your first name or is Ruchika changing it to something else?" Raghu buried his head in his hands as everyone at the table guffawed.

"Shut up Shashank, or I'll stab you with this fork," Ruchika jumped to Raghu's rescue before Raghu said anything inviting further ragging from Shashank.

"See, now she won't let him speak for himself even. Bye bye my fiery friend... thou shalt be missed," Shashank said faking horror.

"I should have come for your wedding. I would have embarrassed you so much, you would have regretted inviting me." Devika jumped to Raghu's rescue.

"Yes, but you didn't na, bloody ditcher. Friends like you and Poncho should be caned," Shashank said slapping my arm. Devika finally smiled looking at me.

"Can we please stop the girly ranting?" Ragini gave Shashank a cold stare, silencing him instantly.

"Now who's the pussy?" Raghu hollered across the table, everyone guffawed again.

"So, Advait, when's the wedding?" Shashank asked as the laughter subsided.

"That depends on her highness' mood..." he said placing his hand on Devika's chair. "...She hasn't agreed on a date as yet. As soon as she does, I'll fly her away to SF..."

I saw Devika's face flush the smile as the wedding date was mentioned; my stomach on the other hand cramped at the thought of Devika going permanently away from me. Even though she wasn't always around in the past eighteen years, I knew at the back of my mind she would be accessible. All through the time Mr Francisco bragged about his life back in SF, Devika and I kept stealing glances at each other. I had missed her in the past two years, but only when she reappeared did I realize the magnanimity of how much I had missed her. Every time she looked at me, there were these unrecognisable feelings that launched mini tornadoes all over my body, making me highly unstable.

"I think we should leave, lest will miss the flight," Advait said to Devika as the lunch wrapped. She profusely coughed cleverly masking her displeasure.

"I'll just say bye to everyone and be back," she replied as her coughing petered out. My eyes followed her as she skittered between Raghu's relatives bidding the goodbyes.

"Hey, it was nice meeting you." I said to Advait as he caught me staring at Devika.

"Same here, brother. If I'm not wrong I've seen you before."

"Yes, probably at Nishi bhaiya's sangeet."

"Yes, now I remember! You are the guy everyone was talking about then..."

"Yes..."

"Let's leave, I'm done," Devika said, thankfully interrupting a potentially awkward conversation.

"Oh sure. Bye Arjun, see you soon?" Advait said, I nodded yes with a smile.

"Bye..." Devika said to me before she turned to leave.

"Are you not going to tell her?" Ragini said as I stood motionless watching Devika walk away yet again. I mutely looked at her, "After what you've put her through, she deserves to know."

"Who deserves to know what?" Shashank asked entering the scene.

"She deserves to know that he loves her..."

"Who are you talking about?"

"Devika." Raghini said, I turned to her stunned.

"Are you out of your mind?"

"No, I am not, but you are blind. What you couldn't see in all these years, I figured it out in a few hours." She poked her fingernail in his chest.

"He knows what I'm saying."

She turned to me. "Tell her before it's too late Arjun, again."

"But..." I said.

"Don't worry. She feels the same about you, don't you know it already?" I smiled, "Now run!"

I hysterically rushed to the parking lot as the fact that I was in love with Devika sank in deeper and deeper. I had no idea why I had not figured that out. Huffing and puffing, I caught up with her before she sat in the car.

"Dev..." I said, barely able to breathe.

"Arjun? What happened?" My furious panting continued.

"I'm sorry..." I said trying to regain control over my breath.

"Sorry for what?"

"Sorry for being a dick to you, sorry for not being there when you needed me the most, sorry for letting you go away easily, sorry for screwing everything we had..." I gasped for breath.

"I was so pissed at God for not letting me have what I wanted that I couldn't see what I already had. I was so confused and guilty and angry at everything, that I could not recognise any of my own feelings."

She was quiet, looking at me with those huge eyes, so I continued, "I can't change the way I feel for Hrida..." I took a few steps towards her, "... but what you and I till now didn't know is what I feel about you is equally devastating. It took me two years away from you and one Mr Francisco to realise what I had lost and what I was about to lose..."

I curled my finger to her pinky finger, "...You. I'll fight every heavily moustached warrior in your family if I have to, but I'm not letting you go away this time. I'm sorry it took me so long to say this, but I love you Dev, not crazily, not madly, but fairly enough for us to last a lifetime..." I noticed the moistness in her eyes. Advait in the mean time had gotten out of the car.

"Dev? Say something?"

"Promise me you'll roll joints for me till death do us apart," she said as she took a step towards me.

"I promise," I said and held her face to kiss.

The End

After the End:

2013

"I might have exaggerated a bit when I said I'll fight all the warriors in your family." I said inching towards Devika as we stood in front of a hundred odd fierce-looking men and women of Devika's family.

I had always considered my internal contortions as the only obstacle in the way of me getting married. So after overcoming my partial pursuit of self-destruction and recognising my feelings for Devika, I thought happily ever after of my story was just around the corner. Little did I know that there were around hundred more people to be buttered before I could drive into the sunset with her. Talking about fighting for your love is one thing, but the thought of literally sword-playing with ferocious men who'd shred you like confetti in the blink of an eye made me piss my pants. Not only men, even the women with their moustaches akin puberty hit boys looked barbarous.

"Pussy you are, but that's what makes you adorable." Devika giggled as her fingers gripped the back of my hand, "Besides they don't really fight for a living these days."

"Are you both going to stand there and keep talking to yourself?" Thundered Digvijay Uncle, Nishi bhaiya's father. On the flight to Gwalior, I had mugged up the names of all of

Devika's three grandparents, eleven uncles, eight aunts their respective spouses and some fifty-six cousins, even maids just in case. I somehow had a knack of consistently getting myself in the utmost complicated situations possible. As though once wasn't enough, I was here again in front of the 'To be Father-in-law' to convince him to let me marry his daughter, after him agreeing to it once.

"Sir..." I said clearing my throat, "... sirs I mean, and ma'ams, and   brothers and sisters..." I said as I looked at everyone. I had no idea what I was saying or what I was going to say. All I could think of then was to turn around and run away. I did turn, but then my eyes locked themselves on Devika who stood behind me, absolute as always, her eyes exuding warmth and love. Something she had done for the past nineteen years. I had an intense urge to smack myself every time I wondered what took me so long to realise how I felt about her. She had been right there in front of me all this while and I couldn't see it. It was only when I lost her that the blood rushed to my brain. It was time for me to man up and face the warriors.

"I-I am sorry..." I said walking up to Devika's father but maintaining a safe distance. "No words can justify what I did, so I can understand the anger and hatred you might have for me. I know you love Devika dearly and don't want to see her hurt in any way. I love her too, it is my love for her that gives me the courage to stand here in front of all of you, and if it's anything to go by, then believe that I'll never let anything break her heart again..." I turned to look at Devika's gleaming eyes. Her smile made my heart pound and I began firing words straight out of it. Fifteen minutes later when I was done with my monologue, except for the 'To-be Father-in-law', the moustaches of all the men and women sitting in front of me were soaked in their tears. I stood there with my eyes fixed on Devika's father for a reaction. He motionlessly stared at the floor for exact three minutes before he got up. It felt like all my innards had begun to run helter-skelter as soon he took his first step towards me, sweat began to drip from every corner of my body. I anchored my feet to the ground to keep myself from running away, but what happened next flipped all of the discomfort within me.

"Welcome to the family..." he said extending his hand towards me. "Lemme know when we can meet your parents."

Devika jumped to hug him. I too wanted to do it but controlled my emotions, lest he would change his mind. Nishi bhaiya satiated my itch to hug as he pounced on me.

"You broke my heart..." Nishi bhaiya said hugging me, I felt few of my bones crumble inside me, "Don't do it again, okay?" his rugged voice choked.

"I'm sorry bhaiya..." I said as he released his grip on me.

I spent next one hour hugging and touching the feet as Devika's father introduced me to everyone. My forehead had never gotten so many kisses all my life. I was overwhelmed with all the love showered on me. I stood there smiling as people pulled my cheeks, clicked photographs, stuffed all sort of sweets in my mouth, asked questions after questions about filmstars, but to my surprise, I had no qualms about any of it. I gelled with all of them as if I forever belonged to the family. I guessed 'The right time' had come. I looked at Devika, covering her smile with her hand, rolling her eyes in mock anger, strands of hair falling on her face. I swear if it was a film, there would be a romantic song playing in the background. I loved her, so much that my heart somersaulted looking at her. All I could think of was hold her close and never let her out of my sight for a single second.

"Thank you..." I muttered looking skywards.

"Done talking to God?" She said as she hugged me.

"Hmm..." I smiled as I turned to face her. Somehow I couldn't get enough of looking at her.

"Thank you..." she said hugging me, "The master shall reward you handsomely for it..." she said whispering in my ear.

"How handsomely?"

"Handsomely enough to fry your brains useless," she said pecking a kiss on my lips. "But that's for later, for now I have work to do."

"Like what?"

"Like flying back to Mumbai and convincing your mother?"

"Shit!"

and the story continues...